A Prospect of London

Also by Julie L'Enfant

The Dancers of Sycamore Street
Hazel Belvo: A Matriarch of Art
Nicholas R. Brewer: His Art and Family
Persistence of Vision (with Jaden Hansen)
Other Realities: The Art of Paul S. Kramer
Pioneer Modernists
The Gág Family: German-Bohemian Artists in America
William Rossetti's Art Criticism: The Search for Truth
in Victorian Art

A Prospect of
London

a novel

Julie L'Enfant

Trebuchet Press

Trebuchet
Press

To Norm, my real-life travel companion.

CONTENTS

THE BAND IN ST. JAMES PARK

Chapter 1

You'll know, if you've ever read any of Emerald Glover's novels, that she always describes the weather in England as cold and gray and wet, but the morning I arrived back in that country, the weather was nice and sunny. Some of the other people on my charter flight—people from North Central Louisiana University in Barston, Louisiana—expressed surprise at the beauty of the weather, for in addition to the general reputation England has for being chilly and gray, the papers back home had been saying that England was having an exceptionally cold, wet summer. But I hadn't believed any of it—I knew what England was like in the summers! It was warm in the sun and cool in the shade. You could tolerate long sleeves in the daytime; then, late at night, you might need a sweater or an old raincoat, such as the one I had been carrying over my arm and now, down on the windy platform where you boarded the train, put on. I was elated by the air. This was exactly the English air I remembered—light, cool, and thin somehow, like air on a mountaintop.

We clambered onto the Gatwick Express, heaving our bags onto luggage racks above the green plush seats. A few NCLU people had chosen this particular car—Edwina Warren settled next to me—but the other people in the car were strangers. I was dizzy with fatigue and confused by the babble of voices. I sank into a seat and closed my eyes, thinking disconnectedly of that scene in Glover's novel where Jasmine is crossing the English Channel, about to see England for the first time, and another of her books where Ariel comes into London and sees the snow. But enough of Jasmine and Ariel, I thought crossly, I want my own characters in London!

When I opened my eyes, the train was clacking along rapidly, and there was an Englishwoman sitting across from me. At first, I thought I might be dreaming, but Edwina was looking at her too. I knew she was English because of her complexion—fair skin with red cheeks (cheeks the redness of which extends all the way down to the jawbone, a type of ruddiness seen often in England but never in the United States, except on the occasional baby), also because of her eyes, which were very, very blue. And she was dressed English-style, in a floral-print dress without any reference to contemporary fashion (it had an Empire waist). The other people in this train car appeared to be transcontinental travelers. They wore rugged wash-and-wear clothing and looked tired, and they were burdened with luggage and coats and other impedimenta. But this woman was going somewhere (London!) just for the day. Despite the chill of the wind, her dress was summery, made of a lightweight fabric (voile perhaps, or, even more English, lawn). All she had with her was a black patent leather handbag on her lap and, down beside her in the aisle where people kept having to step over it, a rectangular basket with some kind of stalk-like vegetables in it. These were red tinged with green, either an especially stout sort of celery or, it occurred to me, something called rhubarb. And stuck among the stalks was a black umbrella.

I nudged Edwina, who pressed her lips together and caused her eyes to sparkle, signifying that she too had perceived the Englishness of the lady with the rhubarb and found her delightful. I was afraid the Englishwoman had seen this exchange but, as I looked back at her, was relieved to see that she did not seem to notice anything, either in the train or out the window: her eyes looked like Wedgewood saucers. I realized that the Englishwoman wasn't going to meet my eyes, so practiced was she in the art of urban travel. She seemed completely unconscious of the fact that people kept having to step over her basket as they went to and fro in the car and was equally impervious to being watched. Nevertheless, I turned my gaze out the window. It was a dazzling landscape. There were green fields and yellow fields, and occasionally there were red brick towns—the backs of houses, that is, each with a garden. From time to time, we stopped at a station, where a crowd of people would advance toward the train. I made this same journey the other time I was in England, but it had been in the middle of the night, and I had gotten the impression that there was nothing between Gatwick and London but a few lonely station platforms. Actually, it was quite populated.

The sun seemed inordinately bright this morning, making the car almost hot, and I could not seem to get away from its glare no matter how I adjusted the window shade. I was not willing to lower it entirely, as it was imperative that I see out. In the distance was a castle on top of a hill, a real castle with battlements and a flag. I looked at the towns and fields, but my interest in the landscape was soon satisfied. It was London I was looking for! From what I had been able to gather, most of my companions on the flight were just going to London on their way to somewhere else. A few were going "down to the Continent," but most were headed for the English countryside. The Lake District was a popular destination, as were the Cotswolds. A few people had mentioned BritRail passes as their way of getting around, but it seemed to me that the majority intended to rent a car and drive around the countryside. They always used those same words: "rent a car and drive around." The charter flight gave us three weeks, and these devotees of the countryside invariably expressed shock when I said I intended to spend the entire three weeks in London. They seemed to think this long concentration on the city, this avoidance of pastoral pleasures, denoted some kind of decadence. Of course, I had business in London—those novels—but even if I hadn't, I would have planned to stay right there.

Those associates of mine from the English Department— Edwina Warren, two instructors named Mavis Adams and Lucy Maddox, the Nicholsons (Charles Nicholson was our chairman), and the Beckwiths, Sid Beckwith being the department's senior member at that time—were staying in London, at the same hotel I was, as a matter of fact. But even they talked of various side trips out of the city. I was the only one who was planning to stay in London the whole time, and I could hardly wait to get there. I had waited eight years. I had been so afraid something would prevent my getting here this time!

Presently there were no breaks between towns, no more patchwork fields or other sunny vistas. The buildings were a continuous wall on either side of the train, and the names at the stations were now the beautiful and familiar names of London's suburbs—Hammersmith, Richmond—which might look gray and ordinary, but which evoked many scenes in my overcharged mind. Now the gray buildings loomed larger, and our train was only one of many darting under overpasses and through tunnels. Most everybody craned at the windows to see the white chimneys of the Battersea Power Station, the broad reach of the Thames, although the lady with the rhubarb sat motionless, not even bothering to look out at these sights. She must have made this trip a thousand times to be so blasé about entering London; she must be very English.

She was the quintessence of the British national character, it seemed to me. She was quaint, even "dowdy," to use the word so often applied to the Queen, and she had that air of stolid preparedness that the English have developed as a consequence of living on a small island so often besieged. Nothing fazed her: why, the train could have stopped and a giraffe gotten on, and the woman would not have flinched; she might not even have shifted her china-blue gaze to it. But the main thing exhibiting her British character, in my opinion, was the umbrella sticking out of the rhubarb. What a careful, cautious person she must be to bring along a "brolly" on such a perfect sunny day.

∾ ∾ ∾

I had come to London the first time in the summer of 1972, almost exactly eight years previously. I had been a junior at Whittaker College then, and London was the first stop on the Whittaker Junior Trip, a five-city tour. We arrived at Victoria Station in the middle of the night. The train ride had not gone well. (Nothing had, really. We had had breakdowns and mechanical failures resulting in long delays all the way from Natchez, Mississippi, the place we'd started from.) The train ride from Gatwick Airport took about four hours. The train would slow down and sometimes, in the black of night, just come to a halt. Somebody had ascertained that a strike was the cause of this snail-like behavior of the train. In any case, we got to Victoria at about three in the morning, English time. It was practically deserted. English people don't work all night as Americans do. There was concern that we would have to spend the rest of the night on benches in the station. However, someone, MacPherson probably, managed to hail a taxi, and eventually, we all got rides.

But something a little discomfiting happened in the process. I had my only experience with snobbery in England (some people think England is a snooty nation, but I never found it so, except this one time). A taxi driver, along with another taxi driver who was a crony of his, strolled among the crowd of weary travelers from Whittaker, clearly savoring this opportunity to evaluate and select their passengers. Some of the adults in the Whittaker group looked quite presentable, but the students looked scruffy, and as the taxi drivers looked us over, picking off one of the chaperons and one or two well-heeled students, I felt acutely how shabby most of us did look in our jeans and T-shirts. Then, the taxi driver I am talking about stopped in front of me and said, with comic incredulity, "You're not goin' to the West End, are you, luv?" and I shook my head no, not knowing which part of the city the West End was but figuring that it was the best part of London and aware that I wasn't dressed for any place fancy. Like everyone else from Whittaker, I was going to the Stanford Hotel, which (I found out later, to my chagrin) was in the heart of the West End!

But this time, the train just zipped into London with no unscheduled stops, and Victoria Station was bright and bustling in the morning light, with the noise from the trains and the crowds of passengers reverberating under the huge, vaulted roof. Edwina and I hefted our bags down from the train, joining Mavis Adams and Lucy Maddox, catching sight of the tall, thin figure of Charles Nicholson, the shorter figure of his wife Allison, and starting after them. Sid Beckwith and his wife Carol joined us as we jostled through the crowds. We had all been to England before (Sid Beckwith most often), but there was no doubt that Charles was our leader. He was new at NCLU, down from the East, a well-known scholar as well as a proven administrator. The charter flight had been his idea. Charles had his detractors, but he did get interesting things going, I thought happily as we went out into the fresh English air in front of the station and joined a queue for the taxis. The taxi situation was much more organized in the daytime, I saw with relief, watching a line of taxis being paired with a line of travelers as if guided by an invisible hand. Actual Londoners were walking down the sidewalk in front of the station, and I was amused to see that every one of them carried a black umbrella on this cloudless morning, just like the lady with the rhubarb.

Edwina and I shared a taxi with the Beckwiths. I had forgotten how spacious London taxis were and how fast. I looked eagerly at the city as we whizzed through the thick traffic. It was the same! I saw it in flashes—a green part here, a gray monument there, and everywhere red buses—and this very randomness seemed to offer greater proof that the city was still intact. I had heard such dire things in the eight years since I had been able to come. There was always some "crippling" strike or some terrorist bombing. London was supposed to be overrun by immigrants from places that used to be colonies back in the days when England was a great power, though the little island country was just not equipped to assimilate so many, a sad fact that led to awful race riots. And then the economy had simply gone haywire since 1972

(I knew this had something to do with Margaret Thatcher and her quarrels with the Labour party, although I did not follow politics). One of my mother's friends had come to London two or three years before and stayed at one of the big hotels near Hyde Park. A cup of coffee had cost three dollars, she reported, and my mother had taken this as the definitive pronouncement on the state of London at the present time (hopelessly out of whack), repeating it every time the name "London" was mentioned, and I had fallen into the gloomy habit of thinking of London as a city doomed to ruin by greed and other ugly human impulses, much as Venice is known to be sinking into the sea. Oh, yes, I had also read that London was sinking: any day now, the Thames would flood it. A few years ago, distressed at all this bad news, I actually asked someone who had just returned from England whether London was "still there." He had given me a funny look before saying, "Of course!" And now I could see why. London was so monumental and busy, so apparently thriving, that when you were in the middle of it, you could not doubt that it would last forever.

"Well, how do you find the dear old town, Caroline?" Sid Beckwith asked as we hurtled through it.

"Wonderful!"

"At least the weather's decent," said his wife Carol, in a martyred tone.

"Decent?" echoed the taxi driver from upfront, though he had a Cockney accent and the word came out something like "day-sunt." He had not previously spoken to us, but now he was looking back at us in the mirror, where I could see his eyes. "You calls this daysunt? I calls it a bloody 'eat wave!"

Sid Beckwith chortled silently, and I exchanged glances of amusement with him and the others, knowing that this remark would be remembered by everyone present and alluded to for years to come.

"You ought to have the weather we just left," said Sid, a bluff, gruff man who looked more like a sportswriter than an English professor. He gave the taxi driver a rundown on Louisiana weather in late June. It was hot, he said, got up to ninety or ninety-five every day, and more often than not, it rained in the afternoon and made steam. Even at night, it was still so hot you couldn't take a walk without getting soaking wet. Here it was warm in the sun all right, but as soon as you got in the shade, brrr, Sid shivered dramatically.

Meanwhile, I stared raptly out the window. I listened as the taxi driver continued the comical exchange with Sid, but what was really on my mind was the hotel. Whereas in 1972 we had stayed at the Stanford Hotel, which was so near Buckingham Palace and St. James Park that the park had seemed to be our lawn as well as the Queen's, nowadays it is impossible to stay at a hotel like the Stanford for less than ninety or a hundred dollars a night. This had to do with the well-known ruination of the economy. You couldn't stay at an ordinary hotel anymore (and that is all the Stanford had been, an ordinary hotel); you had to stay at some budget kind of place. Charles had recommended a bed and break-fast place in Bloomsbury called St. Cuthbert's Hotel. He said it was "delightful" and "the best value in London," and later, his wife Allison had also used the word "delightful." There was a drawback; however, the rooms did not have private baths. "The bathrooms are right down the hall, though. And they're very clean. And there's never anybody in them," she had rather implausibly claimed. The location was ideal, just a few blocks from the British Museum, where Charles did his research and where I was also going to be doing research. I wanted to believe Charles and Allison when they said St. Cuthbert's was "delightful," but I really could not. Apart from my serious misgivings about the bathroom (I had never stayed in a hotel without a private bath), I was leery of anything called a "bed and breakfast place." It sounded so dismal, so austere! It suggested a narrow iron bedstead with a pallet on it instead of a mattress, then a sparse kind of meal consisting of porridge or even "gruel," served up at dawn in dishes made out of the same dingy metal as the bed.

The idea that the Nicholsons' bed and breakfast place was a kind of flophouse in a seedy part of Bloomsbury—some place which provided only basic services, like Hull House—and which the Nicholsons professed to love only because, as instigators of the NCLU charter flight, they had a deep interest in making London out to be affordable. This idea had taken root so firmly in my mind that I was shocked when the taxi, which had wheeled around onto a broad, handsome street, stopped in front of a fine-looking entrance which had "St. Cuthbert's Hotel" imprinted in gold on the fanlight above the door. I thought there must be some mistake. I thought this must be a second St. Cuthbert's Hotel, which the taxi driver had confused with our own more grim establishment, but Sid, who had stayed at St. Cuthbert's before, was climbing out of the taxi, helping his wife out. Then he was helping Edwina and me out, and I stood on the sidewalk amid the bags staring happily up and down the street. St. Cuthbert's was part of a long terrace, which comprised four or five other hotels with fine-looking entrances. Across the street was another terrace, identical to this one, with more hotels. The terraces were three stories high, mainly red brick, though the ground floor was made of creamy stone, and each window on the ground floor had a window box with red geraniums in it.

This was Bedford Place. I observed the tall wrought-iron fences running the length of either sidewalk, shiny black in the morning sun. In this first glance, when I was too tired to observe fine points, I thought Bedford Place looked remarkably like Eaton Place on *Upstairs, Downstairs*. I immediately formed an impression of a series of substantial households, exceedingly well run, just like that of the Bellamys, even if it was 1980, not 1910, and even though they were commercial establishments rather than private dwellings. This impression was so strong it would override much evidence to the contrary.

Chapter 2

Who are you people? Colonials, I daresay. Have you booked?"

These words were spoken in the lobby of St. Cuthbert's Hotel by a tall, somewhat stout young man in an Irish fisherman's sweater and baggy brown corduroy pants.

"Of course we've booked, man," Sid Beckwith said, stepping forward, visibly controlling himself. We had made our reservations months ago. You would have to be mad to come to London in July, the height of the tourist season, without reservations!

"Where is Mr. Renniston, the manager?" Charles Nicholson asked.

"We've seen the last of Mr. Renniston. I'm the new manager, Christopher Sparks."

This Mr. Sparks had a negligent, jocular air and looked very sloppy in the sweater and brown corduroys—he had no shirt underneath the sweater—but he spoke with an arch accent, which I recognized from *Masterpiece Theatre* as "upper class," or at any rate, not Cockney. You could tell at once that Mr. Sparks was not a hotel manager by vocation, as Mr. Renniston had probably been, but that he was working as a hotel manager for the time being either because he was waiting for an opportunity to do what he was meant to do (acting came to mind) or because he was too lazy for anything more demanding. In any case, Mr. Sparks was more playful than the usual hotel manager. He asked our names and, when he heard them, affected great puzzlement, going back into the office and pretending to have lost the guest register.

"Who is this clown?" Sid Beckwith muttered quite audibly as we crowded anxiously up to the desk and looked into the office. St. Cuthbert's was a makeshift sort of hotel. You could tell from the narrow lobby, actually no more than a hallway, that it was originally a residence. The office, back behind the stairs, had probably been a broom closet. As Mr. Sparks rooted around in the papers on the desk, my eye roamed over the items on the counter where the register should be—a rack with postcards in it, a stack of *What's On*, even a few souvenirs in the form of Beefeater dolls with the kind of eyes that close if you lay them down and which now, even though they were standing upright, drooped as if they were drugged.

Mr. Sparks had seemed to be kidding, but now it looked as though he really could not find our reservations. What on earth would we do? How would we ever find another place to stay that was reasonable? A moment ago, we were discussing whether we should go to bed for a while or not. Now there was doubt about whether we would have beds at all! I looked hungrily at the cover of *What's On*. It seemed that we might have to leave—whipped, harried nomads—without even being able to look at its contents. I could see into a room to the right of the office—an orderly and comfortable-looking room, with a television, a fireplace, even a Teddy Bear on the pillow of the bed. At this moment, St. Cuthbert's seemed like the most charming lodgings in the world; tears of longing to be able to stay there filled my eyes.

"Charles Nicholson, from Barston, Louisiana?" Mr. Sparks asked doubtfully.

"Hot dawg!" cried Sid Beckwith, socking his fist into his palm, and we all laughed with relief. While Charles and Sid signed the register, I took up a copy of the guide to entertainment and leafed through it lightheartedly, chatting with Lucy Maddox about tickets. We had to get tickets to things! Mavis Adams asked about tea. Well, said Mr. Sparks, he thought some member of the staff might be prevailed upon to make some tea, maybe even some toast.

There was one slight snag. I had booked a single room, but as it turned out, no single was available, Mr. Sparks said. Would I mind a double occupancy with Miss Warren? The rate was several pounds lower.

"Well, I'd be delighted," my colleague Edwina said earnestly, and my heart sank. I was distressed at the prospect of sharing a room, being a very light sleeper and also a person who needs privacy. Nevertheless, politeness compelled me to say, "Of course! That would be fine!"

"Are you sure, Caroline? We got confirmation of a single for you and a single for Edwina. I'll get Charles to argue with this yo-yo," Allison Nicholson said quietly.

"Oh, no, that's fine," I said, lest I hurt Edwina's feelings. Edwina was such a good person. But, of course, the new arrangements would not incommode Edwina, a stocky, cheerful Midwesterner who looked as though she could make herself comfortable on a wagon train.

"Miss Landry?" Mr. Sparks said as I signed the register, as if he had heard of me before and particularly wished to make my acquaintance. "I have a telephone message for you, Miss Landry!"

"Oh!" I said, struck by fear that it was a message from home. My grandmother had died, or my mother was ill. I would have to take the next plane back to attend a funeral.

Again Mr. Sparks was pawing through his papers. "I just saw it not an hour ago. Ah, here." He came forward. "Someone at the St. James for you, a…" He puzzled over the writing on a ragged-looking note. "Franklin Harold."

"Ah," I said with a mighty sigh. "Yes, thank you."

"Wants you for tea."

"Thank you so much." This was none of his business. "May I use the phone?"

I called Franklin Harold right away while Mr. Sparks took the others upstairs. I should have remembered about the Harolds. Franklin was the son of my grandmother's neighbors in New Orleans (not some kind of lover, as Mr. Sparks seemed to have been trying to suggest with his eyebrows). I knew that Franklin had been in England the last two years and that Mr. and Mrs. Harold were coming to "take him home" after spending some time here themselves. By coincidence, they were arriving in London at about the same time I was. They had told my grandmother they would be in touch.

It was festive, talking with Franklin, whom I had seen only a few times but with whom I felt a strong bond of sympathy, Franklin being, like myself, a bookish person in a family that was not bookish. He majored in history at Dartmouth College and was supposed to have gone to law school but came to England instead for some kind of degree in history or literature at Oxford. In fact, my grandmother told me, he had come over "to write." As I chatted with Franklin on the phone, accepting the invitation to tea at four o'clock that afternoon, taking down directions to their hotel, I wondered whether Franklin had gotten the mysterious degree or written any books. Franklin did not say. He spoke primarily of his parents, who had had a difficult flight over. They were supposed to have arrived two days prior to this, but due to a bizarre accident that befell the airplane before takeoff (a truck had run into it at the terminal), they didn't arrive until the day before at four o'clock. To top it all off, their luggage was lost, and it still hadn't been found.

I was looking forward to seeing the St. James Hotel, which was bound to be one of London's finest (the Harolds would travel deluxe). Afterward, I would walk over to St. James Park, one of the many places in London with special meaning for me. Meanwhile, I was anxious to see my own hotel. I hefted my bags, as there seemed to be no bellboys at St. Cuthbert's. Up past the first landing, I continued to see signs that this was a real hotel and not some completely different kind of establishment, as I had feared. The room I was to share with Edwina looked very much like the room I had had at the Stanford. The bedspreads on the two beds and the curtains were the same shade of orange—"London orange," I now dubbed it—and the furniture was the same light wood. There was a sink in the corner of the room, just the same. Excusing myself from Edwina, who was already unpacked, I put down my bags and went to find the bathroom. This took a moment, as our room was in a cul-de-sac in the irregular pattern of hallways, and it took some exploring to find the bathroom. I saw that it was going to be fine. It was surprisingly big and airy, with an old-fashioned clawfoot bathtub and a view. (No shower, though, which meant we would have to wash our hair in the room, in the sink.) You could raise the window, which had frosted glass in the lower portion for modesty, feel the fresh English air, and see out into some thick green trees. Below was a garden, or square, rather, since beyond it was the rear of another terrace. And above and beyond this terrace, against the fine blue sky, stood some of London's tall new buildings. Yes, the bathroom was going to be just fine, and sure enough, nobody was in it.

∾ ∾ ∾

Edwina belonged to the school which believes that you should go to bed for a while when you arrive in Europe rather than the rival school, which advocates that "you stay up till *they* go to bed." When I returned to the room, Edwina was already dressed for bed in striped flannel pajamas, about to don a black sleep mask. Edwina was engaged to be married in October to an associate professor in the College of Engineering at NCLU, and I wondered briefly whether she intended to wear these manly pajamas after her marriage.

"I guess I'll lie down a minute too," I said uncertainly, going over to the window to close the orange curtains, pausing a moment to look at the view out the front—the elegant terrace across Bedford Place and, beyond that, multitudes of chimney pots on the rooftops of London. Then I crawled under my orange covers. A few minutes later, I heard somebody throwing pebbles against the window. The room was dark, and in my mind's eye, there was a little boy down on the sidewalk tossing the rocks. He was dressed like Oliver Twist.

On the way over to the window, I got a little exasperated at the importunity of the pebbles, but when I opened the curtains, I saw rain. It seemed to be a different day from the one on which we had arrived, a different season. The glass of the window was icy. I raised the window an inch or two, and damp wintry air blew in. The terrace across the street looked grim in the rain, and on the sidewalk below, the black umbrella of some prescient Londoner was bobbing along.

This was just astonishing—after all, I was pretty experienced in the vagaries of the London climate. On the junior trip in 1972, we spent five whole days in London, days which had been so varied and full of experiences, consequently so long, that they seemed to constitute a fair sample of the London summer. One day it had gotten cloudy for a little while and sprinkled (this was London's much-talked-about "raininess"), but the rest of the time it had been warm in the daytime and cool at night, like perfect spring days at home. I remembered long, cool days and long, long evenings. Sometimes it was still light when we came out of the theatre. Louisiana doesn't have much in the way of a twilight—it's dark blue for a while, that is all—but London has a twilight that lasts for hours. I remembered one evening when we didn't go to the theatre but explored Belgravia and Mayfair instead, ending up in that grand square with the American Embassy at one end. Although it was ten or ten-thirty, it still wasn't dark, and it was as if we were being given some supernatural extension of that brief twilight at home.

We went on to Paris, Munich, Florence, and Rome, but all during our time in those other cities, I pined for London. The fact is, I had fallen in love with it, just as you fall in love with a person. Sometimes I tried to figure out the origins of this love, recalling such things as how I had always responded to green parks and golf courses—a certain golf course, not too far from the house where I had grown up in Meridian, for instance; or how I always thrilled to big gray buildings. Of course, I knew that my love for England was directly promoted by reading and studying about it—I taught English, after all—but I really thought it had more to do with certain vague sights, what I called "scenes," than with anything in literature. New Orleans had always been a source of such stimuli. For example, I had always loved Audubon Park, which is only a few blocks from my grandmother's house. I had one of these strong responses whenever I walked all the way across the park to Magazine Street and looked back toward St. Charles. You saw the golf course; you also saw the spires of the Church of the Most Holy Name of Jesus, which reminded me of John Constable's paintings of the church at Dedham Vale. It did not matter that palm trees were part of the vista across Audubon Park, or even that the church at Dedham Vale is gray stone and Holy Name red brick (in fact, the architectural styles of the two churches are completely different). The feeling was the same, particularly on gray days, most particularly on foggy or misty days, which always reminded me of England even while running contrary to my own meteorological experience there. Up close, by the way, Holy Name did not remind me of England at all, and inside, where the Baroque style predominates, it seemed more evocative of Spain, or some other Catholic country, than the country I loved.

But none of this response to buildings or vistas had any definite form until the trip in 1972. It would have been quite possible for me to fall in love with another of the cities we went to—I have a French heritage, being a Landry and having studied French, which predisposed me to love Paris, and Italy had most of the art I wanted to see—but although I read up on Paris, Munich, Florence, and Rome with a thoroughness equal to that with which I had read up on London and felt that I was able to appreciate the glories I saw there, it was London I fell in love with, and London I longed for from the moment I left it. What I was yearning for was rather vague. It was certain scenes: the very streets of London, the parks, certain people. I had passed a man in a snappy felt hat with a feather in it crossing Great Russell Street in front of the British Museum; I missed him dreadfully. I kept thinking about an Italian family I had seen in a coffee shop near Hyde Park one day, a good-looking young couple, very tan, with two shiny-haired children. They did not look Italian—the woman was blond—but they spoke the lovely Italian language to each other and to the children, who were beautifully behaved in the coffee shop. This was the sort of European family whose Christmases are featured in *Vogue*. The woman wore a becoming shade of red lipstick that didn't wear off when she ate (it had to have come from some expensive and esoteric Italian line of cosmetics), and the man was wearing a suit with white socks. I knew that my father would never have dreamed of wearing thick white socks with a suit—that would be risible! Even the boys at Whittaker would know better than to wear white socks with a suit. Yet on this Italian man, who was probably a count, the socks looked exactly right.

Sometimes I felt as though all London were a stage setting for my instruction or even just delight, as on the Sunday we were in the city and practically everything was closed, traffic much reduced, and we saw the amusing spectacle of an American rock star riding down a broad empty street on a flatbed truck with his sidemen, all yelling and waving as if this dignified Sunday in London were Mardi Gras. Things like that haunted me, and ever since then, my love for London has been growing. I read English novels and collected books on travel in England. I was also devoted to *Masterpiece Theatre.* I never missed an episode if I could help it and was deeply upset if I had to miss it or was interrupted while watching it. It actually hurt my feelings when people criticized this program or made fun of it, as they often did. It seemed to be a byword for stuffy, pompous, and lifeless culture, although it did not mean *culture* to me: it meant a glimpse of England every Sunday night, a glimpse of London when I was lucky.

But something had brought this love for London to a climax, and now, standing at the window, looking out at the rain, I remembered another occasion in 1972. Early one evening, we were on our way to a play at the Haymarket. Going across St. James Park, we noticed that something was going on in the Mall, the broad avenue that leads to Buckingham Palace. We went over to join the crowd, made up of humble-looking folk, many of them white and pasty, with fat babies that didn't cry. It was a military parade, but the soldiers were not the modern sort, but rather picturesque soldiers in what looked like costumes of the past—red uniforms with bushy shakos, some with such exotic touches as animal skins draped over their shoulders. The units seemed to represent different parts of England's former empire, the places with wild animals—Africa or India.

Some of the units carried musical instruments rather than rifles, and while we pressed into the nice crowd to see them pass, something splendid happened: one of these musical units, the members of which happened to be draped in tiger skins, started playing a march. Now, this was not a simple, foursquare march such as an American marching band would play, but a melodious march with a subtle rhythm and a teasingly clever harmony. The band was marching rather slowly, employing a hesitation in its gait—sort of dragging its feet in a certain way that matched the rhythmic subtleties of the tune. Feeling compelled led me to learn the name of this work, and I started running alongside the band, trying to read it from their tiny sheet music.

I kept on following the band, some of the other people from Whittaker trailing along after me. The crowd got thicker near the palace as if something important was about to happen. I asked a policeman, who replied, "The Queen's birthday, Miss, trooping the colour." He looked droll as he said this as if I had asked something very silly, such as, "What is that big gray building behind the fence?" Exalted at having stumbled on such an important public event (we wouldn't have come on purpose, of course—that would be "touristy," like attending the Changing of the Guard), we maneuvered through the people to the place where the military units were amassing. Presently the Queen herself appeared on a palace balcony—she was far away, but you could tell it was the Queen—along with Prince Philip, and was it the Queen Mother? I descried a blue hat. They looked like tiny dolls waving their little arms. With tears in my eyes, I waved back.

I hadn't thought much of this experience at the time—so many remarkable things had happened in London—but then something brought it vividly back. This was about nine months before, in the fall of 1979, my second year in Barston. I was attending a concert given by the NCLU concert band, and they played Gustav Holst's English Suite No. 1. I was momentarily confused as to whether this could be the same Holst who had written *The Planets*—I had thought that Holst was Scandinavian or German (Gustav?)—but this piece sounded so English from the very first bar, and it brought back St. James Park. There was that wandering first part, deep in the brasses, then that sprightly march with the smart rapping of the snares, the splendid screaming of the clarinets. Then, when the first part and the second part combined in a brilliant contrapuntal relationship, I saw again the march down The Mall, which combined the clever syncopated music and the deliciously dragged-out gait of the soldiers. I knew that the band in the tiger skins hadn't played English Suite No. 1. They had played some simpler march, the name of which I had forgotten. Still, the spirit of the English Suite No. 1 was so similar that I burst into tears right there in Wilkerson Auditorium and had to fish around in my purse for a Kleenex. *I had to get back to London* (a necessity which I had failed to recognize until that moment), and when I got to London, I would sit in St. James Park and listen to a band.

Chapter 3

I can't wait to get out of London," said Mrs. Harold, a plump gray-haired woman, wagging her head back and forth as if London had already driven her to distraction. "We would have left today if it weren't for the luggage."

"You can't dislike London!" I burst out as Mr. Harold threaded his way through all the chintz-covered chairs and seated himself over in the corner at a delicate escritoire to call the airline. I knew Mrs. Harold was upset and needed humoring, just as my own mother needed humoring on occasion, but really, I could only go so far. I couldn't completely ignore the truth! What could London possibly do to irritate Mrs. Harold, particularly when she was staying at this hotel tucked back in the innermost recesses of the most august quarter of the city—why, it was like staying in the vault of a bank!

The St. James Hotel, where I met Franklin and his parents for tea, was off Jermyn Street, lined with gentlemen's clubs and interesting shops distinguished by being not the least showy, obviously catering to the gentlemen who belonged to the clubs and even (you saw so many royal warrants) to the royalty that lived nearby. I thought it very appropriate that the Harolds' hotel be in this vicinity because the Harolds were royalty of a kind. Mr. Harold, a lawyer, had been King of Carnival in New Orleans a few years before. He and his family lived in an impressive pink stucco house on Lafayette Place, a dead-end street right around the corner from my grandmother's house on Palmer Avenue. I didn't exactly know what being King of Carnival entailed, apart from riding on a float on Mardi Gras day and waving a scepter. Nor did I understand how you got to be King, though I thought it had something to do with public service; also, you had to come from a "good family," whatever that meant. But I admired Mr. Harold as a fine, substantial person with great moral power.

Actually, I hardly knew the Harolds—I just knew them as people who came to my grandmother's annual open house on Christmas Day. But this is what I mean by Mr. Harold's "moral power." One time a couple of years before, when I was down in New Orleans visiting my grandparents, there was a commotion in the neighborhood in the middle of the night, a clamor from a record or tape player playing at top volume. It was a Richard Pryor concert, actually, and it was so loud you could hear the bad words even with all the windows closed, as windows must be at night in New Orleans. Everybody in the house had awoken, including my grandfather, who was very ill at the time. My grandmother called the police, and the racket stopped after a while.

The next day I was helping my grandmother weed the flower beds in the front yard when Mr. Harold came by, walking his dog. He stopped a moment to talk about the offensive incident, and he said that he too had called the police. "We can't have that kind of disturbance in our neighborhood, Mrs. Landry," he said to my grandmother, exhibiting such a serene assurance in their common right to peace and tranquility, and their ability to maintain it, that I had the pleasing image of Mr. Harold coming out of his house in the middle of the night, his scepter raised, to restore good order.

I had always loved visiting New Orleans. I had wanted to go to college at Newcomb, where my mother and grandmother had gone, but my father had been opposed to this, my mother too, and I ended up at Whittaker College, high on the bluffs of the Mississippi River in Natchez, Mississippi. Whittaker was very good academically, it was said, perhaps even better than Newcomb, and Whittaker had offered me a full scholarship. After college, with nothing better to do, I went on to the University of North Carolina, where I got a master's and Ph.D. in English literature. Then I got the job in Barston. Since then, I had driven down to New Orleans several times for my grandmother's traditional Christmas Open House, which she continued after my grandfather died. That is where I had seen the Harolds over the years. I hardly knew them, really, but when you're abroad, it seems essential to get together even with acquaintances from home who happen to be in the same place you are, and now I listened as Mrs. Harold went on.

"London is terrible. The traffic, the people. We're leaving as soon as we can for Stow-on-the-Wold. Stow-on-the-Wold is a little village in the Cotswolds, you know. There's an old country hotel there where we've been going for years."

"Mmm," I said, nodding sympathetically but actually feeling slightly irritated at this mention of the Cotswolds, that favorite of people who rented cars and drove around. I had seen many pictures of the Cotswolds and believed I knew their charms: quaint villages with thatched-roofed houses and rolling hills with sheep. I failed to understand why anyone would prefer straw and sheep to London. The very name "Cotswolds" was faintly annoying to me now. The person who pronounced it sounded as if he had marbles in his mouth.

"Mother and Dad really don't like London," Franklin put in from over by the fireplace. "But I feel like you, Caroline. I've spent a lot of time in London, especially this past year. I've come in almost every weekend for the theatre and museums."

"Do you stay here?" I asked Franklin in the intimate way we talked (although we barely knew each other), so different from the ceremonial way you had to talk to Mrs. Harold.

"Lord, no," he said with a laugh, indicating that his budget was not to be confused with his parents' budget. "I have this little place in Kensington, quite a nice little hotel for the price."

"Where are you staying, Caroline?" Mrs. Harold inquired from her chair, where she sat like Queen Victoria.

"St. Cuthbert's Hotel in Bloomsbury. Actually, it's a bed and breakfast place," I felt compelled to add.

"One of those places with the bath down the hall?" Mrs. Harold said with a stare.

"It's not bad! No one's ever in there—hard as that is to believe!"

"Some of the b and b's are quite nice," said Franklin by way of support.

"The thing about this one," I went on bravely, having associated myself with this outré place, "is that it's right near the British Museum. I'm doing some work there."

"Really!" Franklin cried. "What kind of work?"

"They *say* the bags are coming now," Mr. Harold said on his way across the room to rejoin us. But he was smiling gently to show that he did not believe the airline, which had botched everything else, and which could be expected to be lying now, although this need not concern his family or their guest, he seemed to be saying. He was a prominent New Orleans attorney, and he might speak softly, but he carried a big stick.

Just then, the tea tray arrived. It was impossible to hold any kind of sustained conversation for a while because the tea trays required so much maneuvering and cooperation. Franklin was given the responsibility of pouring the tea, as Mrs. Harold was far too upset about the bags, and Mr. Harold began to pass the food.

"Have a scone, Caroline. And butter. Franklin, pass the butter to Caroline."

I ate the scone, then a cucumber sandwich. I was worried about eating too much, as this was ceremonial food, really; you weren't supposed to come at it like a starving dog, but Franklin was also eating enthusiastically, and Mr. Harold was sampling this and that. Mrs. Harold was not eating anything. Like many plump women, she seemed to disdain the idea of food.

"Well, I don't think this tea is very good, Winston. It isn't hot," Mrs. Harold complained.

Mr. Harold held his index finger aloft, like a figure by Leonardo. Miraculously, this caused the waiter to materialize. Mr. Harold said the tea was not hot; please, he said, bring another pot. Then Franklin asked me again what I would be working on.

"Oh!" I said, hastening to chew and swallow a buttery little sandwich. "Some research, some possible research on this writer named Emerald Glover."

Franklin had never heard of her. "Was she British?" he asked.

"No, American."

"Living over here?"

"Well, she did. She lived in Red Lion Square at one time, but I think she must be dead." I had gone to Red Lion Square earlier that afternoon, despite the rain, and Emerald Glover's address was an architect's office, which seemed to bode very ill for my research. I didn't remember Emerald Glover's building from 1972. I had seen Red Lion Square before, when MacPherson had taken us there to see a place William Morris had lived (a better-preserved literary landmark), and now the thought of MacPherson, who used to come regularly to London and who might still come regularly, caused my heart to turn over.

"What sort of books did she write?"

"Well . . ."

"Who is this, Caroline?" Mrs. Harold interrupted. Like my mother, Mrs. Harold was always about four beats behind the conversation. It seemed to be part of her dignity. And when I told her the name, she asked me to spell it, just as Mother would have.

"I don't think I've heard of her," Mrs. Harold decided, "but then I have so little time to read."

"She published four novels in the 20s and 30s. The interesting thing is, I think she may be from Louisiana. Her first book was set in Louisiana, but then, apparently, she moved to England before the First World War."

"She came to England and wrote?" said Franklin, looking stricken.

"Winston, wasn't there a woman writer from Metairie named 'Emerald Glover'?" Mrs. Harold said.

"Oh, thank you," he said to the waiter, who appeared with the new pot of tea. "Now, Frances, what did you ask?" She repeated her query about Emerald Glover and spelled the name. Mr. Harold thought. "You're thinking about Emma Gilbert," he said after this. "I don't believe we know an Emerald Glover."

I tried to tell them a little about Emerald Glover—it was rather interesting how I had discovered her, I thought—but even though Franklin obviously wanted to listen, the exposition was not easy. In the way of parents, Mr. and Mrs. Harold, while expressing extreme interest in what the young people were talking about, in fact, kept interrupting or even changing the subject, and the talk, while we had tea, most often had to do with the tea itself, or the luggage. The luggage was honestly the only subject in which the senior Harolds were interested.

But the thought of Red Lion Square, and MacPherson, had reminded me of another literary landmark I saw in 1972: 52 Gordon Square, the most famous address of Virginia Woolf. I had gone off by myself to find Gordon Square one afternoon, and as I stepped into the street to cross over and take a closer look at the blue plaque, a taxi came out of nowhere, passing so close that it brushed my skirt (whoosh!) Why, I was almost mowed down, I thought in amazement as I stared after the taxi, which wound down at a stop sign, then wound up again and whirred away. I suppose I looked left before stepping out in the street, rather than right, a matter of instinct, although I don't know for sure, it happened so suddenly. I stood there a minute, shaking, then stepped back on the sidewalk. At that moment, I was entirely alone in London—the Whittaker people were at the British Museum for the afternoon, and I had played hooky. I realized, in the wake of the taxi, that if I *had* been run over, the authorities would find out my name and home address from my driver's license, but nobody would have known where I was staying or with whom I was traveling. I would just have been this dead American girl, shipped home in a box. Finally, I pulled myself together and carefully crossed the street to look at number 52, but it hardly made an impression on me, I was so rattled by my brush with death.

I shouldn't have told anybody about it—I was AWOL at the time, and the incident was a dramatic illustration of the risks you took going AWOL—but I told MacPherson, who, although he was a chaperon and bound by the rules of the trip to condemn, even punish solitary expeditions, I had reason to believe would sympathize with my adventure. Rashly, then, I told him about it as a sort of joke, referring to the taxi that almost ran me down as a "killer cab," and he said one of the penetrating things for which he was famous. He said, "That's what you get for being starry-eyed!" *Starry-eyed*, he said, with what might have been a gleam of irony (you were never sure with MacPherson). At least I thought this remark was "penetrating," though I did not know what it meant, exactly, and had to puzzle over it with a friend or two.

Chapter 4

At one point, I turned to Franklin to ask what his plans were. He said he had decided to go back home and go to law school. He was entering Tulane in the fall.

"Oh, splendid!" I exclaimed, although I saw that this represented a defeat for Franklin. He wanted to write, not practice law, and I believed fervently in Franklin's vocation for writing even though I had never seen a line he had written. Franklin had changed a good deal since I had seen him last, which would have been at an open house five or so years before when he was still in high school. On that occasion, we had had an absorbing talk on Goethe, both of us, by coincidence, having just read *The Apprenticeship of Wilhelm Meister*. It was an intense discussion, pleasurable in its contrast to the idle chatter of the other people at the party. I remembered how Franklin had stood, drinking eggnog, trembling slightly, his face and neck taking on a peculiar mottled appearance. Franklin was thin and serious looking, with that sensitive skin which was a display of his sensibility. Now he was taller and seemed less wispy, but that might be because of his clothes, which had the aura of the tailor with a royal warrant. Franklin had on a tweed jacket and loose-fitting brown pants. I had an idea these might be "flannels."

"You have to study at a law school in Louisiana if you're going to practice in the state," Franklin explained intensely, blushing. "Louisiana's legal system is unique, you know."

"The civil law," Mr. Harold put in.

"I thought about teaching history as a means of support while I try to write," Franklin said, leaning forward, looking at me searchingly, "but the teaching profession seems so horrible nowadays. I wanted to talk to you about that."

"Oh, it's horrible," I confirmed. "Jobs are really scarce. I'm lucky to have mine. And you have to publish—criticism, I mean, not fiction. We had a fine man who wrote fiction but wasn't interested in scholarly work, and they let him go this spring."

As I explained these conditions, an unpleasant feeling was developing in my stomach. It had to do with Jerry Braswell, the man of whom I spoke. After he was fired, he went out to New Mexico "to write," and he was probably starving by now. I myself would be up for tenure review in a year or so. I had published one short article (only a review, really), and I was trying to turn my dissertation into a book, but it was just sitting on my desk at home, a lifeless heap. I was here to do work on Emerald Glover, but it would likely come to naught. There was a real chance that I would be turned out, like Jerry Braswell.

There was another reason I had bad feelings in connection with Jerry. We had been dating for over a year when he got the bad news, and when it came, he asked me to leave NCLU with him. This was tempting—I cared for Jerry—but after a few days of turmoil, I had said no. The thought of the desert and Jerry trying to write—well, it seemed so bleak. I still hadn't sorted out my feelings about this. In particular, I had not sorted out what part MacPherson had played in this decision, but sometimes it seemed to me, that spring and summer, that I had been an idiot to turn Jerry down. There was such a dearth of eligible men in Barston, Louisiana, that sometimes it seemed to me, at age twenty-nine, that my romance with Jerry had been my last chance at love.

"We want Franklin to keep on with his writing," Mrs. Harold said querulously. "We just wish he'd give us a page or two to read!"

Franklin sprang up and walked over to the fire, his hands in the pockets of his "flannels," where he began to pace back and forth in a brooding manner.

"How's your grandmother, Caroline? I mean, how is she really doing?" Mr. Harold inquired tenderly, taking no notice of this. I said she was doing fine, considering.

As we talked, I observed as much of the life of the St. James Hotel as I could. I took particular notice of a slim woman in a beautiful suit. She came breezing in, carrying a purple shopping bag from Liberty's, greeting the clerk at reception. Her accent sounded Italian, but she was blonde rather than dark, reminding me of the wife of the count in white socks. She went back to the elevator, where she stood a few moments, repeatedly pressing the button and sort of prancing around. The suit was interesting: the jacket was red wool and very short, just to the waist; the skirt was black, with knife pleats, and it was rather long. Neither of these silhouettes would have been stylish at home the previous winter, but I knew that this was a woman of some higher style. Her hair, for example, was in a ponytail high up on the back of her head, the way little girls, or cheerleaders, wear it, but this did not look incongruous: it simply made her look more rich and carefree. Even the weather did not seem to have bothered her.

She carried no raincoat or umbrella. In fact, she was wearing flimsy little black patent leather sandals. She must have had a taxi or limousine take her from door to door.

Observing her, I recalled a woman I had seen earlier at St. Cuthbert's as I was leaving: a small, neat Japanese woman who looked enviably well-equipped for the sudden storm. She was standing outside on the little porch of the hotel, wearing a nice raincoat and galoshes, and she was shaking out a huge, strong-looking umbrella that I wished I knew her well enough to borrow. We smiled at each other. I knew her for a teacher; it was also apparent that she was somebody thrifty and sensible, somebody who valued, above all things, the life of the mind. Moreover, I knew at once that she was representative of the kind of people who stayed in Bloomsbury.

But presently, it was five-fifteen and time to go. As it happened, just as I was taking my leave of the Harolds, the wayward bags arrived. The manager came up to Mr. Harold and murmured something just as the first bag was wheeled through the front door on a dolly by a porter from the airline. The porter brought in a second bag, then groveled before Mr. Harold, who was magnificently mild and courteous, even giving the porter a tip but waiting to express his pleasure about having the bags back in their possession until the porter had left. Then the four of us stood around looking admiringly at the two bags—great huge things, bound with leather straps— as if they were works of art. Apparently, the Harolds always had porters to handle their luggage when they traveled; they couldn't possibly have lifted the bags themselves.

"I'll walk Caroline to the bus stop," said Franklin as we said goodbye around the luggage, which looked like two dolmens at Stonehenge.

❧ ❧ ❧

As we went down the little lane away from the hotel and up Jermyn Street, it was no longer raining but was still cloudy and very cold. I had given up any idea of going to the park. All the shops and offices on St. James Street were closed now, and there was nobody around except one derelict tottering up the other side of the street drinking out of a paper bag. I had forgotten how early London closed in the evening.

We walked up to Piccadilly. There was a little more life up there—a few pedestrians, some traffic, but no buses at the moment. We walked up Bond Street and over to Regent Street, where we looked in the windows of Liberty's, a place I was anxious to get back to. Then Franklin showed me Carnaby Street, which had been so avant-garde at one time but now just a little alley-like place with a carnival atmosphere. There was a good health food restaurant down here he wanted to point out since you had a tough time finding healthy food in London, according to Franklin, who cited this as the city's one and only drawback.

"I envy you, just getting here," Franklin said, getting a little mottled on the face and neck. "There's so much going on."

Walking down Carnaby Street, I asked Franklin more about his writing. He had tried to write, he said with an anguished expression, but he just couldn't get anything much out. He would write a page or two, then tear it up. Time was up, and he wasn't getting anywhere. Now he was going to have to support himself. The decision to go to law school had been preceded by much inner turmoil, but he finally made it in the belief that it did not mean giving up writing. He planned to practice somewhere quiet, he said, maybe in Covington or Mandeville. He would practice law in the morning and write in the afternoons.

"That sounds so nice. I wish you much luck and success," I said, having the pleasing image of the rusticated Franklin contemplating life in some old-fashioned-looking office across the lake, his feet up on an antique desk, warm sun coming in the window.

"No, no, I'm still flailing," Franklin said, stopping in the middle of Carnaby Street, shaking his head miserably.

On the bus back to Bloomsbury, I pondered the terrible word "flailing." I was making a brave show of having work to do, but, in fact, I was flailing too. If I could do anything I wanted to, I would be a writer, just as Franklin wanted to be, but I had no talent. I had tried to write a story once, but it had been a miserable experience. I had just drifted into graduate school in English and then gotten a job teaching English because all I really wanted to do in this world was read fiction. I really had been lucky to get the job in Barston, which was near enough to my family without being too close. I had a pleasant life in Barston. It was a clean, neat town, and, while it did not have much to offer apart from the university (a rather plain place with red brick buildings), everyone agreed that it was free from the problems of big cities like New Orleans. It was certainly safe. And the school was fine—the department was really going places under Charles's leadership—even though at present my teaching responsibilities were mostly required courses for freshmen and sophomores, what they called spadework. There was not much demand for more specialized upper-level courses, as very few people majored in English at NCLU, where the big major was engineering.

On the whole, my students were mediocre. You couldn't even get them to appreciate Jane Austen. The previous fall, when I'd been laboring to teach *Emma* to a class of sophomores, one of them came up afterward and said, kindly, "I can tell you really like this book, Dr. Landry, but we . . . , well, they had time to read long, drawn-out writing like this back in the nineteenth century, but we just don't have the time."

"I see!" I said perkily, unable to come up with any suitable rejoinder to this egregious statement. Later that day, I saw this scholar in a car on campus, driving slowly down a hill, trailing a girl walking down the sidewalk. He was whistling at her, a long, low wolf whistle, and I couldn't help hoping he would run into a bridge abutment.

Of course, not all my students were mediocre, but this sort of boy set the tone. I thought people I had gone to school with at Whittaker were far better students, although even they didn't measure up to my ideal. My idea of "students" came from some young people I had seen at a Prom Concert in 1972 at the Royal Albert Hall. The group from Whittaker had sat up in the balcony, but these other young people stood en masse on the floor below, *stood* for the entire performance. When the conductor came out, they roared. When the orchestra played "Pomp and Circumstance," they sang along, each one seeming to know the words—I never even knew it had words—and throughout the concert, they responded to everything with a show of passionate enthusiasm. They were held in by ropes, but they pushed against them, and sometimes it seemed that they were going to break through in their hunger for aesthetic experience. When I asked MacPherson who they were, he said carelessly, "Oh, students." Students! The word had a noble sound, suggesting the kind of young people who in earlier times would have stood for hours to see some hero of theirs pass down the street in a carriage, even in a cold rain, I thought now, looking out at Piccadilly from the bus.

But such passions seemed anachronistic now when the word "student" made you think of drugs. I turned to a consideration of the gentle, sheltered life Franklin needed to foster his writing, but I knew NCLU couldn't offer that. He would be so discouraged by the students and then, too, so oppressed by the pressure to produce scholarly work.

But I didn't want to think about my life back home here in London. Looking out of the bus, I heartily wished that I could simply explore the great city without any responsibilities or worries, like the lady with the ponytail. But there was no getting out of it: tomorrow morning I had to go to the British Museum. I had to "learn the terrible truth," as I thought of it then.

PART TWO

THE SEARCH FOR EMERALD GLOVER

Chapter 5

The first time I had ever seen the name "Emerald Glover" was the previous fall in a biography of one of the Stracheys. I had undertaken to review this tome, along with eight or nine other new books on Bloomsbury, for the NCLU literary journal *The Piney Review*. I was not looking forward to reading it, having had, by this time, a surfeit of Bloomsbury lore. Actually, I was just looking at the pictures when my attention was caught by one taken at a house party at Garsington, the country home of Lady Ottoline Morrell. Everyone was in costume in the picture: Lady Ottoline was a Turkish pasha, Lytton Strachey was Pierrot, and so forth. But amid the regular Bloomsbury crowd, there was an unfamiliar woman, small and bright-eyed, wearing a long, ruffled dress in the antebellum mode and a broad-brimmed straw hat. The book did not offer much information about this mysterious character. The caption named her as Emerald Glover, and the text mentioned her only in passing as "a novelist from the American South."

Intrigued, I checked for works by this unknown writer in the NCLU library and was surprised to find listings in the card catalog for four books—*Sunset on the Savana, Café of Sorrows, Guns at Noon*, and *Plantation Trace*. I was even more astonished when I actually found all four books way back in the stacks. The four Glovers were packed tightly on the shelf and so dusty it looked as if they hadn't been touched in years. I extricated one of the books and opened the spotty pages. Unfortunately, it had no jacket with information about Emerald Glover, nor did it have a blurb from a jacket pasted in the front or back. There was no introduction. The publisher was some obscure firm in Philadelphia named Farquhar and Sons, the date 1924, but it had originally been published in London in 1922, and that was all I could learn before I began to read, leaning up against a wall in that forgotten wing of the library, my nose swelling up from the mold. I had feared that Emerald Glover's books were historical romances (those titles!), but as I read, I realized that this Emerald Glover had done some good, clear writing, and the descriptions rang true.

I checked the books out, finishing the first in the series, *Plantation Trace*, sometime early the next morning. Its protagonist, Marie, grows up in a little town in Louisiana which had once had a fine plantation but which is now just a poor farming community with just a church and a couple of stores. Marie's father is a farmer so poor that Marie wears dresses made out of flour sacks.

"Have you ever heard of Emerald Glover?" I asked the editor of *The Piney Review* the next morning. This was Ed Schwartz. "She wrote this novel called *Plantation Trace* that first came out in 1922, and it's set in Louisiana, probably south Louisiana," I said, recalling Spanish moss on the trees.

But Ed had not heard of her, nor had anybody else in the department, including Gladys Baker, the resident expert on Louisiana literature. I knew, of course, that Emerald Glover might never have been to Louisiana, might simply have set her story there, but from the first, I believed that *Plantation Trace* and the other three books in the quartet were autobiographical. Certainly the heroine, who had a different name in each novel but who was definitely the same intriguing girl, had the sound and feel of a real girl in Louisiana. I found her very appealing. She read a lot, and she cut off her own hair one time, just as I had done (to quote the mother of Marie, "It looks like the rats have been suckin' on it.") She was more adventurous than I had ever been. In *Plantation Trace* she smoked little cigars and often slept in the woods. In *Guns at Noon* (1924), about the Great War, she worked in a London hospital nursing the troops. She called herself "Jasmine" in this book, and it ended with her marriage to a handsome English officer. In *Café of Sorrows*, published in 1930, the spunky girl, now "Ariel," took part in the decadent literary life of post-war England and France, mainly France, although there were some scenes which took place in England, a few in London, and one at a country house which sounded very much like Garsington. (I thought I saw portraits of Virginia Woolf and Lytton Strachey in certain attenuated, acerbic figures who were not nice to Ariel.) Finally, in *Sunset on the Savana* (1935), the heroine, now "Rachel," found herself totally disillusioned with Europe and turned her back on all of it, going to Africa to raise flowers. She was alone in this last book: Jasmine had married an Englishman, but Ariel had left him to go to Paris, where she had a number of lovers; Rachel, however, was disillusioned with men as well as with Europe and emigrated to the highlands Kenya, where she worked on a flower farm.

They were not particularly original, these four novels, but I had been studying the Bloomsbury Group for so long I was tired of originality. Besides, the books were beautifully written, in my judgment, and I liked the stories too. Emerald

Glover had traveled everywhere without protection or support; she wore unusual clothes, even men's clothes at times; and she loved many men, then left them without apparent regret. Indeed, she did not seem to have an ordinary conscience, except, in the way of writers and other artists, for the big things like war and peace.

This was a rather arid time for me professionally, and it occurred to me that Emerald Glover might conceivably be the subject of a scholarly work. Exploration in the files and indices of the NCLU library did not turn up any books or scholarly articles about her. I did find a few reviews in old magazines (these were really moldy), but they were the casual, discursive type of criticism, the sort of old-fashioned stuff that just discusses the plot. As far as modern literary scholarship was concerned, Emerald Glover was extinct. For the first time in a very long while, I felt some scholarly excitement. But I had to check further, of course: I wrote that publisher in Philadelphia, though I doubted very much that such a firm still existed. I also wrote people I knew at LSU and Tulane, as well as at universities in Mississippi and Alabama, even Georgia, in case Emerald Glover had just said "Louisiana" in the books to disguise real people and places but was really from one of those other Southern states and well-known there, with statues of her and things named after her, or even a home place open to the public.

As it turned out, none of my colleagues at other universities had any information on Emerald Glover, but after three or four weeks, I received this letter from Philadelphia.

Dear Professor Landry:

In response to your inquiry about Emerald Glover, I have gone through our files and have come up with some information that might be of help to you.

The only contact our firm ever had with this author, who was published originally in England, by the way, was to send royalty checks to her in London at 51 Red Lion Square. Perhaps she died there, or at any rate moved, as the last two checks our firm sent to her were returned marked "Addressee unknown."

I have become quite intrigued with this Emerald Glover as a result of your inquiry and put your question to my father-in-law, William Farquhar, who, even though he is ninety years of age, has a good memory and a strong interest in the past. He remembered the name Emerald Glover and remembered her books, which he has in his library at home and which gave him, he says, "the liveliest pleasure." He even remembers having a "romantic interest" in Emerald Glover and wanting to meet her, although he never did.

By the way, it may interest you to know that the sales figures for Emerald Glover's four books were very low: her total earnings for them was $425.73, which was computed on the basis of ten percent of each volume sold. It appears that the series had been a much bigger seller in England, as indicated by a letter in our files from James P. Murdoch, the London literary agent who handled Miss Glover's affairs with us and also with her English publisher, Cockerham & Gatehill, Ltd. Unfortunately for your purposes James P. Murdoch died in 1940, and Cockerham & Gatehill went bankrupt in 1946, according to our records.

I wish you success in your endeavor. If I can be of any further assistance, I am at your service.

Very truly yours,
Thomas P. Collins

She was published in England; she lived in London for a while! This new information set me dreaming about going there to do research, which in my mind consisted of looking around old bookshops or going up steps to some grand door in Red Lion Square, raising a brass knocker. But the main thing (for I received this letter the previous fall) was to sit on a bench in St. James Park, listening to a band. It seemed like a pipe dream to me at that point, but when I mentioned the idea to Charles, he took it very seriously, whisking me into his office, asking me questions, and writing down my answers on a legal pad attached to a long clipboard. He said the British Library was the place to look into this. It had a copy of everything published in the British Isles, also an extraordinary collection of papers relating to those publications, including letters, diaries, and manuscripts. If Emerald Glover had ever published in England, there was good reason to believe that all her work and papers relating to her work would be in the British Library.

"I'll write and find out," I said efficiently.

"Oh no, no, no, no, no," said Charles, with a light laugh (he was very wise in the ways of the scholar). "The British Library doesn't have time to send lists of their holdings to scholars all over the world. Why, they might not even *have* a list of all their holdings! That's how much the British Library has!"

The only sensible thing to do was go to the Reading Room of the British Library, which was in the British Museum, and see for myself, Charles said, telling me then that he was seriously looking into the idea of a charter flight to take NCLU people to London the following summer. Travel was essential to the research of a university. I could not believe it at first. I had wanted to go back to England every summer since 1972, but first there was graduate school, when I was either going to school or working to pay for school, and then there was my job at NCLU, which began in the summer of 1978 and had included heavy duties the fall of 1979. I had not really been anywhere of significance since the summer of 1972. And now Charles spoke of London as a scholarly obligation, going on to speak about thrifty travel arrangements and possible grant money to foot the whole bill. And in due course, I did get a substantial grant; he did set up the charter flight; I made reservations and got actual tickets I could hold in my hand. I even began to believe in the research a little, fantasizing about finding some cache of materials on Emerald Glover, which would serve as the basis for a hefty book.

Actually, this fantasy of a cache was not too farfetched. Edwina Warren, now the world's leading authority on Lady Hermione Hart, had started out with a manuscript she had found one summer in the Bodleian Library. She planned to spend most of her time this trip in the British Library, which had recently acquired more of Lady Hermione's papers. And I knew another story about a cache. Not too long before this, I had met a friend of the Nicholsons at one of their cocktail parties: Jasper Billings, a professor of English at the University of Texas and the internationally known authority on the Victorian poet Ernest Hobson. He told me of an important experience he'd had while researching his celebrated biography. He had gone over to London to see what the British Library had on Hobson, the way you have to do. Presenting himself to the guard at the Manuscript Room, he said something such as, "I'd like to see what you have on Ernest Hobson," and the guard had said, "Well! If you're interested in Ernest Hobson, you'd better have a look at what's in this drawer!" Whereupon the guard had fetched a big fat stack of letters to and from Ernest Hobson, the existence of which Professor Billings had not even dreamed before that moment. "A gift from heaven," said Professor Billings, looking upward.

Of course, I did not really believe in such a cache of materials. I usually imagined getting all the way over to the British Library and finding nothing but the same four books the NCLU library had, then having to wonder how I could look busy for three whole weeks, and whether I would be honor-bound to give the grant money back, and of course whether, given the failure to corner my own writer for scholarly research, I could hold on to my job. I woke up at three o'clock the morning after arriving in London in this horror-stricken frame of mind. The evening before, I had been so tired upon returning from having tea with the Harolds that I had gone straight to bed, thinking I would sleep forever. But here I was, wide awake at three o'clock in the morning. I sat straight up in bed and saw Edwina lying over in the other bed, secure in the knowledge of the cache awaiting her the next morning, snoring raggedly.

After a few minutes of trying to go back to sleep, I got up and opened the orange curtains. It was actually getting light. The sky was dark gray over the terrace across the street, but just over the chimney pots, the sky was slightly pink. People always talk about the rooftops of Paris, but I thought these rooftops were far more beautiful. It had been raining—the street was wet—but the growing pinkness over the chimney pots suggested that the sun might come out today.

In about six hours now, Charles was going to escort me over to the British Library (you couldn't just walk in, of course), and together we would find out the terrible truth. I worried about this for a while but then got cold and crawled back under the orange covers, sinking into a refreshing sleep.

CHAPTER 6

Edwina went on ahead to the British Museum the next morning. She had been terribly cheerful at breakfast, I reflected as I waited for Charles in the lobby of St. Cuthbert's, but then Edwina was always cheerful. She had her life in excellent order. Her wedding to the engineering professor was set for early October, and the invitations, already addressed, lay in neat stacks on her dining table back home.

Her professional life was in excellent order too. After all, she was the authority on Lady Hermne Hart, an obscure eighteenth-century Englishwoman who, unbeknownst to anyone, even members of her own immediate family, had written poems and kept diaries. Edwina made her initial discovery of Lady Hermione's works on her junior year abroad from St. Mary's, a girls' school in Indiana. She edited the poems, whatever that means exactly, publishing them with an introduction by herself. Already established as a scholar, Edwina went on to graduate school at Yale, publishing more and more of Lady Hermione's work, which continued to surface here and there in libraries and at auctions. Somehow Edwina had managed to get a hammerlock on Lady Hermione, whom she always referred to in just this familiar way—"Lady Hermione"—as if she were a personal friend, which in a sense she was, having, from the grave, provided Edwina with the material with which she was so steadily advancing her career. Edwina had come to NCLU in 1977, one year before I had; and the spring just past, at the same time as Jerry Braswell was fired, Edwina was promoted to associate professor, with that most sought-after of prizes, tenure. In contrast to myself, Edwina had not been able to wait to get to the British Library this morning, where a newly discovered diary awaited her.

Now Charles came down the stairs buttoning his Burberry raincoat, adjusting his Burberry scarf. I felt a thrill of nervousness when I saw him.

"Good morning, Caroline."

"Good morning, Charles. How are you this morning?"

Like Edwina, Charles was in tip-top shape. He was tall and thin, with bright brown eyes and a thick brown mustache that reminded me of the brush with which the girl who served us breakfast swept away the crumbs from the tablecloths. He saw my difficulty with the umbrella and said, with some gallantry, "Here, let's use mine." He started to open his giant multi-colored model, the kind you take to the stadium.

Charles had been the chairman of the English Department at NCLU for a year now, replacing old Dr. Harkrider, who had finally retired as chairman after some forty years. Dr. Harkrider was a local man who had himself gone to NCLU as an undergraduate back when it had been called the College of North Central Louisiana and was just a simple school rather than a "university" with graduate programs and important research. Dr. Harkrider had not seemed to be concerned with "research." We became friends. England was one of the things we had in common—Dr. Harkrider and his wife were also ardent Anglophiles and would have come on this trip had Mrs. Harkrider not been ill—and I still went over to the Harkriders' on Sunday afternoons sometimes to have tea and admire their camellias. In fact, it was the Harkriders who were keeping Ottoline, my cat, while I was gone.

Dr. Harkrider had been a popular teacher as well as a popular chairman—"Tea at the Harkriders" had been a monthly event—but of course, now it was a new day, and in looking for his successor NCLU had wanted not only an able administrator but a scholar of national or even international reputation, someone to "bring the department into the twentieth century," as someone had put it.

The man they found was Charles Nicholson, vice-provost of a small college in Connecticut and a leading authority on Tobias Smollett. He was a graduate of Williams and Harvard; his wife, Allison, was a graduate of Vassar College. I found the Nicholsons very congenial, and not the least condescending about the town of Barston, or the school, although I looked for signs of condescension, recalling that Easterners I had met in graduate school at the University of North Carolina seemed to think that Chapel Hill was on the southernmost border of civilization. Conscious of how far south of Chapel Hill the little town of Barston was, I wondered why Charles and Allison Nicholson had been willing to descend from New England all the way to this nether point on the globe, much as I always wondered how English people back in the nineteenth century could bear to leave England for India or Ceylon. But, like the English, the Nicholsons seemed to make the best of it.

They bought an old house on Main Street and were still in the process of redoing it (this was fairly original for Barston, the idea of doing over old houses in the central district not having previously occurred to the citizens of Barston). Also, Charles had started a soccer team for their two boys, and Allison could often be seen driving the members of the team around town in her resplendent blue Volvo station wagon with its immaculate mud flaps and gleaming chrome luggage rack that winked in the sun. Professionally, too, Charles made many changes in the direction of improvement and progress. Some I did not care for—the "tenure track," for example—but most of them I did, like a lecture series he started and, of course, the charter flight. Charles had his detractors (Jerry Braswell, for instance), but he made things happen: if it weren't for him, I thought as I went out the front door of St. Cuthbert's, sheltered from the rain by his huge, strong umbrella, I wouldn't be here right now.

As we walked down Bedford Place, Charles inquired solicitously about whether I was rested after the long trip, how I liked the hotel, what plays I wanted to see. I chatted easily with Charles, but at the same time, I felt terribly nervous. There were many ways I could distinguish my case from that of Jerry Braswell, who not only had not published anything in the way of literary scholarship while he was at NCLU but openly did not give a damn about publishing anything scholarly, but just then I felt like the most unworthy candidate for promotion ever to come under review. Charles believed that no one should stay at NCLU more than four years if he or she had not written two substantial critical articles or, better yet, a "book-length publishable manuscript," and since I had been there *two* years already and had published only that review, I felt that behind this facade of pleasant conversation, he must really be thinking, "This is it! There better be something of value in this Emerald Glover project, or Caroline Landry is washed up in my department!"

But I had something else on my mind besides tenure: I might see MacPherson in the British Museum. I have mentioned that MacPherson was along on the junior trip from Whittaker as one of our chaperons, although I'm afraid it was absurd to put MacPherson in charge of anything. He was a novelist rather than an academic, and he had been writer-in-residence at Whittaker the previous year. He had been to England many times—in fact, he had been a Rhodes Scholar—which is why he was made a chaperon, I suppose, and I imagined he would continue to come to England on a regular basis. Of all the things I felt I was putting myself in the way of by coming to England, MacPherson was one of the chief, I admitted to myself as I negotiated the puddles on the sidewalk and the rivulets by the curbs, trying, meanwhile, to carry on an intelligent conversation with Charles. I tried to stay my nerves by focusing outward on Bloomsbury. "Bloomsbury" sounds so floral and lighthearted, but actually, this part of it around the British Museum and the University of London looks like a collection of banks.

We reached the museum. Proceeding over the broad forecourt and through its monumental Ionic columns, we entered the front hall thronged with people in wet raincoats to find the tiny office where I filled out the form for my ticket to the Reading Room. We showed our tickets to the guard at the door, and I stood on the threshold, gazing up at the great round room, with its rows of high-backed desks radiating from a central station and, up the walls, countless rows of countless books. I dimly recalled a passage in *Orlando* where Virginia Woolf compares the dome of the British Museum to Shakespeare's brow and asserts that the Reading Room is "pure mind," or some such metaphor (anyhow, the analysis is quite brilliant). I also recalled the oft-repeated fact that Karl Marx read here every day during the time he was in London, which—although I did not know very much about the work of Karl Marx and did not admire what I knew—also seemed very impressive at that moment and added luster to the fantastic domed space.

A few moments later, feeling somewhat like a treasure hunter who has come thousands of miles over the cruelest terrain (treacherous seas, hostile deserts) and who at last has his hands on the casket for which he has searched so long and lifts the lid, I consulted a large scrapbook for "Glover, Emerald." I had been afraid there would be no entries for Emerald Glover (this would be the worst, this would be like an empty casket, with worms in it), but in fact, there were four entries for Emerald Glover, one for each of the books in the quartet, entries which looked almost exactly like the four cards in the NCLU library. I felt a cut of disappointment, for I had dared to hope that Emerald Glover had published more books in England, where she was appreciated, than in America, where she wasn't. Nor were there any books about her, thank goodness.

"Just the four novels," I whispered to Charles, who was standing by. "Nothing more."

"Shall we walk over to the Manuscript Room, then?" he whispered gravely, escorting me through room after room of literary treasures in glass cases, the wooden floors creaking like the floors of an old country store.

"I'd like to see what you have on Emerald Glover," I said to the guard in the Manuscript Room, in hopeful paraphrase of Professor Billings. I exchanged a significant look with Charles. The guard went away, and as I waited for his return, I could see Edwina ensconced at a table with papers spread out all around her, hard at work, like a squirrel storing nuts for the winter. I longed to be able to join her, but the guard came back too soon, carrying no cache.

"Sorry!" he said in that chirpy English way, with no note of apology. "Nothing on that person here!"

∾ ∾ ∾

"I was afraid of that," I told Charles dolefully.

"Oh, well," said Charles, "there are still plenty of places to look," as if to say, even if there is no cache of treasure, you can still seek veins of precious metals in the rock and work them with a pickax. He walked me back to the Reading Room, mentioning some of the major indexes to English periodicals and newspapers. Then he took his leave to pursue some Smollett inquiry.

I knew I should take up the pickax, so to speak, but I did not have the strength. In fact, I was suffering from jet lag, although I didn't think of this at the time. I merely thought myself inadequate as a scholar when I compared my lethargy to the zest with which Charles had marched away toward his task, not to mention Edwina. Feeling a little inferior, I decided to go to the coffee shop before tackling the first index. At first, I couldn't find the coffee shop, which seemed to have moved, but a helpful guard directed me through the King's Library (a long, grand room which housed the first books ever printed), then down some stairs and out a door, down some other steps akin to a fire escape, which put you outside for a few wild moments in the damp, gusty wind. The new coffee shop was extraordinarily nice, I thought as I got some tea, but then I always did love the coffee shops of museums.

The coffee shop was crowded, and I looked at the patrons with interest. I was on the *qui vive* for MacPherson, who liked to hold forth in coffee shops. But he was not there, and I relaxed a little. The patrons were surprisingly homogenous.

The people back in the halls of the museum had seemed to be tourists, mostly, but the people in the coffee shop seemed to be scholars. I based this conclusion on the solitariness of these people (most sat alone), also the scruffiness. (Charles, who wore navy blue blazers and tan or gray trousers with a knife-sharp crease, was that rare bird, the elegant scholar.)

I drank my tea and watched the scholars, rather hoping that I too would not be immediately classified as a scholar, wondering what or whom they were here to study. Obviously, these scholars, many of whom were brown-skinned, had come from all over the world. I was just musing like this when suddenly I had the horrible thought that one of these scholars might also be here in pursuit of material on Emerald Glover. This was a reasonable possibility. I knew there was worldwide interest in English literature (I could remember articles on Virginia Woolf by people from the most surprising places such as Japan, Brazil, Iceland, for heaven's sake). Why had the idea of a rival for the Emerald Glover material not occurred to me before? How could I have thought I was the only one to have noticed that enigmatic picture in the Strachey biography? Now I imagined some young man in the jungles of Ceylon (I knew it was "Sri Lanka" now, but I still thought of it as Leonard Woolf's Ceylon), some young man in a village in the jungle, some nascent scholar staring in fascination at the picture of the enigmatic white woman in the big floppy hat, the novelist from the American South, meanwhile chewing on his thumbnail and plotting how to get to London and the British Library. I gulped down my tea and leapt up, looking fearfully at all the heads bent over their tea. I ran back outside, up the stairs, past the incunabula.

In the Reading Room, I located the most recent issue of the main periodical index Charles had mentioned, figuring there had been just enough time since the appearance of the

Strachey biography for one of these enterprising scholars to have published an important article, but there was no listing for "Glover, Emerald" in the spring of 1980 or fall 1979, nor yet in the summer of 1979. I began to relax when I reached spring 1978, as this antedated the provocative Strachey tome, which was the only publicity Emerald Glover had received in modern times, as far as I knew, and I was tempted to jump back to 1940 or so, that is, a couple of years after Emerald Glover's probable death. But I decided against such expediency; I decided to be thorough, the image of Charles writing things in his neat little zigzag writing on a sheet in his clipboard coming to mind. I didn't want to have to backtrack later. And so I looked carefully through this index, volume after volume, rather as if I were panning for gold, when suddenly my eye was caught by "Glover, Emerald," and a reference to an article called "Artists of Northumberland." It appeared in something called *Our England*, the issue for March 1965.

Must be a daughter, I thought with interest. Of course, a daughter probably wouldn't have the very same name, I reflected as I went to the main desk in the Reading Room to request this copy of *Our England*. More likely it was a niece who was named after her famous aunt, or a granddaughter. In any case, it might be somebody I could talk to about the original Emerald Glover, I thought, recalling that Ernest Hobson had a grandson who invited Professor Billings for several happy weekends at his country house in Wiltshire. While I was waiting for the back issue of *Our England*, I envisioned Emerald Glover's niece or granddaughter, a ruddy-cheeked and obliging countrywoman who just happened to have this old trunk that had belonged to her American forebear.

Our England was not a scholarly publication but rather a picture magazine with a large format, something on the order of *Life*. It had been bound into a volume so heavy and bulky I could not flip through it until I had lugged it back to my seat. There, I saw that it was a magazine that celebrated "the countryside" that everybody loved to drive around so much: the landscape, the villages. It also had features on people such as war heroes and historical figures, even literary characters. At one time or another, *Our England* had probably presented a pictorial feature on the Harolds' Stow-on-the-Wold.

When I located "Artists of Northumberland," I got a jolt. One possibility that had not entered my head was that the artist of Northumberland was Emerald Glover herself. But there she was. I was looking at a picture of a dainty crone-like lady in tweeds bending over an easel, holding onto a canvas, and there was simply no doubt that those bright eyes were the same bright eyes I had seen before. She looked very old, seventy at least, and, apart from the eyes, very frail. Her back seemed to have a hump on it; at any rate, she held her head at an unusual angle. She was perched on a hill with the easel, the patchwork countryside spread out beyond.

I plunged into the brief article:

> Northumberland is a place of infinite variety. Some of Britain's wildest scenery is to be found in its moors and crags, whilst some of its gentlest scenes are to be found along the winding river valleys of this northeastern county. It is a quiet corner of the land, almost completely unspoilt. Yet, we remember, it was the locus of some of the bloodiest moments of our history with conflicts between the Northern Peoples, the Romans, and the Danes. There is Flodden Field, where, in 1513, many brave Englishmen and Scotsmen, including King James IV, met their death . . .

But I soon began to skim rather than read, anxious to get to the part about Emerald Glover. I saw her name. It said she lived near Pelwichton, "a lovely old village that had escaped modernisation." She favored the landscapes around

Pelwichton, "the fertile valley of the River North Tyne," and she had painted a notable series of "colourful landscapes featuring Hadrian's Wall." She was an American who had published some novels in the 1920s, the article said, but she was as attached to her village in the North as if she were a native. She loved the outdoors and always painted in the open air. And that was all the text said about Emerald Glover—it then went on to an artist who specialized in Norman architecture. I looked back at the pictures, first the picture of Emerald Glover, which bore the caption, "Miss Glover at her easel on a slope of Whin Sill. The painter's greatest problem is the wind!" Then an example of Emerald Glover's painting, called *View from Housesteads*, which was full of quadrangles and looked simple, not unlike one of Cézanne's landscapes. This simplicity might, as in Cézanne's works, disguise great artistry, or it might just look like this on account of the patchwork scenery.

Emerald Glover alive in 1965! I was flabbergasted. I had never thought Emerald Glover lived beyond the 1930s, mainly because of the novels themselves: Ariel in *Café of Sorrows* and Rachel in *Sunset on the Savana* had had debilitating chest complaints suggesting tuberculosis, which had no cure in those days. But beyond this was the fact that Emerald Glover had dropped out of sight after *Sunset on the Savana*, not publishing anymore, not even collecting her royalties. She might have committed suicide, like Virginia Woolf or Sylvia Plath, only nobody ever knew. Yet here she was, only twenty years ago, and an artist, too! Could such a good writer become a good painter? Some writers painted: D. H. Lawrence, for example, Hermann Hesse, Jean Cocteau—

"Found something?" Charles whispered in my ear, causing me to start.

I displayed *Our England*.

"Pelwichton," Charles murmured. "Aren't you lucky? That's in marvelous country. Allison and I drove through there once. You ought to run up there. She might still be alive!"

"I hardly think so," I said, looking again at her picture.

"I'd write, if I were you, or try to call."

"Oh, of course I'll write, I'll write today," I said, frowning, hoping Charles didn't doubt that I was conscientious about my scholarship. A scholar at the next desk said "Shhh!"

Writing to Pelwichton was just a formality, of course. The article was only fifteen years old that day in 1980, but it seemed to belong to the distant past: for one thing, the magazine had an antique look, more like the 30s or 40s than the 60s (the British spelling—"whilst," "colourful"—contributed to this antique air). In any case, twenty years was a long time to me: in 1965, I had been twelve. Besides, if Emerald Glover weren't dead, by some miracle of nature, she would be exceedingly ancient by now (at least eighty-five) and probably bedridden, maybe even senile. I had an idea that she was unsociable: those bright eyes, which had been clever looking in the Strachey biography, maybe a touch mischievous, now looked a little wild. It might also be significant, I thought, that the pictures by the other artists of Northumberland were nice village scenes, or landscapes with animals, whereas Emerald Glover's pictures had none of the people or sheep of Northumberland, just its bare rocks and fields.

"How do you find out if somebody's dead?" I asked Charles.

"I'm not completely sure!" he said with a laugh. (There had never been any doubt about Smollett.) "Best thing is to check for an obituary."

I spent the rest of the morning following this suggestion, also checking other indices and sources of information as suggested by the attendant, an Indian man not intrigued by the mystery. All the while, I was braced for further surprises in the British Library, but nothing more came my way.

Chapter 7

Down at the end of Bedford Place, on Great Russell Street, was a red mailbox with one slot designated "London" and (I loved this) the other, "Away." The next morning I put two items in the slot for "Away."

Dear Mrs. Glover [on St. Cuthbert's letterhead]:

I have long been an admirer of your work and, in fact, am at present doing research on it at the British Library. I will be in England until July 19 and would very much like to meet you and talk with you about your work, if that is at all possible.

You may reach me here at St. Cuthbert's hotel. The telephone number is _________.

Yours sincerely,
Caroline Landry

Dear Mom [on a postcard from the British Museum picturing the Sutton Hoo helmet]:

There's a lot to do on my research project on Emerald Glover, but I assure you I am relaxing and having a good time too. We're going to see *The Mousetrap.* It's been

     A Prospect of London

running a hundred years because it's so clever. Weather
cold and wet, but I'll enjoy the excuse to shop for a British
sweater. You'd love the stores.

Saw some Newcomb pottery in the British Museum!

Love,
Carrie

The note to Emerald Glover had been hard to write,
had, in fact, required several drafts. First of all, any writing
was difficult for me. Then, this particular writing task
seemed to be an empty exercise, as Emerald Glover was no
doubt long gone. Actually, this whole question of visiting
Northumberland made me uncomfortable: down deep, I
believed a true scholar would have hopped right on the
train, regardless of any correspondence, for even if Emerald
Glover were long dead and gone, at least the scholar could
see where she had lived, maybe find people who had known
her, run down all her associations. But I would not do this,
I decided, arguing internally that Northumberland had
nothing to do with Emerald Glover's four books, which did
not use Northumberland as a setting, indeed were probably
written long before she went there. But the simple truth was, I
didn't want to leave London ("Away"). I also argued to myself
that I was accomplishing a great deal every day in the British
Library investigating the reviews of Emerald Glover in various
newspapers and magazines back in the 20s or 30s, which were
nothing very interesting but which were certainly the kind of
material upon which to base something to publish.

I dutifully stayed at the British Library until two o'clock
every day, never leaving a moment sooner, but at two o'clock
on the dot I sprang out of the door and got down to what
I really wanted to do: explore London. Every day that first
week I planned to go to another major museum such as

the National Gallery or the Tate, but sometimes I also went shopping. I had to have some warm things—a shop on Great Russell Street yielded the first and most essential of these, a sweater and a cap (Fair Isle style with a red border)—and I wanted a new raincoat since it looked like I'd be using it often. For this, I went to Harrods, where I bought an Aquascutum raincoat and a sturdy English umbrella.

Harrods was so interesting I went back twice more. It is well known how vast Harrods is and how it deals with everything you need from cradle to grave, but I saw that it was more than just a store. It was like a museum of contemporary life that displayed the finest goods in the world. I stood at the pen counter and wrote my name on a pad with a Mont Blanc Meisterstück pen, and one day I tried on a suit from the House of Chanel and a suit from Lanvin. These were too rich for my budget, but I did buy two dresses off the rack, as they say. The Food Halls had fish from foreign seas, flowers from foreign fields, and the "jewellery" department had jewels so expensive that the prices were presented in Arabic. One day in Harrods I saw the most famous young American actress of the day, not a common "movie star" but a serious actress who had gone to Yale and who, although she could be anywhere in the world she chose, was striding through Harrods with a shopping bag from the Food Halls, wearing blue jeans and big sunglasses. You also saw sheiks in white robes and, never with the sheiks, but in groups of their own, veiled women I took to be their wives, glamorous Arab women in Western dress. In one of the tearooms, for example, where I loved to sit over tea, the women would chatter with each other in Arabic, voices in a high register, turning occasionally to consult with beautiful dark-eyed children who had been off somewhere else but now ran up to say something urgent as if they were at a playground.

I also loved the Harrods version of ordinary departments. Hardware at Harrods is very absorbing, particularly the section for "knobs and knockers," where wealthy English people buy the handsome fittings for their doors. Harrods also had a photographic studio, like many department stores back home, but where American studios would display a portrait of an ordinary person or family selected because they were photogenic, Harrods displayed a photographic portrait of King Hussein.

Another thing I did was poke around the area near St. Cuthbert's Hotel, "my neighborhood," as I liked to think of it. There were some wonderful shops right around the British Museum and London University—bookshops, of course, though I was determined not to buy a bunch of books as I had in '72, knowing now that books were like lead weights in your suitcase. Later on, I would permit myself to look for copies of Emerald Glover's books in second-hand bookstores, but apart from that, I would resist all books, I vowed. I would just stay out of bookstores and browse in other kinds of stores like the narrow little shops on Montague Street that were clearly not meant for tourists but rather for the highly civilized people who lived and worked around there. One of these was a stationer's. I went in there one afternoon and spent a long, happy time, finally purchasing several treasures manufactured in England: an unusual ballpoint pen, three thick stenographic pads with the impressive name of "Cambridge Reporters Notebooks," and three tiny notebooks with pictures of early models of the red London buses on their little covers. The reporters' notebooks were for my research, of course, but also for my important thoughts. Right there on the sidewalk in front of the stationer's, despite the rain, I took the new pen and opened one of the ring-bound notebooks to write the words "light," "air," and "the lady with the rhubarb."

Meanwhile, I just soaked up London. Sometimes I actually had wild thoughts of staying. Some of the old terraces in my neighborhood had flats "to let." I went so far as to write down the name of a real estate agency that handled some of these flats with the idea of calling them one day, asking about prices, although I never went so far as that. I knew that Bloomsbury was no longer a place where you could get a flat for a few pounds a year, as Virginia Woolf or Emerald Glover had done. No, now this was a luxury area that only institutions and associations could afford. And how would I support myself over here? They hardly needed an American to teach British literature. Why, the very derelicts in the squares probably knew Shakespeare better than I did. Of course, you could marry a British citizen. In 1972 we had talked a lot about the possibility of "meeting somebody" on the trip, and some girls *had* met boys, or vice versa. (Some of us had struck up a conversation with some kids from the University of Manchester at the Prom Concert, for instance, and this had led to an actual date for some girls less shy than I, even the exchange of a few letters.) I wondered whether I would be willing to marry somebody in order to stay over here. Probably not, I decided. No, I would have to take the route of a work permit and papers that would allow me to stay awhile. I had heard stories about Americans who had tried this. One couple I had known in Chapel Hill had tried to move here and open a bookstore in Hampstead, but they had gone home after a year. And I had read in the paper about a girl who was part owner of a successful record store in Middleton who had actually moved to London for a few months before her business in Middleton, which had been supplying her with the fabulous sums you needed to sustain yourself here, had failed and she had to return home. Anna, the girl who served us breakfast, was from New Zealand, and she could stay only a year, she had told us, before she had to find a place where she afford to go back to college.

A couple of evenings, I went to the theater with some of the Barston people. Nothing really good was on, apart from *Nicholas Nickleby*, which was completely sold out—everybody agreed that the theatre in London was in sad decline these days, nothing like 1972, when you had fifteen or twenty plays to choose from and the tickets were a pittance. One night some of us went to *Monty Python and the Holy Grail* at a cinema in Leicester Square. But one evening, I just went off by myself to walk around Chelsea. It had been raining all day, but it was not raining as I stood on Shaftesbury Avenue waiting for a bus. The sky was even a bluish sort of gray, and there was a fresh, damp wind. It was almost twilight.

Across the street from the bus stop was a theater where a revival of *Oklahoma!* was about to open (this was the kind of leftover season they were having in the London theatre that summer—*Oklahoma!* was on, and *The King and I*). As I watched for my bus, I heard, over the screeches and hoots of the London traffic, a good baritone voice singing "Oh, What a Beautiful Morning." I looked up and saw a man in a second-floor window, moving around the brightly lit room as he sang. Then, as if sensing himself watched, he came to the window and looked down at me, grinning. He was handsome, with dark hair and a dark mustache. He continued to sing with his arms stretched out. He appeared to be nude! Oh, he probably had on a towel, but I couldn't see it from down on the street, and it was obvious from the way he was spreading his arms and grinning that he wanted me to think he was naked. So I laughed and pretended to cover my eyes, waving as I boarded the bus.

Chelsea, with its pretty terraces and flowery gardens, looked just as I had once expected Bloomsbury to look.

I got off the bus at the Chelsea Embankment, by the river, found Cheyne Walk, then went up Cheyne Row. Blue circular plaques distinguished the houses where famous people had lived. I had made a list of famous addresses—Rossetti's house, Whistler's house, Carlyle's house—but I soon forgot all about the list in the pleasure of wandering the narrow little streets, just taking the blue plaques as they came. The houses were attached to each other, but the rows were more informal than the terraces in Bloomsbury, and more artistic, I thought, as the roofs of the houses varied in height. Whereas in Bloomsbury, the owner of each house could express his individuality only in the color of his door and the type of door knocker, here in this community of artists and other interesting people (I was sure that each resident of Chelsea was such a person), the whole house seemed to express the delightful taste of the resident, particularly by its color, even though it was part of a row. Some were painted a lovely soft color—blue or rose or green or yellow—with no house, seemingly, the exact same shade as any other. Every one of the houses had a flower garden.

I went up and down the streets, whichever way I felt like going, stopping whenever I turned a corner and saw more ordinary housing such as a red-brick terrace, turning back into the more picturesque quarter. But after a while, the twilight faded, and a soft mist or drizzle started, and I saw that it was time to orient myself and find a bus. I took out my map. As I made my way back to the Embankment, I saw the most memorable house of all.

This particular street in Chelsea had something I had never seen in London before: some detached houses, that is, houses standing by themselves on what at home would be called their own lot, although here it would surely be called something else. The house I liked was a two-story, covered with brown shingles. This made the house all the more unusual. One day Sid Beckwith explained why most buildings in London are stone or brick: practically everything in London had burned down in the Great Fire of 1666, and after that, new buildings had to be made of non-flammable brick, stone, or slate. Well, here was a house that broke the rule, or was exempt for some reason. It was behind a hedge about six feet tall. You could not see it clearly from the sidewalk but could only catch tantalizing glimpses through the leaves. But if you jumped up to see over the hedge, you could spy a man and a woman having dinner in a brightly lit room. The house had a thick stand of trees around it, and in the gloomy dusk it seemed to be in some Scandinavian wood rather than the heart of London. I lingered there, jumping up and down to get a better look. The dining table was long, with the couple dining intimately at one end of it. And—this was fascinating—over in a far corner, near a fireplace, was a music stand with what must be a score open on it. This was where some world-renowned musical virtuoso lived, I concluded, or some famous conductor.

But presently, I went on and found my bus, climbing up to the top, as was my habit, making my way down to the front. I always found bus rides completely absorbing in London. You seemed to dive right into traffic; that is, the flat face of the bus would shove right up to the next vehicle in the heavy traffic of the London streets. And while the driver down below was probably aware of a wide margin of safety, I would think, up above, that we were surely going to collide. Bicyclists down below seemed to be in particular peril from the huge darting bus and also from taxis, which were distinguished by their speed and apparent recklessness. The underground was also very exciting: I always felt half lost in the crowded Tube stations, dazzled by the posters for unfamiliar British products as well as posters for all the plays and films you could go see (even mediocre American films looked irresistible in these advertisements), ruffled and stimulated by the fierce winds that came up the escalators and stairs and out of the black tunnels from which the train would zip. All of London was dominated by transport. The streets had this special smell of diesel exhaust, which I knew was probably poisonous but which I nonetheless inhaled rapturously at every opportunity, calling it "Eau de London." And you could always hear a jet passing overhead, the peculiar sound (a plunging, tearing sound which came to you unevenly, sometimes loud, other times soft, nothing like the straight course of the plane you could see, and different, somehow, from the sound of jets flying over other places) indicative of the countless people coming into London or having to leave it.

Frankly, I was amazed whenever I talked with anybody for whom just being in London was not a sufficient end in life. The first time I rode the underground on this trip, I encountered such a person. I had bought my token in Holborn Station and was standing at the turnstile looking for the slot to put it in when a man, who seemed to come out of nowhere, took it out of my hand, inserted it in the proper place, and ushered me through. "First time on the Tube?" asked the man, whose actions might have been thought intrusive or even rude had he not been a fellow American and, furthermore, an American man of substantial position, an executive. He was a fit, silver-haired man in a fine suit, very much on the model of Mr. Harold, and he carried a briefcase so well-used that it testified to long years of being in charge.

"This time, yes," said I, to show I was no rube.

On the way down the two remarkably steep escalators in Holborn Station, the American executive took this opportunity to confide in a compatriot. He was with an oil company, he said, and had been living in London two years. Before that he had lived in Paris and Athens and some other glamorous cities on the Continent, but all he really wanted, he told me, was to get back home to Houston. He wanted to go to an Astros' game and eat a hot dog. Well, I *was* confounded! I suppose I could see how you would get tired of living here. The winters were dark and damp, I had read, and the plumbing would probably get to you after a while. In this man's case, there was the additional factor of his having already spent several years abroad in other places which undoubtedly had their own peculiar inconveniences, but Houston! Louisiana was at least a green state but Texas was brown and sunbaked, to my mind, and Houston, where my brother Mike and his family had lived for five years, was a chromium and steel sort of city surrounded and crisscrossed by hot expressways. How could you be in London, so gray and full of character, and miss Houston? I wanted to interrogate the man about this, but at the bottom of the second escalator, he scurried off in some other direction, looking at his watch like the White Rabbit. I often thought of Alice in Wonderland in a Tube station.

One other person I talked with that first week was homesick: Carol Beckwith. Of course, the Beckwiths were a special case, both of them from Barston or little towns near Barston, older people of about sixty years of age who had never had children. Indeed, Sid was one of the few really local people left in the department, by which I mean people who had graduated from NCLU or LSU, and I thought of him as the last of a dying breed now that college teaching was so different, now that NCLU no longer even considered hiring local graduates, and now that the faculty had people from all over the country, including the most glorious parts of the East, who were apparently eager to teach down at NCLU. Now Sid *did* love

London. His area was seventeenth-century British literature (he didn't have his own author, in the modern manner), and he loved to read first editions in the British Museum, then go out and look at old churches, Sir Christopher Wren being his special hero. But Carol did not share these enthusiasms. Instead, she took up residence in the hotel in a way that was different from everybody else. In the mornings all the rest of us had breakfast and went out somewhere, either to work in a museum or library or to visit another museum or point of interest. But Carol would establish herself in what by now we all called the telly room as if she were in a sitting room at home. She wore an at-home sort of outfit, which included an old cardigan sweater and bedroom slippers. She took her pot of tea in there and *The Times.* I know she went out in the evenings—she and Sid were always attending chamber music concerts at the Wigmore Hall or plays at the National Theatre. The Beckwiths were also high on Gilbert & Sullivan, always telling the rest of us we just had to go to the Sadler's Wells Theatre to see the "D'Oyley Carte," which, although it had a handsome royal blue poster that was among the most eye-catching in the Tube stations, they said was in financial trouble and about to go bankrupt. Anyway, Carol may well have gone out later in the mornings or in the afternoons, but I know for a fact that she followed several British soap operas, and I had the impression that she spent the whole day in the telly room, which was lit with just one dim lamp these dark, wet mornings. I stopped in for a moment one day, and Carol, a spindly person with limp gray hair, confessed that she was "a little down." "I always feel a little lost the first few days," she said. "I can't stop worrying about the house."

That too confounded me, because from the vantage point of London, like this, my own dwelling in Barston—indeed, Barston itself—did not seem to exist. I tried to visualize Barston. Really, apart from the red-brick university, Barston was no different from other towns in north Louisiana. It had a main street with old-fashioned storefronts for businesses selling things like feed and religious books, and its most imposing buildings were the Savings and Loan and the funeral home. Away from the main street, there were several different neighborhoods, the most prosperous of which was sort of out in the woods (this is where the president of the Savings and Loan and the director of the funeral home lived), the rest of which were very modest. The typical house in Barston was built right after the Second World War and was a white frame with a screened-in front porch. The Beckwiths lived in such an unremarkable house. On the other hand, most single people, like Mavis Adams and I, lived in one of the few apartment buildings in town, the Bienville Towers. Fairly new, the Bienville Towers had balconies and green shutters intended to evoke the architectural atmosphere of New Orleans. Having none of its own, Barston had to evoke the atmosphere of someplace! There was very little to do in Barston, apart from movies, an occasional play at the university, the band concerts, now the lecture series.

The only time I even thought of home that first week in London, apart from when Carol Beckwith made that amazing remark, was on Friday, which happened to be the Fourth of July. I had not even realized that it was the fourth until I was paying for my dresses in Harrods, and the clerk said something like, "Well, this must be a special day for you!" It took me a few seconds to figure out what she was talking about. When I got back to the hotel late that afternoon, I saw a crowd of Barston people in the telly room, engrossed in the news. (A lot of people regularly watched the news and even the programs in the evening: television was quite respectable since it was the BBC, and everything, even reruns of terrible

American shows like *Starsky and Hutch*, had the air of being educational.) When I joined them, murmuring greetings and exchanging comments on the awful weather (somebody had actually seen sleet), there was something on about Prince Charles. The people from Barston did not take the monarchy seriously, of course, but they watched respectfully as the well-spoken announcer reported some speculation about a certain girl of the British aristocracy who might become the long-awaited royal bride.

Carol Beckwith, engaged in some knitting under the lamp, commented, "He'll never find anybody that meets all their qualifications. Such a girl doesn't exist."

No, there's certainly no such girl, everyone agreed.

Then there was something about the Fourth of July over in America, and footage was shown of a celebration in Washington, D.C. There had been a parade earlier in that far-off time zone at the White House, and now we saw soldiers dressed in Revolutionary War garb, which is to say torn, ragged clothes, with a ragged little boy out in front playing the piccolo. I knew this was historically accurate. The revolutionary army had been bedraggled and tatterdemalion; they could hardly afford splendid uniforms such as the British have worn through the ages. And in fact, this poverty and informality had worked in their favor. I remembered from school how the English line, dressed in eye-catching red coats, marched right into the fire of the less formal revolutionaries. But as I saw the re-creation of this revolutionary army on the BBC news, I could not help but feel, with a sigh, that America was a simple, inferior land and that Louisiana, in particular, was provincial and without interest.

PART THREE

THE MIRACULOUS DRAUGHT OF FISHES

Chapter 8

Number 14 was my favorite bus in London. I can still see the route in my mind: down Shaftesbury Avenue, around Piccadilly Circus, down Piccadilly, past Green Park on the left, the terraces of Mayfair on the right, past the Hard Rock Café, where you could always see students of the modern type lined up to get in, around the Wellington Monument, past Hyde Park and the great hotels beyond Hyde Park. Then you entered Knightsbridge, my favorite area of London, if I had to choose just one, with the brown prow of Harrods visible among the densely packed stores up ahead. Up ahead was what I held to be the best museum in London, the Victoria and Albert.

The V&A was unlike any other museum. In the first place, it was out here in this green residential area, away from other museums and public buildings, more private in atmosphere, more domestic than any other museum I knew. Of course, it was literally "domestic"—you found furniture and clothing here as well as the usual pictures, and the crockery and other artifacts were not things dug out of the earth by archaeologists but familiar, recognizable articles such as you might find in a stately home. But apart from that, the V&A had a unique atmosphere which I thought of as home-like. It did not have bright, open rooms, one leading straight to another, like the usual museum; rather, it had small, softly lit rooms in no discernible pattern, like a maze, and each room seemed to be a secret chamber. You just wander in the V&A, I recalled, every once in a while emerging into a dark, chill hallway with French doors open to a bright green courtyard.

MacPherson had taken us out to the V&A one day that first trip, and my return here brought him vividly to mind. Robert MacPherson was not a regular professor at Whittaker but our writer-in-residence at the time. He was very well known. I think it was I who first noticed the resemblance between MacPherson and D. H. Lawrence: MacPherson had the same kind of boyish, wise-looking face, the same slight build. And the resemblance was not all physical. MacPherson was also from a mining town, but in Kentucky rather than Nottinghamshire, and his first novel, *Beyond the Mountains*, was about growing up in this town and getting away from it. It dealt rather explicitly with sex, I should add. On top of this, MacPherson was married to a woman somewhat older than himself who had been married before, and this marriage, like that of the Lawrences, had a celebrated storminess. The general understanding was that MacPherson's wife had a great deal to put up with in MacPherson, who drank quite a bit and had a romantic aura of instability about him. Part of the legend of MacPherson was that he had "cracked up" in class one day some time back in the 60s when he was teaching at another school. He had just walked out of the room, so the story went, and left town for a couple of weeks. Anyone but MacPherson would have been fired for doing a thing like that.

His wife was really beneath him, we thought. Mrs. MacPherson was not beautiful; in fact, she was rather blowzy. Nor was she particularly intelligent by campus standards. (One time at a tea given by the English department, when somebody mentioned Lytton Strachey, she said, with a giggle, that this sounded like a brand of girdles.) But it was widely assumed that the bond between these two dissimilar people was sex. An important aspect of the MacPherson legend was that this union was passionate—like Frieda, Mrs. MacPherson was supposed to have run away from her first husband with her second—also tempestuous, as MacPherson was believed to have run away from Mrs. MacPherson several times, including the time of the legendary crackup. But Mrs. MacPherson had taken him back.

We believed that MacPherson's wife had made every allowance—no telling what MacPherson had done on his odysseys—and it was easy to believe in this all-embracing tolerance on her part when you saw her standing around at a party, arms folded over her stomach, smoking, listening to chitchat, giggling at the same time as she blew out some smoke. There was a gaiety about her that might come from understanding everything about her brilliant, erratic husband and forgiving it, or—and this was equally likely—from understanding nothing about him. Or, the gaiety might come from a source entirely different from the understanding. My idea about this different basis sprang from a remark Mrs. MacPherson made one time at a student party. Some of us had just seen the controversial Bertolucci film *Last Tango in Paris* and thought it just too exciting for words, but Mrs. MacPherson said she thought it was boring. It just showed people doing what she did every day, she said, giggling and taking a drag on her cigarette. The remark produced a silence that was a mixture of shock and admiration, and it planted in my mind the image of MacPherson in a raincoat, pressing Mrs. MacPherson up against the wall of an upper room in their big untidy house. It also deepened my general impression that they enjoyed a marital life of great intensity and originality.

And indestructibility. It seemed to have survived every kind of incompatibility and disillusionment. Furthermore, it seemed to provide MacPherson with something his nature required: an "essential matrix." I came up with this phrase after going to a party at the MacPhersons' house and getting a first-hand look at the household, which consisted of the incongruous couple, her three children from the previous marriage (now teenagers), their two children together, and several rowdy dogs. Mrs. MacPherson treated her husband with the same jocular affection with which she treated the children. MacPherson, for his part, looked sheepish at home, and rather pleased. My conviction that this messy, cheerful setting was MacPherson's "essential matrix" was strengthened by a remark I heard that evening. Some people were talking about another professor at Whittaker, a Dr. Benson who had just left his wife and family for a graduate student at Ole Miss. "What a shame," Mrs. MacPherson remarked seriously. "He's lost his home." And MacPherson, standing nearby, nodded somberly in evident agreement. I understood that Mrs. MacPherson provided MacPherson's "home," which was beyond value and irreplaceable. He might stray, but he would come home, wagging his tail behind him.

Mrs. MacPherson did not go on the junior trip. She did not care for England, it was said. One summer, according to another chapter in the legend, their family took a cottage in the Fen Country, but Mrs. MacPherson thought it was "too cold" and packed up after a couple of weeks, went home, declaring that she would never go back to England. Thus on the trip in 1972, MacPherson was without his wife, and we students had the full benefit of his presence. All the students agreed that MacPherson was the most stimulating teacher at Whittaker, which was just in Mississippi but was nevertheless known for its unconventional, provocative teachers. Yet, it was not merely MacPherson's presence in London that made me fall in love with the city. That had to do with the city itself, the ineffable spirit of the place that made me feel it to be my spiritual home. MacPherson was a catalyst, however, the way he knew England inside and out.

Now, entering the V&A, I recalled the day we had come out here with MacPherson. We had clustered around him right inside the door while he enumerated the things we could not miss—the Constable collection, the William Morris things, and the Raphael cartoons. The cartoons weren't very funny, he'd said wryly, explaining for the benefit of those who hadn't had art history yet that the "cartoons" were full-size studies for a set of tapestries depicting the Acts of the Apostles, which now hung in the Sistine Chapel, where we would see them in a couple of weeks. The group split up then—we were college students and too mature to follow around after MacPherson or Miss Walker, our other teacher, like ducklings—but a certain number stuck with MacPherson in a casual sort of way. Back in the out-of-the-way room where they keep the Constables, MacPherson discoursed brilliantly on that artist's work. He had been to all the places Constable painted—Salisbury, Dedham Vale—and he told witty stories about trying to get across the water meadows in the one place, his encounter with some cows in the other. He also directed our attention to Constable's tiny notebooks displayed in glass cases. Constable had made the most painstaking studies of clouds and other aspects of nature on his honeymoon, a time when even the most dedicated artist might be forgiven for taking a holiday, MacPherson said out of his deep knowledge of art as well as the mysteries of sex.

Now I found the grotto-like place with the Constables and went in. I, too, loved Constable now. I had no interest in going to the countryside but was enchanted by these representations of it, which were so elegant and gay. And there was the church at Dedham Vale, which still reminded me of Holy Name. But all the while I was enjoying the Constables—going up close to inspect a little dog in one picture, seeing that in reality, it consisted of only four daubs of paint—I recalled something that had happened here in the V&A that day in 1972. It had taken place in the room with the Raphael cartoons, a room quite different in atmosphere from other rooms in the V&A. Where most are dim and secret, this one is bright and grand, a great high-ceilinged salon for the display of those great works of art. I had gotten separated from MacPherson and the group trailing after him somewhere in the labyrinthine museum and ended up by myself on a bench in front of the cartoon I liked best, *The Miraculous Draught of Fishes*. This depicted Jesus in a boat on the Sea of Galilee with the fishermen who would become his disciples. A serene Jesus was on the left, saying something to the big strong fishermen on the right, who were leaning toward Jesus in various attitudes, two of them withdrawing their nets from the water. The composition was riveting—the diagonals of the fishermen, the horizontals of the sea, and the town back there on the shore, with other figures on the shore also in well-composed attitudes. And the colors were wonderful, aquamarine and terra-cotta. The cartoon was so monumental, and yet so alive. It was interesting that the single tapestry on display in the V&A was also *The Miraculous Draught of Fishes* and that it was so inferior to the cartoon. Of course the medium was different. The cartoons were done in some kind of paint, but the colors looked so soft and mild that you thought they were done in pastels, that soft artist's chalk that comes in such pretty colors. The tapestry, on the other hand, looked bumpy and coarse. Furthermore, the wondrous composition of *The Miraculous Draught of Fishes* suffered from being reversed. In the tapestry, the cautionary Jesus was sitting over to the right and all the muscular fishermen leaned forward from the left. This must have been what Raphael had in mind all along, but it looked backward to me.

Anyway, in 1972 I was sitting on a bench in front of *The Miraculous Draught of Fishes* when MacPherson entered the room and came over to the bench, sank down beside me, and said, "Caroline, lovely Caroline! I want to see you. May I see you later?" in this urgent, ardent way. No one else was in the bright, open-seeming room at the time, except someone way down at the other end whose back was turned, and I felt overcome, quite ravished. Just as I opened my mouth to say something (what?), Sally Johnson came into the bright room. "Sally!" I said, as though Sally Johnson were just the person I had been waiting for, and MacPherson simultaneously slid off the bench, also greeting Sally with a little wave and going on out of the room with an energetic-looking jog. The whole thing probably took two seconds. I felt just like I had after the killer cab passed too close, guilty too for some reason—but Sally said, "Where's *he* off to?" then seemed to forget all about it. It took me longer to forget about it, as it both thrilled and terrified me to think that MacPherson might actually be interested in *me*. MacPherson was a famous person; he was married. Nevertheless, in the next few hours, my imagination took this incident and elaborated on it to the point where I was actually wondering what my life would be like as MacPherson's next wife. In truth, I had no idea at that time what to do with my life, and the idea of being the wife of a famous writer (never mind that he had another wife, a home), being his muse, keeping his house, coming to London with him of a summer, was deeply exciting. It was a dangerous idea—I did not go so far as to picture introducing MacPherson to my mother, but I was actually willing to be the next scandal at Whittaker, which fostered scandal in its innocent way.

Meanwhile, MacPherson seemed to have left the museum, and after a time, the rest of us also departed and returned to the hotel. Presently it was discovered that MacPherson had checked out of the hotel and headed north—on a motorcycle. Miss Walker was hysterical, but the other students just shook their heads admiringly. As for me, I was in a state of profound agitation, being forced by the circumstances to believe that I was somehow the proximate cause of MacPherson's disappearance. He did not show up again in London, or Paris, nor yet in Munich; he did not show up, in fact, until shortly before our departure from Rome. As a matter of fact, nothing further ever took place between MacPherson and me. That fall, he did not return to campus, and later we heard he had checked into some hospital "to dry out." After that, I concluded that MacPherson's abrupt departure from the tour, as well as the cartoon incident which preceded it, had probably had more to do with an incipient breakdown of general proportions than with me in particular.

MacPherson became even more of a legend at Whittaker after he was gone, and alumni still talk about MacPherson when they meet. I remained intensely interested in him, reading reviews of his books when they came out, seeing the film version of *Beyond the Mountains* twice (it was terrible). I constantly imagined that I might see MacPherson again. He was the kind of person who would turn up at Tulane, and I could imagine my grandmother, who was in all sorts of organizations, receiving MacPherson at some function, MacPherson kissing her hand. I halfway expected to run into him in London, and now, in the V&A, it seemed to me that he might come around the next corner, or be the man looking in the next glass case. In this frame of mind, I left the Constable room to find the Raphael cartoons.

They were in the same great salon, and there I circulated around *The Acts of the Apostles*, pausing before *The Miraculous Draught of Fishes*. It still thrilled me, but I was so different from the girl who had admired it before, a girl so mute, so green! I was alight with the possibility that MacPherson might come in now; I wondered how I would act, what I would say. But I wasn't going to meet him today, of course. I believed I could feel his presence in London, but at the same time knew he probably wasn't anywhere near Great Britain. He was probably off in a desert somewhere or on the top of some mountain.

Presently it was time for lunch. A bit let down, I left the cartoons and, with the help of guards who stepped out of the shadows here and there, found the lunchroom. It was down in the basement. I had not seen it before and was surprised by its complete lack of charm. It did not have a cloistered air like the restaurants or coffee shops in the Tate or the National Gallery; rather, it was enormous, hot, and noisy, like a school cafeteria. In fact, as I entered the lunchroom, I thought of the sign for a small café on a highway between Alexandria and Barston when I went the back way that said "Dinning Room." But this *was* a "dinning room," I thought. You could walk through the V&A and hardly ever see another person apart from the guards, but then you came down here in the basement to the lunchroom, and there were a thousand noisy people, which added to the mystery of this museum.

I got something to eat, then turned to face the babbling crowd under the hot lights. I looked for a table. I also looked for MacPherson. He wasn't there, but I did see a man I had seen in the breakfast room at St. Cuthbert's, a dark-haired man who wore turtleneck sweaters and who I surmised was a playwright. He was sitting about halfway across the room, in the same attitude as I usually saw him in the breakfast room, smoking a cigarette and studying his fingernails. I turned in another direction lest he see me, despite the fact that he might be an extremely interesting person and I was forthright and direct now, rather than girlish. I felt vaguely guilty about avoiding this opportunity to meet and talk with a genuine Englishman. But perhaps it was the playwright's hair that put me off. It was straight and rather long, as befitted a playwright, and while it had been clean and shiny the first time I saw him, it had gotten dirtier every day until now it was downright oily. I knew that Europeans had broader notions of cleanliness than Americans and that in Europe, it was considered more civilized somehow not to spend your time bathing and washing your hair, but still, I was put off by this, or used it as an excuse.

After lunch, I went back out into the cool, quiet hall and searched out the works of William Morris. MacPherson had been keen on William Morris, and in fact it was through MacPherson that I came to have the possession that I valued the most, a William Morris wall hanging. MacPherson told us you could go to Liberty's on Regent Street and buy fabric printed on the very same blocks that Morris & Company had used years ago. I did this after MacPherson disappeared. I found the Honeysuckle pattern, bolts of it, just sitting in the upholstery department like some ordinary fabric, and I bought a yard. Back home, I had it stretched in a frame, just as you stretch a canvas. I have often said that if my apartment were burning and I could snatch only one thing before escaping from the flames, it would be my William Morris wall hanging. William Morris was all over the V&A. There was the Green Dining Room, which used to be where you ate, in better days, but which was now just an empty room with his wonderful designs on the walls. Elsewhere was a piano embellished with Morris designs. I also revisited a collection of his inimitable fabrics, which I looked through, losing track of time.

When I finally emerged from the V&A that afternoon, traffic was heavy on the Brompton Road and the nearest bus stop had a long queue. I joined the queue and waited through the arrival and departure of three buses, none of which was a Number 14. Then suddenly, on impulse, I broke away from the queue and started walking. It wasn't raining at the moment, the air was chill and invigorating, and after the pressure of all those reveries in the V&A, it felt great just to stride down the street. The traffic was so thick in Knightsbridge that often-times I was moving faster than the vehicles, and I enjoyed getting a closer look at the buildings and store windows I had simply passed in the bus.

At first I thought I would just walk until I came to a less crowded bus stop, but the stops in Knightsbridge were really thronged; besides, I got warmed up and began to enjoy the walk itself. It began to take on the character of a feat or stunt that I would enjoy telling about. I would walk all the way back to Bloomsbury. Later, when I told the ladies from Barston, they did not seem to believe me. Surely you could not walk from South Kensington to Bloomsbury! Such a long walk contravened the laws of nature, they seemed to think, and I realized I might as well have claimed to have walked up the side of a building.

Chapter 9

The Gospel at St. George's Bloomsbury that Sunday morning was about the blind beggar Bartimaeus, whom Jesus healed. The priest used this as his starting point for reflections on the homeless people of London, a number of whom could be found in the streets and squares of Bloomsbury. I had noticed these derelicts in Bloomsbury Square, which you had to cross to get from the hotel to the Ristorante Italiano, where I had been eating dinner almost every night, or to get over to the Holborn Tube station. They sat on benches in the square with their possessions stacked next to them in green plastic garbage bags. Often they had bottles of whiskey or wine, but this alcohol was apparently just for innocent refreshment, as these men and women never seemed to be drunk. They often visited together and appeared to enjoy a pleasant, well-organized derelict society. I had never seen derelicts quite like this, even in New Orleans, where they tended to fall down in the street or lie soddenly in doorways; nor did I remember seeing such people as this in London in 1972. I had taken particular notice of them this week as the only sign, apart from the high prices, that England was having any economic trouble. London looked so solid and prosperous, except for these derelicts in the squares. Mavis and Lucy had mentioned them one morning at breakfast, wishing to warn Edwina and me not to walk through the squares alone, the implication being that one of them might grab us, try to rob or rape us, but I had not taken this warning seriously. These derelicts simply did not seem aggressive and dangerous; they seemed more like urban hoboes, just resting and having a good time amongst themselves.

Yet they were a problem to this priest, for they resided, as it were, in his parish. He described a recent conversation with one. He had not wanted to stop and talk with the man but felt he must, he said. And here it seemed to me that the priest was confessing not only a disinclination to spend his free time in pastoral duties but also a certain distaste for the beggar himself (clearly the priest was a man of culture); nevertheless, he did stop and talk. There were many ways the derelict could go about improving his situation, the priest averred (and I was sure this was true, as England was still practically a welfare state, despite the efforts of the current government to reform it). But the priest came away from the encounter convinced that the derelict did not want to change. This Bloomsbury beggar had no faith like Bartimaeus, the priest seemed to say; he was an inadequate beggar. Even so, the priest clearly deplored his own powerlessness to inspire the unfortunate man. I felt very warm toward the priest and deeply sorry that he was working here in a parish—Bloomsbury suddenly seemed very gray and inhuman—with more bums than churchgoers.

As if to dramatize the pitiful condition to which this church was reduced—and this the Church of England, the state church!—an old lady came forward and began passing along the pews, taking up the collection in a small pocket-like affair made of green felt. I recalled how even at my small Episcopal church in Barston, we took up the collection in commodious plates; here, a fragile-looking old lady went around with a green felt pocket. Both Edwina and I inserted a few English bills.

∾ ∾ ∾

The only English people I had talked to that first week in London had been hotel staff or museum staff or clerks in the stores (Napoleon called England a nation of shopkeepers, and in my experience, it would seem to be true), and this is the main reason I went to church with Edwina—to meet some English people. Thank God I did. Otherwise, I probably would not have met Mrs. O'Leary.

After church, we were invited to "stay behind for coffee." The tiny congregation gathered back in a corner of the church. A slight woman with short brown hair, crimped in the style of the 40s, came forward and pressed our hands, introducing herself as Mary Ann Milford, offering us coffee and biscuits, which were actually cookies. Miss Milford had a white, anxious face, and when, in the course of the introductions, I said we lived in the state of Louisiana, Miss Milford fell back in an attitude of astonishment, much as if we were apparitions emerged from the crypt.

"Why, our other visitor is from Louisiana, too!" Miss Milford said, pointing out another member of the party, a stern woman in a black felt hat.

We shook hands with our fellow Louisianian, a tall, old-fashioned-looking person about seventy-five or eighty years of age. Her name was Dora O'Leary, and she was from Jonesfield, a town that happened to be about twenty miles south of Barston. She had been on the NCLU charter flight, too, although we did not remember seeing her, nor she us. Edwina and I did most of the talking and all of the explaining; Dora O'Leary said little, just looked amused.

Miss Milford hovered nearby in obvious excitement. "We had a man from Dallas, Texas, last week. You might know him. His name was Williams, or Wilson—Williams, I think—"

"Hmmp!" said Dora O'Leary. This was a piercing hum, starting high and darting rapidly down, as if to say Miss Milford lacked good sense.

"Texas is an awfully big place," I put in rapidly, worried that Miss Milford might think Louisianians rude. "It probably looks as if we're right next door, but we live a couple of hundred miles from Dallas. We're not neighbors in the usual sense. England is so much smaller," I rattled on even though I knew that the norm of courtesy in England was completely different from the norm of courtesy at home. Back home, you keep on talking when you're uneasy or trying to apologize. If you think you've hurt somebody's feelings, you might keep talking for an hour. English people would say just one word—"Sorry!" Of course, Yankees, at home, would say nothing at all. I figured Dora O'Leary was Yankee in origin.

Miss Milford, too, seemed curious about this formidable person's provenance. "Would you be Irish?" she said, imitating an Irish brogue.

"Certainly not!" Dora O'Leary declared stoutly. "My late husband was Irish" (so it was "Mrs."), "but I have no patience whatsoever with those madmen. My family name is Loganson."

Miss Milford now faded away, and Mrs. O'Leary turned her attention upon Edwina and me. "What do you do, young ladies?"

"We teach at NCLU in Barston," Edwina said. "Department of English."

"*I* went there, a hundred years ago," Mrs. O'Leary said with a grim smile. "They called it the Normal School back then, of course. I got my teacher's certificate in two years. I've been friends all these years with the Harkriders. I don't guess you know the Harkriders."

"Of *course* we know the Harkriders!" I cried. "It was Dr. Harkrider who hired me!"

Mrs. O'Leary asked me to repeat my name a couple of times for her inspection. "French, I guess," she said disapprovingly. "From south Louisiana?"

"No, I grew up in Meridian, Mississippi. I have family in New Orleans, though. My father's family was originally from Houma," I said, pronouncing this last place name carefully ("Hoo-ma") to distinguish it from Homer, a town in north Louisiana not too far from Barston. This was a crucial distinction, understood immediately by anyone from Louisiana, between the north part of the state, which is predominantly Protestant, and the Catholic south. It was not as marked a division as that between Northern Ireland and the Republic of Ireland—there had never been any armed conflict—but still, it was an important distinction, and feelings about it ran high.

"Catholic?" Mrs. O'Leary inquired, one eyebrow rising.

"No, Episcopalian. I grew up Methodist, but I love England so much I joined the Episcopal Church."

"That's better," she said, and I knew she shared the prejudice of many Protestants in the piney woods of north Louisiana who thought that Catholics had horns and hooves. Mrs. O'Leary looked like the sober, respectable Protestant ladies you see in Mississippi and north Louisiana. She wore rimless spectacles and plain clothes that looked as if they had been ordered from the Sears catalog: a dark green dress made out of serge or gabardine with the durable sheen of serge (the word "bombazine" came to mind), and stout walking shoes, the kind that lace up and have a high, thick heel. She wore her hair, which must have been very long, in thin braids wrapped around her head. At first glance, you might think Mrs. O'Leary was a member of one of those religious sects that require its womenfolk to wear three-quarter length sleeves and no makeup, never cut their hair, but I saw that Mrs. O'Leary was not the type to let any church dictate to her. This individualism was undoubtedly the basis of her antagonism to the Catholic Church, which she would probably call the Church of Rome under the assumption that the pope ruled the lives of its members from his Vatican stronghold. It was interesting that I should encounter Mrs. O'Leary in an Anglican church. I liked the Church of England because it was English; Mrs. O'Leary was probably attracted to it because its founder sacked the monasteries.

Meanwhile, the few other members of the congregation had gathered around us with their coffee and biscuits, and now the ancient lady who had taken up the collection thrust herself forward to ask, "Are you three ladies traveling together?"

"Never saw these young ladies in my life until this morning," Mrs. O'Leary said.

"You're traveling alone, then?" Miss Milford asked Mrs. O'Leary.

"No, my nephew is with me. He went hiking out in the countryside this weekend. I'm staying in London. Too old now for traveling around. Besides, I'm not interested in *scenery*," Mrs. O'Leary asserted. She seemed to be about seven feet tall. Her severe-looking spectacles gave off flashes of light, but behind these were large brown eyes which were surprisingly mild-looking when you looked straight back at her. She might even have been pretty once, I thought, before she got so monumental. "I taught literature for forty-five years," she went on. "But now I'm trying to see something of the world. After I retired, I went to Greece and Italy, then China. Last year I went to the Holy Land. Britain's a young country, in comparison."

"Not all that young," said the priest. "Have you been to our new City of London Museum? There's an excellent view of the old Roman wall."

"It's on my list," said Mrs. O'Leary, peering down at the priest, who stood a good six inches shorter than she. "You're a mighty good preacher, Reverend Davenport," she said. "I don't blame you for gettin' fed up with those hoboes. I saw 'em yesterday, just sitting in the park like good-for-nothin's, as able-bodied as you or I."

"A terrible social problem," Father Davenport murmured as he turned to Edwina and me.

"How do you do, Father. I'm an Episcopalian, and I'm so glad to be here this morning," Edwina said, pumping his hand.

"I'm a Methodist, Reverend," Mrs. O'Leary continued. "I thought it was right to come to the Anglican Church when I was in England because John Wesley was an Anglican until the day he died. Did you know that John Wesley was an Anglican, never *was* a Methodist?"

"Yes, I do recall," the priest said, with a mild smile, taking a cup of coffee from Miss Milford.

"There wouldn't a been any Methodist Church if the Anglican Church hadn't been so pig-headed about ordaining ministers for the colonies. We might all a been Anglicans in America, though I'll be frank, Reverend—your service is a mite Catholic for my way of thinking. And I don't know *where* you get your hymns. You ought to use more of Charles

Wesley's hymns. The tunes are better, and a body can sing 'em without being a musical genius."

As Mrs. O'Leary held forth, I was smiling in a friendly way at the Anglicans as if to say, all Louisianians aren't so critical! But presently, Fr. Davenport changed the subject, asking about our flight over and where we were staying.

Mrs. O'Leary said she and her nephew were staying at the Florence, another of the hotels on Bedford Place. I thought it might be nicer than St. Cuthbert's. At first, all the hotels in the terrace had looked alike to me, all very nice (such is the collective power of a terrace), but by now, I had noticed that not all the hotels were maintained equally well. The best ones—the Florence and a place called the Cumberland Club—were extremely well kept. Sometimes they were obscured by green scaffolding, with men crawling over their facades to repaint the woodwork or perform other maintenance work. The worst ones, on the other hand, had dead geraniums in the window boxes and piles of green garbage bags (the same type the derelicts used for luggage) on the sidewalk out front. The worst hotel on the block, the Waverley Arms, actually had a "vacancy" sign hanging by its front door. St. Cuthbert's was somewhere in between. It was nicely painted, but the workmen employed to keep it in good repair were not as assiduous as the workmen at the Florence or the Cumberland Club. Right now, for example, they were remodeling some bathrooms, and the fixtures they had removed at the first of the week were still piled on the sidewalk.

"The Florence is a fine hotel," Fr. Davenport commented, then turned to Edwina and me to ask where we were staying.

"St. Cuthbert's."

"Are you getting any rest?"

When we looked puzzled, he said, "You don't know the legend of our St. Cuthbert?"

St. Cuthbert had been a bishop in the North Country back in the seventh century, the priest told us. When he died, he was buried at the priory on Lindisfarne, the Holy Isle, but he had requested that if the monks ever had to leave the Holy Isle, not to leave his body there but to take it with them. Sometime in the ninth century, the Danes sacked this monastery, forcing the monks to flee, but they remembered the request of Bishop Cuthbert and took him along. They had no place to go, however; they just wandered for two centuries with their holy burden. (Now I realize that this peregrination was done by several generations of monks, but as Father Davenport was telling the story, I imagined a single band of wandering monks.) At last, the bishop was laid to rest in Durham Cathedral, where he remains to this day. The remarkable thing, though, was that during all this time—from the time of his death in the seventh century to the time he was buried in the eleventh—his body *never decayed*. The English were still Catholics in those days, of course, and at some point, Bishop Cuthbert was declared a saint.

"You don't really believe that, do you?" Mrs. O'Leary said in a tone of Protestant asperity.

"It stays quite cold all year round in Durham and Yorkshire," said Father Davenport drolly. "In any case, I always think about the poor bishop being bundled around the countryside for two centuries before finally coming to rest."

I chuckled appreciatively now at the name of our hotel, but I was thinking of something else: a little church on a road outside Barston called the St. Rest Baptist Church. It was some sweet, pious country people's idea of sainthood or saintliness, but before I could mention this interesting contrast, Mrs. O'Leary took up the theme of saints.

"I wondered whether you Anglicans believed all those farfetched legends. At least you don't have statues in the churches. The Catholics act like those statues are magic lanterns, rubbin' on 'em, even kissin' 'em! I saw statues in Italy with their feet rubbed down to nubs. I declare, it made me want a dip a snuff!"

The little congregation of St. George's laughed politely. By now, the coffee was all gone, but before we dispersed, Miss Milford was anxious to introduce each of the other members. First was the ancient lady who had taken up the collection, then a slight man with a thin mustache who turned out to be the organist, then a mannish-looking woman with long, frizzled hair wearing a black satin motorcycle jacket. Miss Milford was a secretary at some branch of the Civil Service, she said, while her friend, Agnes Jones, the woman in the motorcycle jacket, worked at the Cumberland Club. This latter woman was gigantic—she was bigger and stronger-looking than Mrs. O'Leary. Although her job was not specified, I got the idea from her size and rough appearance that she worked "below stairs." I did not learn what the organist and the old lady "did" but had the definite impression that there was a tremendous gap in education and culture between Fr. Davenport and his little flock. They were at pains, by the way, to explain why there were so few people there, each one of them, at one time or another, saying something about "the changing nature of Bloomsbury" (so many people working in Bloomsbury at the British Museum or London University but so few actually living there), or "the troublesome period of transition the Church of England was in these days." They were also eager that we three Louisianians come back to the church, and when they found out that we were going to be in London two more weeks, urged us to come to a special Vespers service "Thursday next." It was to be a joint effort of

St. George's and the Benedictine order of monks, having to do with the opening of an exhibition at the British Museum on the Benedictines in Britain. As we talked about this, pledging ourselves to come, I watched Fr. Davenport, wondering whether this was an honorable post for him or whether he had been passed over for more desirable assignments for some reason and was just stuck here. It was a magnificent church, but it didn't have a real congregation.

Mrs. O'Leary put on a coat which was also suggestive of Sears and tied up her head in a wrinkled old scarf. The other people were beginning to put on coats and rainhats and other armaments against the cold, wet weather which we now had to go out and face and which, although I certainly found it stimulating, like the rare wintry days in Louisiana, I was getting just a teeny-weeny bit tired of, if truth be told. Mrs. O'Leary looked so stolid as she put on her things—so unconscious of being in London alone at her age (why, she might slip on the steep steps outside and break her hip!) that I felt a surge of affection for her, even though we had just met and she was not, of course, immediately lovable.

I turned to Edwina. "Maybe we ought to . . . "

"Invite her to dinner with us?" said Edwina, who was not a Southerner but who was very thoughtful and hospitable, nonetheless. Edwina was the kind of person you would want for a neighbor in a hurricane.

"Mrs. O'Leary," I said, going over to her. "If you don't have plans for dinner tonight, we'd like to invite you to join us at the Italian restaurant not too far from here. It's near our hotel . . . "

"Why, that's mighty nice of you girls," Mrs. O'Leary said, looking unexpectedly human. "I'd be pleased to. You can meet my nephew."

CHAPTER 10

The Ristorante Italiano was not a fancy place, nor was the food even all that good, or so said Edwina and the other people from Barston, who had tried this place the first night or two, then moved on to other restaurants in search of more sophisticated adventures of the palate. But I had stuck with the Italian restaurant because it was warm and dependable, not too expensive, located just a few steps from my Tube stop, Holborn Station, also the bus stop that I used. And there was another element to my attachment to the ristorante: it wasn't a tourist place, but rather somewhere Londoners ate on their way home from this part of the city. It was a "neighborhood restaurant," and I was pleased to think of it as *my* neighborhood restaurant—something I had always wanted to have in Barston but did not have. As I approached the ristorante in the evening gloom, the lights glowed gold above the café curtains, and I would enter the small dark vestibule, close my sopping umbrella and remove my wet raincoat, all the while smelling the wonderful aroma of Italian food, hearing the murmur of people already eating. I would also hear, in a kind of descant, the louder voices of the staff, who were genuine Italians from Italy and therefore always shouting at each other in their mother tongue, although they would speak to the patrons more civilly in beautifully accented English.

Unlike the one Italian restaurant in Barston (Bono's, which specialized in pizza), this ristorante was really authentically Italian. It looked just like the restaurants I had seen in Florence and Rome, with red-checked tablecloths and menus with the simple stripes of the Italian flag on the cover, red, white, and green. But there was one rather touching difference. This ristorante in London had English placemats—those hard melamine placemats with hunting scenes on them, "Stopping the Earth," for example—also English prints on the wall, these too of hunting scenes. And it seemed to me that the Italians who owned this restaurant displayed these scenes, which had nothing to do with Italy, as a kind of tribute to England, an overt statement that they were pleased to be here, much as a tourist getting off the plane in Hawaii dons a lei. Since I was usually by myself in the ristorante, I had looked a good deal at this decor. Outside, above the green café curtains, you could see a parade of black umbrellas, some going one way, some the other. It was interesting to watch two umbrellas approach each other, converging without any appearance of hesitation as if they would surely collide and get all entangled until, at the last moment, one would lift, the other dip. Londoners seemed to know some arcane umbrella etiquette, just as they knew how to ride across from each other in trains, or even sit at a table with you in a crowded eating place without requiring you to carry on a conversation, and so much else about living well together in a limited space.

"Well, their Chicken Cacciatore's fairly edible," Edwina said that Sunday evening as we took off our wet things in the foyer. We had spent the afternoon in the National Portrait Gallery—I examining an exhibit of Bloomsbury photographs downstairs in the twentieth-century wing for the face of Emerald Glover (not finding it), Edwina gazing once again on the little-known portrait of Lady Hermione Hart by Sir Joshua Reynolds.

"We're looking for an American lady tonight," I told the headwaiter, who recognized me by now. "Tall," I specified, holding my hand way up.

"Thees-a-way!" said the headwaiter promptly.

"Well, there you are. Thought you'd gotten lost," called out Mrs. O'Leary, rising from a table amid the murmuring Londoners. A man of about thirty was with her. "Miss Warren, Miss Landry," she said, "I'd like to present my nephew, John Loganson."

The nephew rose to meet us. He had a smooth, pleasant face and grayish-blond hair with the texture of Spanish moss. He was wearing a thick gray sweater with a collar and looked athletic. We shook hands and told him our first names as he pulled out our chairs.

John had spent the weekend in Norfolk, the fen country on the eastern coast. The weather had been terrible, "just like this," said John, who spoke slowly and had an interesting voice, which sounded squeezed somehow, as if it were coming out of an old radio.

"Were you camping?" asked Edwina.

"Tried to, but I ended up at inns most of the time," John said.

"That's too bad," Edwina said. Edwina was a great camper out. She often spoke of her many summers at Camp Wanamaukee in Wisconsin, and even now, as an adult, she tended toward vigorous vacations. (Edwina was the kind of person who could turn out a meal in an old Hi-C can.) I, too, tried to make some sympathetic sound at the mention of "inns," but I myself would have gone to the inn in the first place. I didn't care for camping out and had never done it since my Girl Scout days. Tramping through the woods was not my idea of a good time, anyway. My idea of a good time was to eat a dinner that someone else had cooked, then have tickets to something.

I ordered the minestrone, which came hot and was, I felt, very salubrious these cold, wet evenings. I also ordered spaghetti and a glass of red wine, which was salubrious too, even if it was warm and grainy. As I surrendered my menu to the waiter, I felt Mrs. O'Leary's gimlet eyes on me. She sniffed. Too late I remembered that temperance was a big part of the credo of north Louisiana Protestants and that she would find wine at our table to be offensive. I had been tactless, I feared.

"I'll have the Chicken Cacciatore and minestrone, and a glass of red wine," Edwina said obliviously. "I recommend the Chicken Cacciatore, Mrs. O'Leary."

"A glass of red wine, please," said John at the commencement of his order, with an air of happy innocence. He had noticed the look, I was certain, and now he looked at me with a deadpan expression. John was droll. You might make the mistake of thinking he was slow because he spoke so slowly, but he just had that wry humor so characteristic of our part of the country.

"I hope you have milk," Mrs. O'Leary challenged the waiter. "We old folks have to drink milk if we don't want our bones to give way."

"Your bones will never give way, Aunt Dora," John said with a grin.

During dinner, John, Edwina, and I traded autobiographical information. John had grown up in Jonesfield, then gone to LSU, where he had studied music. Now he taught instrumental music there, having gotten his graduate degrees at the University of Illinois. His specialty was the bassoon. Names of people Edwina and I knew at LSU were mentioned, connections established. Edwina asked questions designed to discover whether John had tenure (he did) and whether he was married (he was not).

"You know, it was amazing, my running into your aunt this morning," I commented, with a glance at Mrs. O'Leary, who had just been sitting by while we talked without smiling, like a turtle on a rock.

John said he had met somebody in Norfolk that week-end who was from the obscure town of Ventress, Louisiana, a person who had graduated from NCLU in May.

"Europe's full a people from north Louisiana right now," Mrs. O'Leary said, as if irritated by this childish talk of coincidence. "A whole plane full came over last week, don't you know."

Edwina asked what John and his aunt had done that afternoon. They had gone to Sir John Soane's house, he said, going on to remark that he had enjoyed it immensely but always got more tired in museums than anywhere else on earth. He'd rather climb a mountain than try to see everything in a vast museum like the British Museum.

"Have you seen the mummies?" Mrs. O'Leary said suddenly to Edwina and me, as if this were a pop test. She did not say *she* was tired or appear to be tired in any way.

"Not this trip," I said. "Which is funny, since I go to the British Museum every day. I'm doing some research."

"Really? On what?" John asked. He was finished with his meal by now and had turned sideways in his chair, where he sat with one leg crossed over the other. He was wearing those suede desert boots so many college teachers wear.

Warmed by the wine, I confided, "I'm doing some work on a writer I believe is from Louisiana, though to tell you the truth, I'm not sure yet. Her name is Emerald Glover and . . . "

"I'm related to her," said Mrs. O'Leary, and sniffed.

"*What?*" I cried, being prepared to go through my usual spiel about who Emerald Glover was and how I had discovered her. I felt as if I had jumped off a cliff in some rickety glider contraption and been swooped up by an eagle.

Mrs. O'Leary sniffed again. "She was a cousin of mine. Now, I don't remember much about her—she left home when I was just a young 'un, but I heard about her when I was growing up. There were always stories about Emerald. She sent copies of her books to her mother, and when Jewel died, they ended up in the library. Course I read her books in the library."

"Aunt Dora's been a librarian at the public library in Jonesfield all these years, besides teaching English at the high school," John said admiringly, swinging his boot.

"I don't believe it," I said, with a glance at Edwina, who was gazing at me with glowing eyes, much as if she had just learned that I was engaged. "Are we talking about the same person? Her name is Emerald Glover—G-L-O-V-E-R—and she wrote four novels in the 20s and 30s, fifty years ago. Now the first one is set in a little town in Louisiana, but I haven't been able to determine which one . . . "

"It's Jonesfield," pronounced Mrs. O'Leary. "Not exactly, of course, but then it's a work of fiction, and you have to have some leeway with the facts. I always thought she wrote well, but she sure wasn't kind to the people back home."

"No," I mused, remembering the young heroine of *Plantation Trace* and how stultified she felt.

"I didn't know we had a writer in the family, Aunt Dora," said John, smiling with possible irony. "Are you sure?"

Mrs. O'Leary glared at him. "Now listen, John Abbot Loganson, Emerald Thomas was my Aunt Jewel's oldest girl. Then there was Pearl and Ruby. Emerald was five or six years older than I, which would put her born about 1895, give or take a year. She left Jonesfield right before the war and went to New York—she wanted to be a writer and must a thought you couldn't write in a place like Jonesfield, though Mrs. White's done it all these years. Mrs. White's written some fine poetry . . . "

Here John swung his leg a little faster and sighed.

" . . . that you don't think much of, I know," his Aunt Dora went on, looking at John as if he were a juvenile delinquent, "and you probably wouldn't either," she said to me, "probably too *sophisticated*, but in any case Emerald ran off from home and married some Englishman and published, what is it, four novels. She did well. At least she made a name for herself."

"Well, her name is practically forgotten outside Jonesfield," I said, heart pounding. "I can't believe you're actually related to her. Think about all the coincidences that had to take place for me to meet you."

Mrs. O'Leary sniffed at the coincidence. "A lot of people in Jonesfield knew her better than I did. You'd a been luckier to run into them. Course most of them must be dead. There's Mrs. Bolton, now. She might remember Emerald."

"She's ninety-six, Aunt Dora," John said.

"This is awfully interesting," I said. "Do you know whether Emerald Glover is alive?"

"No, I don't," Mrs. O'Leary said, "I haven't heard tell of her for years. It's been thirty years since I read her books."

"She was alive in 1965," I said, telling them about the article I had just found. "But she was awfully old at the time. I don't think her health was good."

"I thought she settled in England, but I lost track of her after the war, when Aunt Jewel passed on. But she had some kind of illness even as a girl," Mrs. O'Leary said. "She was a feverish sort of girl. My mother and Aunt Jewel used to talk about her—worry about her being off no tellin' where and not a strong girl. I have a clear memory of cousin Emerald lying in a porch swing, sick. She had long red hair that hung through the slats and dragged the floor."

"I wonder if she could still be alive," I said.

"Hmmp," pronounced Mrs. O'Leary skeptically. "Emerald's father's people were all short-lived. Her father died back before the First World War of heart trouble, and Pearl and Ruby both died young. Course she's half Loganson, due to Jewel—your grandmother's sister, John, my aunt. I suppose she might go more than four score. You've looked into it, I expect, Miss Caroline?"

"I wrote," I said, wincing to show that I realized how futile this was (not wanting Mrs. O'Leary to say "hmmp" again). "I just wrote a note and addressed it 'Pelwichton, Northumberland,' mailed it Thursday. I can't say I expect to hear anything."

"Wouldn't it be something if you did?" said Edwina. "You could go up and see her. Publish a great interview. Get her to authorize a biography. You'd be *the* expert on Emerald Glover."

"I could bag her and take her home," I said merrily. "I think I might be promoted to full professor if I took her home."

Mrs. O'Leary took no notice of this academic horse-play. "You're going to have to come to Jonesfield when you get back and look around. There's a lot you'd be interested in."

"The birthplace," intoned John. "The first schoolroom."

"Well, seriously, Caroline," said Edwina. "You're onto something here!"

"I can't get over it," I said later over coffee. "You know, I drive through Jonesfield just about every time I drive from New Orleans to Barston."

John groaned sympathetically, for I was referring to the notorious road connecting south Louisiana and north Louisiana, a sort of patchwork route which was partly interstate and partly dangerous old two-lane highways. Louisiana didn't have a north-south interstate for some reason (politics, no doubt), but the fundamental reason seemed to be that Louisiana was a backward state. Except for New Orleans, which was like San Francisco or even a Continental city and hardly seemed part of Louisiana, the state was truly backward, it seemed to me, only Mississippi and possibly Arkansas being more backward. In any index of a state's status—whether per capita income, literacy, whatever, Louisiana was always at or near the bottom.

You got a strong sense of this backwardness driving north through the state. Not too far past Alexandria you had to leave the interstate and get on a murderous two-lane road going through primeval swamp, then more two-lane roads that took you through the rolling piney woods. This was the prettiest part of the drive (some of it was even national forest), but there was nothing in the way of civilization except several nondescript little towns. You had to be careful not to get caught in their speed traps, although usually it wasn't even possible to speed on account of the log trucks, which crept along loaded with piles of logs that looked as if they were about to burst their chains. Jonesfield was one of these towns, distinguishable from the others only by the presence, on its north side, of a factory that made brown paper bags and sometimes smelled like rotten eggs.

After dinner, everyone reached forward to claim his or her own check, but Mrs. O'Leary snatched all the checks, then reached for her purse, a large, flat-sided patent leather affair with the kind of clasp that makes a loud snap. It was so formidable in the way it opened and closed, in fact, it reminded me of Mrs. O'Leary's mouth. She rose.

"Oh, Mrs. O'Leary, ma'am," Edwina and I called after her in protest as she marched away with the checks. But Mrs. O'Leary was approaching the cash register. I could see that she was closed to any entreaty, that the only way to get the checks away from her would be to tackle her among the diners. She was so big in her plain serge dress! She had a belly, but it did not seem to be soft; rather it seemed to be some kind of buttressing.

"John, I don't want your aunt to pay for my dinner," I said urgently as we trailed after her.

"I don't either!" worried Edwina.

"Dora will do what Dora will do," John Loganson said philosophically. "And don't try to reciprocate. You'll make her mad."

"Well, thank you, Mrs. O'Leary, thank you," we said out in the tiny foyer as we put on all our raingear, bumping into each other in the dimness.

Outside, it was raining and almost dark. We walked back to Bedford Place together, Mrs. O'Leary and Edwina charging ahead under one umbrella, John and I following more slowly under mine, crossing Bloomsbury Way and Bloomsbury Square. Bloomsbury Way sounds like a remote, flower-strewn path, but actually, it is a wide and busy street, with phalanxes of taxis hissing at you. Bloomsbury Square was even harder to negotiate, as the square was so wet and muddy that even the derelicts had gone somewhere else.

"I hope you like London," I said, feeling horribly stimulated by the evening and its revelations, knowing I would never go to sleep. In fact, I had had trouble sleeping the whole week I'd been here. "I'm sorry about the weather," I added, feeling responsible for the mire of Bloomsbury Square.

"Oh, no, I love it," said John. "I've been here a couple of times before."

"What's your favorite thing?"

"The opera. I'm crazy about opera," John said. "I'm hoping to get tickets for the Bellini Festival. We actually know somebody who's singing. Tom Kelly, from Jonesfield. Ever heard of him?"

I confessed that I hadn't since I knew hardly anything about opera.

"He's been working in Germany the last few years, the way you have to do to establish yourself, especially if you're an American, but he's finally got a break—he's in *Puritani*. He's supposed to get us tickets."

"Wow."

"I wanted to be a singer," John told me as we reached Bedford Place. "But I just didn't have the voice. My voice coach at LSU told me flatly I'd never make it. So I took up the bassoon instead. Not many people major in bassoon. In graduate school, I discovered a love of teaching, and that seemed a natural path for me. Everybody in my family teaches. My mother taught math before she retired, my father taught history."

Every hotel on Bedford Place looked handsome at night, with their lights all on, and the streetlights among the plane trees gave off a hazy yellow glow in the rain. In front of St. Cuthbert's, Edwina and I accepted an invitation to meet the people from Jonesfield for dinner the next evening in the Italian restaurant. I had not wanted to spend time in London with people from Louisiana, but perhaps because of our strong mutual interest in Emerald Glover, there did not seem to be any question of our simply saying good-bye and going our separate ways, as the Harolds and I had done.

Chapter 11

Each morning at St. Cuthbert's, as I went down to breakfast, I would pause a moment near the reception desk to check the letter rack provided for guests. I was looking for a letter from my mother or grandmother, although I didn't really expect to hear from them; I even went through the motions of looking for a letter from or about Emerald Glover. But there was never anything for me, just the same letters that had been there ever since I checked in, which I suppose were for people who had long since checked out or were away for a while, driving around the countryside.

Then I would pass on into the breakfast room, after pausing one more moment to glance into Mr. Spark's room, which was always neatly made up, Teddy Bear in place on the bed, open to view. Mr. Sparks—what a character! One morning as I came down the stairs, I heard what sounded like the clucking of a chicken. It was Mr. Sparks, who was having breakfast with the staff. When he saw me, he drolly clucked again. He was quite the social leader. In the evenings, he had certain members of the staff and even some guests to watch television in his room. He made a great show of always being on the prowl for women. Once when I was at the desk to get my key, Mr. Sparks emerged from his room, wearing his Irish fisherman's sweater and shiny brown corduroys. He had worn this outfit every day.

"Had dinner, Anna?" he said, looking around me toward Anna, the girl from New Zealand who served us breakfast.

"Yis, I hive!" she said merrily, not even pausing as she passed.

He promptly put the same question to a guest in the hotel, a mysterious girl who looked as if she came from the Middle East and who, like Mr. Sparks, wore the same clothes every day—in her case, a clinging knit dress in a leopard-skin print. She did not answer, just looked startled and ran off.

This guest was interesting. She was never at breakfast but always in the telly room in the evenings. She seemed very friendly, always smiling promptly whenever you looked at her, but she never replied to greetings. (Carol Beckwith said she had given up trying to converse with her.) None of the Barston people had ever seen her go anywhere or come in from anywhere; rather, she seemed to be installed in the hotel permanently. I had the impression that she was somebody's mistress, being paid to wait here on his pleasure. Such a situation was more suited to an area of London like Bayswater, I thought, or St. John's Wood. We were in Bloomsbury, the neighborhood of the British Museum and the University of London, and almost every guest seemed to have some intellectual or artistic interest, such as the putative playwright in the turtleneck sweater.

Except for the French couple, the two other people at St. Cuthbert's whose primary purpose seemed to be amour. I had seen them first in the breakfast room on Saturday morning, noticing them because they were speaking French and because they seemed so absorbed in each other. I imagined how they must have come over from Marseille or Boulogne to London for the weekend, pressing against each other in the Hovercraft, running away from her husband and his wife, unable to go to Paris lest they be recognized. The French couple had not been at breakfast Sunday morning, but I had seen them come in later, pressed against each other, murmuring French with great intensity. They were not a handsome couple—the woman was rather masculine-looking, like so many European women (she would have hair under her arms), and he was smaller than she, with a large, hooked nose. As I approached the breakfast room on Monday morning, I wondered whether they would still be there. I believed they were the people who had occupied the bathroom for such a long time the evening before when I had come in from the ristorante just dying for a hot bath. It had been a couple— you could hear them splashing and laughing; you could hear them speaking French. At first, I had been amused by the aquatic tryst, but I was less amused when I went back fifteen minutes later and found them still there. This seemed a little excessive; this departed from the spirit of the hotel! The fact was that somebody *was* in the bathroom, from time to time, but no one stayed long.

But now I went on into the breakfast room and cast a practiced eye around the tables. (No French couple—they were back with their spouses in Marseille.) Edwina was beckoning to me from a table near the window. As I went over, I saw the playwright in the turtleneck shirt out of the corner of my eye. He was watching me, I thought, though I pretended not to notice.

"My usual!" I called out carelessly to Anna.

"Good morning, Caroline!" said Edwina. "Sleep well?"

"Mmm," I said noncommittally. (Actually, I had awoken a few times—Edwina snored.) It was so pleasant in the breakfast room. Sheer curtains on the long windows looking out to the street blew inward, bringing that fresh thin London air into the room. I looked forward to the little metal pot of hot tea, the rack of toast.

"What did you think of John Loganson, Caroline? He's cute, isn't he?" Edwina said, eyebrows raised earnestly.

"He's very nice. I liked him."

"He likes *you*, Caroline. He clearly thinks you're attractive."

"Good morning, ladies! May we join you?" This was Charles, interrupting this interesting topic.

"Why, certainly. Yes, of course!" Edwina and I exclaimed to our boss and his wife. It was unusual, and rather grand, to have both the Nicholsons down at breakfast.

"The most wonderful thing happened yesterday," I said. "I ran into a woman at church who's from Jonesfield, and it turns out she's related to Emerald Glover—her first cousin. Her nephew is here too. They don't know much about Glover, nobody's heard from her in years, but at least now I know where she's from. It gives me something to go on."

"Good girl!" Charles said, as if I had exercised some scholarly skill in meeting up with Mrs. O'Leary. Allison Nicholson was not sure which town Jonesfield was and had to have it described to her.

"I guess you heard about Sid," Allison said after this excitement had subsided.

"No, what?" I asked, pleased that Charles had been impressed.

"He was mugged yesterday afternoon."

"Mugged?" Edwina and I cried in unison.

Whereupon the Nicholsons told the incredible story of how Sid Beckwith had been about to get on a train at the Gloucester Road Tube station when someone blocked his way and another person pushed him from behind in a frustrating manner. That kind of thing could be expected late at night, but this happened on a Sunday afternoon when there was a crowd on the platform. Something made Sid feel for his wallet (it was gone!), whirl around, and see three boys running away. Sid took after them and caught one, but the others escaped. A bystander helped him restrain the thief until the police arrived.

"He lost seventy-five pounds!" Allison said, lifting one eyebrow.

"My gosh, what was he walking around with that much money for?" Edwina exclaimed. "Where on earth was he going?"

"To some concert somewhere," Charles said with a big sigh, as if this were the most nonsensical behavior on the face of the earth. "Of course, it was incredibly dangerous to go after them. They might have had knives or guns."

"Oh, not guns, Charlie," Allison said, looking ill.

"I think they might have had guns," Charles said impressively. "I've read about this. They have little gangs now that work the undergrounds. One blocks your way onto the train, another one comes up behind and empties your pockets. Of course, you're hurrying to get on the train before the doors close. Most victims don't even know what's happened."

"It's getting as bad as New York City," said Allison. "Oh, Charlie, I hope the Tubes don't get like the New York subways."

"Of course, they won't, darling! The English would never permit that to happen!" Charles declared heartily. I imagined a panoply of officers of the court, all wearing wigs.

"These gangs, though, these punks," said Allison. "They were those awful punks, Caroline. You know the kind—they have pink or yellow hair, leather clothes."

"Oh, them," I said. "The ones whose hair looks like those little dyed Easter chicks."

"They're vicious, though," said Charles, laughing.

"Oh, I know," I declared. I realized that although England appeared to be perfectly safe (unlike New York or New Orleans), it had its dark underside. I knew London used to be so dangerous in the eighteenth century that the venerable sage Dr. Johnson never went out at night without a big club, and that even now, long after the establishment of the wonderful metropolitan police force, Britain had a bizarre and violent element (I had read *Clockwork Orange*).

"You need to be careful with people like that," Charles said significantly. "I'm not sure Sid knew how to handle the situation." He said no more, but he was clearly referring to the fact that Sid was from north Louisiana and, let's face it, a rather countrified person who liked to hunt and fish. Sid had come to London a number of times, but I could see that Charles doubted whether he had ever been to New York City. Sid did not react to the mugging with the skilled passivity of a New Yorker, Charles seemed to suggest, but with the artless local impulses of chasing and grappling.

"And, of course, you shouldn't carry all that cash," said his wife.

Charles shook his head over the folly of the Louisiana man. "His passport was in the room, thank God."

"Carol wants to go home," Allison remarked.

"He wasn't hurt, was he?" I asked. This had just occurred to me.

"Oh, no! He's fine," Charles said, implying that Sid Beckwith was not too sensitive. "But you know Carol—she worries. . . ."

"We really ought to go to Greenwich with Sid and Carol on Wednesday," Allison said.

Allison was referring to a day trip to the maritime museum in Greenwich proposed by Sid Beckwith, one of his enthusiasms, along with Wren's churches and chamber music, being naval history. He and Carol had asked all the Barston people if we wanted to "go down to Greenwich," but nobody had, at the time, everybody having ten other things they wanted to do.

"Are you going, Caroline?" Allison asked.

"I wasn't going to," I said, grimacing to indicate my extreme reluctance to undertake such a journey. I had been avoiding all trips out of the city, although I had been invited on several, such as the day trip to Canterbury for which Mavis and Lucy had just departed. It seemed incredible that they could go to Canterbury and get back in time for dinner and the theatre this evening (just the one-way trip had taken Chaucer and his folk weeks), but they were taking a high-speed train. You could get anywhere in Great Britain in just a few hours, they had said. Distance was so different in England, which was so tiny compared to other important countries: you had to alter all your ideas about space. (I had the idea there was something of interest every few feet in the countryside; there would have to be, to pack it all in.) Time was also different here, I had come to see. You did something important, something that you would remember all your life, morning, noon, and night. In England, time was packed, like the countryside.

"How far is Greenwich?" I asked, this particular side trip seeming to be my duty, somehow, because Sid had gotten mugged.

"Oh, just down the river. Not far!" Charles assured me.

Edwina said she might leave Lady Hermione for just that one day, and I conceded that I too could go.

"Let's say we'll go, Charles," Allison said.

"All right, darling. Caroline, you might like to ask the people from Jonesfield," Charles said expansively, in the spirit of generous, warmhearted solidarity brought about by what had happened to Sid.

❧ ❧ ❧

I did, and they accepted. They, in turn, asked me and Edwina to go to the opera the next evening. Tom Kelley had come through with tickets to the opera. In fact, he had been able to get a box due to a last-minute cancellation, and it seated four.

There was news of other successes at dinner that evening. Both Mrs. O'Leary and I had found one of Emerald Glover's books. While John had been going to the box office on Floral Street, Mrs. O'Leary had been combing second-hand bookshops. She had found *Plantation Trace*, which, over my objections, she presented to me (she "had no use for it"), though I insisted that John keep it for the time being since he had said how interested he was in reading his relative's work. I found a copy of *Café of Sorrows*. I had not intended to shop for the quartet quite yet, but that morning at breakfast, I asked Charles to recommend some good sources for the odd and out-of-print; then, as we were walking to work at the British Museum, I abruptly decided to skip it just this once and start the hunt. Surely this was a legitimate scholarly errand, I thought, as I extricated myself from Edwina and tried to cross over to Russell Square without getting run over, then headed on into the upper reaches of Bloomsbury. It was a wonderful day—cold, but not raining, with a high white sky. I found no Glovers in Bloomsbury, but I didn't mind. It was a good excuse to take a bus out past Knightsbridge to the Fulham Road, where there were also supposed to be a lot of great old bookshops. I found *Café of Sorrows* in one of these.

I also had a jarring experience while I was out there:

I ran into somebody from home. I would have preferred to remain anonymous in London, anonymity being one of its delights, but in the Fulham Road, I came face to face with the Sorensons, a couple I had known in Chapel Hill, and there was nothing to do but exclaim and hug.

"Amy! Jim!"

"Why, Caroline, I don't believe it! What are you doing over here?"

I had to explain about my research. The Sorensons then explained that they had been on sabbatical from the University of Kansas this spring (they lived in Lawrence, as I knew from Christmas cards). They spent the first three months toiling at Oxford in order to free themselves for a tour of Europe the last three months.

"How wonderful!" I cried.

"Oh, yes, oh, yes," said Jim sardonically. "If you like living out of a suitcase week after week."

"We can't get our clothes clean. We have to wash them out in the sink every night," Amy complained. Amy and Jim were both tall, unglamorous people who looked very much alike (one wag in Chapel Hill had remarked, before their wedding, that Jim Sorenson was marrying his sister). They looked Nordic. Indeed they had always reminded me of characters I had read about one time in a children's book by a Scandinavian author, boy triplets with the rather unpleasant names of Snip, Snap, and Snur. And now, as if they had in fact been born at one birth, the Sorensons were wearing identical outfits: jeans and polo shirts and rumpled raincoats.

"Oh, well," I said cheerfully, "you're in London now. Where have you been? What have you seen? What museums have you gotten to?"

"We are so sick of museums," Amy said. "You walk in one and it looks like all the others."

"We went to the British Museum yesterday and walked right back out," Jim said. "All those pots."

"What we like to do is go to drugstores or grocery stores and talk to people," said Amy. "Find out what they can buy."

"You do?" I said incredulously. My interest in the people of England had been completely satisfied by the camaraderie at St. George's Church. I mainly thought of English people as supremely lucky to have been born in this country, to be here before I came, get to stay after I left.

"We've been walking around Chelsea this morning. We thought we ought to hunt up Sir Thomas More," said Jim.

"Chelsea—I spent a happy hour there the other night," I said fondly.

"Chelsea's gotten so chi-chi the last few years," said Amy, like Snip or Snap.

"Well!" I said. We were at that awkward juncture in the meeting of acquaintances where you have to make some move—either say good-bye or propose lunch—and I didn't want to break bread with people who turned up their noses at Chelsea. I looked at my watch and produced a little start. "Oh, my, I'd better run. But it was great seeing y'all. Look me up if you're ever down south."

"We plan to go down to New Orleans next year. We might just stop in Barston," Amy said.

I said goodbye and quickly put some distance between myself and the Sorensons, wondering whether they had been that dreary in graduate school. I found myself on Sloane Street and started looking for a place to eat. Presently I spotted a shop with a Victorian-looking sign that said "Swansea's, Purveyors of Extraordinary Things for the Larder." Inside I smelled the sharp, acrid aroma I associated with the French Market in New Orleans or the Food Halls at Harrods. I could make a picnic of bread and cheese! This is what people who went to France did. I could do it too, I thought, examining a row of sausages. The Sorensons had agitated me a little. Was I a superficial visitor to London? Was I just a tourist?

Swansea's had cold cider in cans with charming pictures that looked like an excellent picnic beverage. I also discovered a barrel full of ready-made sandwiches that bulged with beef or ham and frills of lettuce. I chose one of these and some Woodpecker cider, and the clerk put my purchases in a charming shopping bag which, like all London shopping bags, was cute enough to keep. Now I needed a place to eat.

With an eye out for the Sorensons, I headed back down Sloane Street toward a green square I had seen. The street seemed very cold after the warm and fragrant grocery store. The sky had darkened and (oh, drat!) here came the familiar drops, just a few, though, just a few. I walked rapidly, looking forward to a park bench under a London plane tree. But the square was locked. A second square was also locked. In this more posh part of London, the squares were for the exclusive use of the residents, it seemed (no derelicts here). I felt rebuffed. My feelings were hurt—irrational, I knew, but was there no place for my delightful picnic? I took out my map of the city. Sloane Square was not too far away, and as it was pictured on the map exactly like Russell Square and Bloomsbury Square, I had reason to hope it was public. I headed that way.

Sloane Square turned out to be a concrete area with traffic whizzing around it, but it was pleasant nonetheless. There were some trees and benches to sit on and even a fountain spraying water into the wintry air. At least one derelict sat on each of the benches (here was their place), and so I perched on the edge of the fountain. The derelicts watched with undisguised interest as I withdrew my lunch from the Swansea's bag, and, trying to ignore them, I ate and drank, watching the traffic, which seemed (apart from the red buses and black taxis) to consist only of costly cars such as Rolls Royces and Daimlers.

The cider was surprisingly potent. I had expected mere apple juice, but this was some sort of lighthearted beer. Soon my head was spinning, and I felt surges of joy. Shivering a bit, I took out my copy of *Café of Sorrows* and opened it up, right at the part where Ariel has a terrible argument with her lover in the bistro in Paris (a scene filled with the most satisfying agitation). I read fifteen pages before I looked up, dazed, and remembered where I was.

Chapter 12

My first impression had been that everybody but our-selves was in formal dress, but now I saw that some people, who must have come straight to Covent Garden from offices in W1 or W2, then some neighborhood restaurant, were in ordinary business clothes. I saw that there were even some people in completely inappropriate clothes. One young woman in dramatic makeup was making herself very conspicuous in the lobby, moving from one group of people to another, laughing loudly, as if she were at a cocktail party in somebody's home. She was wearing a white cotton jump-suit that was probably *haute couture* but which still looked like overalls. I also noticed a man and a woman enter the lobby wearing khaki clothes designed for a safari. The man even had a camera around his neck! They were gawking at the lobby as if they had stumbled into some ancient tomb. We watched in horrified fascination as the man went over to the box office and said into the bars, "What's playing? Is it the whole opera or just highlights?"

John rolled his eyes. It was embarrassing, as this crass couple was obviously American. Other people in the lobby, who had probably had their tickets for months, who, indeed, had the air of having inherited their tickets, turned to stare at these gauche people who had just wandered into the Royal Opera House expecting to catch the next show.

An imposing man in a frock coat now stepped over to the box office. Clearly, he was in an official capacity here at Covent Garden—perhaps he was an usher or even the manager—but he had the hauteur of a butler, also a hint of the bouncer. "Sir, Madam," he said in this wonderfully snooty way, just loudly enough for all the ticketholders to hear, "the opera being performed tonight is *I Puritani* by Bellini. It is part of the Bellini Festival and the tickets are very, very expensive. But that is irrelevant now, as they have been sold out for months. There may be a few tickets for standing room, but if you purchase one of those, you must stand throughout the entire opera, which is very, very tiring. And you must be perfectly quiet."

The khaki-clad Americans gaped at the man in the frock coat as if he were an exhibit at Madame Tussaud's. When his speech was over, they stood there another moment, then walked away. He had succeeded in dissuading them from further attempted commerce with the box office, his tone of voice when describing SRO having made it seem like the most undesirable situation in the world, like walking the deck of a submerging submarine. But they continued to look around, apparently not even embarrassed. They crossed the lobby to look at some posters and could be heard to ask if they were for sale. Next, I feared, the man would crouch down and start focusing his lens.

Mrs. O'Leary looked disgusted. "New York Jews!"

"Not so loud, my dear," murmured John.

"Well, it's true. A bunch of Jews from New York were on my trip to the Holy Land. They're just different from us. Course I know Jesus was a Jew, but still. . . . "

"Why don't we go on up?" John said, steering us up some stairs to another golden lobby. Our box was down a dark hall from this, near the stage, with a view of the orchestra pit. We also had a fine view of the house, which was very ornate, with much crimson and gold, but smaller than I expected. It was horseshoe-shaped, its three tiers of boxes ringed with clusters of little lamps with red shades.

In our box were three chairs, plus a stool. John mounted the stool, in spite of arguments by both Edwina and me that, as the opera buff, he should have a real seat. But John was a gentleman, I reflected, as we settled down to read our programs. I had assumed that *I Puritani* was about the Puritans in America, a sort of Thanksgiving opera, but it had to do with the English Civil War. The plot was complicated, and even though the characters were supposed to be English, they had incongruous Italian names. As well as I could gather, *I Puritani* was about a Puritan woman, Elvira, whose true love Arturo seems to betray not only her but also the Puritan cause when he aids Queen Enrichetta, the widow of Charles I. When I read that Elvira lost her mind over this, I felt some foreboding. John had referred to this opera as *bel canto*; he had also spoken of Dame Esther Northfield, the star of the evening, as a supreme exponent of the *bel canto* art. The idea of the arcane art of *bel canto* in the service of a mad scene made me dread complex, clamorous music that would jangle my nerves.

"Tom's got a big part," observed Mrs. O Leary, peering at the program through her rimless glasses. Tom Kelly sang the baritone role of Riccardo, whom Elvira rejects.

The members of the orchestra had been gathering in the pit down below, and presently, the house lights went down. But the little lamps stayed on, scores of glowing pink points around the three tiers. The conductor, Sir Harold Thomas, made his entrance, but although I knew he was very famous and I was seeing him now, in person, I was more thrilled by the lamps. The lamps stayed on during the entire overture, which created the most delightful sense of intimacy, like lamps in a little girl's room. And to my surprise, the overture was light and tuneful, like Mendelssohn. I smiled around at John to let him know that I loved it, but his eyes were fixed on the curtain. He was up on the stool with his back pressed against the wall. He had to sit this way to see, as we were at a right angle to the stage, and now as I turned back to the house, I noticed that every box had a man on a stool in just this position. It was a position of the utmost attention, yet it was perforce a casual-looking "L" shape (bringing the phrase "lounge lizard" to mind). I also noticed the standees, way up above everybody else on the top row of the house, lined up elbow to elbow against a rail, like passengers on the deck of a ship. The audience was as still and quiet as a photograph. People didn't even cough at Covent Garden.

When the overture was over, the lamps went out, to my regret, and the curtain rose. Colorful soldiers sang a throbbing manly chorus; then, there were church bells and a lyrical hymn sung by people offstage. Then Riccardo came out. Mrs. O'Leary notified everybody of this by saying "Tom Kelly! Tom Kelly!" and shaking our arms; John and the people in the next box went "Shhh!" The singer from Jonesfield was a handsome blond man with a beard, and he had a substantial aria, the first of the opera, which he performed exceedingly well.

The next scene brought the entrance of the heroine Elvira, who was, of course, sung by Dame Esther, a large woman with a lantern jaw. Everybody clapped thunderously before she even opened her mouth. Her aria displayed her very great voice in difficult runs and trills. But I was as interested in the orchestra as the singers. The famous conductor seemed to be having a particularly good time. His face, lit by the light from the stage, had an ardent expression. But he was not solemn about his work. He seemed to be engaged in continual badinage with the musicians in the orchestra, particularly the concertmaster. Somebody played a wrong note or missed an entrance—some small thing went wrong—and, instead of being severe with that person, the conductor smote himself on the forehead with the palm of his hand in a comical way. The musicians exchanged glances and laughed. Sometimes the conductor simply sat back on a tall stool, his legs stretched out, and negligently wagged the baton back and forth. But, of course, this was not laziness: it was a case of the orchestra's being so good, the singers so famous, that they could simply take care of themselves.

After some interplay between the tenor and a mezzo-soprano (Enrichetta, the Stuart queen), Elvira came on with a bridal veil and sang a bright, cheerful, and very difficult song. Soon she was joined by the tenor and mezzo, also the bass (her uncle), and the four of them proceeded to sing a quartet involving the most astonishing vocal acrobatics. The music was so gay and rhythmic it was impossible not to jig up and down. I was jigging up and down, very gently, from the waist, keeping time with my head, and I saw that Edwina and Mrs. O'Leary, and everybody else in the house, even the lazy-looking men on the stools, were also jigging this way. Toward the end of this quartet, the singers seemed like a dozen acrobats all flying through the air at once, and when it was over, the audience broke into cheers.

The singers stood frozen during the prolonged clapping and shouting, and when order was restored, Arturo went off with Enrichetta disguised in the veil (this was the elopement), and Riccardo manfully pulled a sword. He then sang an aria, which was tuneful and pleasing, although he was supposed to be in high distress. There was good, firm applause, and just as it was dying down, Mrs. O'Leary shouted, "Yea, Tom!" I felt a thrill when Dame Esther came back on the stage and realized that her fiancé, the tenor, was gone (I could tell from the way John stiffened that this was going to be good). This was the mad scene. Although I had expected hysterical discord, this madness expressed itself in a gentle, swinging song, performed by this very great voice. Once I looked around at John. He was wincing in pleasure, her voice was so great.

Presently the chorus joined in, and it sounded like a whole choir going down a Venetian canal in a line of gondolas, or (since they were pretending to be in England), perhaps I should say a whole choir going down the Thames on a barge. But the focus remained on Dame Esther, who could always be heard above the other singers, and when the mad scene was over, some men in the audience shouted "Brava!" or even just "Ha!" the split second she finished, in that instant before the clapping started. I wondered if it was deliberate, that insertion of the shouts. It seemed to be. The men seemed to have been holding their breath in order to shout in just that blank moment to show how enthusiastic they were about Dame Esther's great artistry, like wedding guests who wait outside the reception, their throwing arms drawn back, to pelt the couple with rice.

∾ ∾ ∾

At the interval Edwina, John, and I got up to stretch our legs. Mrs. O'Leary preferred to stay in the box.

"I'll show y'all the Royal Box," John said, escorting us out into a hallway and around to a door leading back into the house.

"This is the Grand Tier," he said. "There's our box. Look down the row. The last box, closest to the stage, is the Royal Box. See the crest? No one's there tonight. If I were the king, I'd be in that box every night."

We could see Mrs. O'Leary in our box, her head drooping.

"I think your aunt's asleep," Edwina said. "What a dear lady. She's amazing, for a person her age."

We took turns using John's opera glasses to inspect the little people threading in and out of the seats on the floor way below, also the boxes across the house, which were fascinating, like those sugar Easter eggs that are hollow, with scenes inside. Many characters appeared in Covent Garden's boxes, some people sitting and looking through opera glasses, perhaps back at us, some sipping drinks. You saw comings and goings, greetings and farewells. In one box on our side of the house sat a noble old lady in a diamond tiara; a young man came in and bent down to kiss her. In another, a man stood up, saying something to two people still seated before turning around and leaving the box. The man was MacPherson.

"Caroline! What's wrong? You look like you've seen a ghost!" cried Edwina.

"No, no," I said, my heart beating hard. "I just thought I recognized somebody."

We went back out in the hall now, which was thronged with opera goers. All the while I was arguing with myself that this sighting of MacPherson had been a figment of my imagination aroused by the music, and I was glad of this: I wouldn't want to meet him tonight. It occurred to me that

I might have changed, for the worse! (The stars might have gone out of my eyes!) I had convinced myself of this when I heard a familiar voice say, "Caroline! Is it Caroline Landry?"

"Why, hello! Hello!" I exclaimed, not having to simulate shock. It was MacPherson, standing right there and throwing me into a tumult. What could I call him? He wasn't a "Dr." and "Robert" was much too familiar. We had just called him "MacPherson" at Whittaker (he was such a brilliant anomaly), but that seemed too swaggery now.

"Beautiful as ever," he said to me.

"Hello!" I repeated, blushing. (We were shaking hands; his hand was quite cool.) "I'd like you to meet my friends. Edwina Warren. Edwina teaches with me. And this is John Loganson. John's a musician."

"Edwina, John," said MacPherson, shaking their hands. MacPherson looked smaller (perhaps this was only in contrast to the sturdy-looking John); he also looked wrinkled, even wizened. The phrase "dried out" came to mind. But then he was probably fifty years old, I realized. Yet much hadn't changed. He had on what might possibly be the same clothes he had worn around Whittaker—a rumpled tweed jacket and black pants that were an inch or so too short—"pipestem pants," we used to call them. And he had those blue eyes. Well, this was it! It had happened!

"Not *the* Robert MacPherson, the writer?" Edwina exclaimed.

"Well," he said with a nervous sort of laugh, darting a look my way. "I have to say yes."

"I've read all your books," Edwina declared. "I just love the *Teasdale Saga*. I read *The Turncoat* just this spring. You know, *Sons of Glory* is set in my period. It's so accurate. You must spend a lot of time on research."

"Well," murmured MacPherson, "one tries."

"What are you doing over here this time?" I inserted, gratified that Edwina admired my old hero but not sure that this was a compliment from a literary point of view. Dusty old poetry was Edwina's academic specialty, but on the coffee table in her apartment, you would see those fat paperback novels, the kind with buxom heroines on the front, their dresses partly torn.

He said, "I'm living over here a while, till the money runs out."

"Living in London?" I exclaimed.

"You always were fond of the place, weren't you?" he said with a smile.

"I can't believe you're living here," I said, so envious that I felt actual distress at the idea.

MacPherson went on to say he had sublet a little flat in Chelsea on Cheyne Row, near the Embankment. The rent was "frightening."

"Is Mrs. MacPherson with you?" I asked casually.

He closed his eyes and shook his head sadly.

"Are you researching a new book, Mr. MacPherson?" Edwina said adoringly, while I grappled with the idea that he might be divorced.

"I haven't been doing much writing, as a matter of fact. I have several irons in the fire. One thing—they're interested in adapting some of my stuff for TV, and I managed to get in on the scriptwriting."

"For *Masterpiece Theatre*?" I asked, not sure I could bear it.

MacPherson laughed. "I doubt that. It's Granada TV. I'm not sure what'll become of it. They might throw it in the dustbin. I've also got another thing going—an interview program. But you, Caroline. What's become of you? What have you learned about life?"

This is the kind of question MacPherson would ask, looking intently at you with his light blue eyes. My tumult increased. I had forgotten completely, this evening, about my life at home—my threatened job, my unpromising research—and now, remembering, I made a comical face expressing total despair. "Oh, I've just been working. I got degrees in English at Chapel Hill and I've been teaching at North Central in Barston. I've worked every summer—this is my first real trip since '72."

I craved MacPherson's good opinion of my unremitting industry, but he shook his head and said, "All work and no play . . . "

"I'm supposed to be working on Emerald Glover over here," I resumed lightly, to suggest how much time I spent otherwise. "She was an American who lived in London in the 20s and 30s."

"Emerald Glover. Emerald Glover. Didn't I just read something about her?"

"Oh, I don't think so."

"I think I did see that name—she was one of the Red Lion Square crowd, wasn't she?"

"She did live in Red Lion Square . . . "

But by now, a bell had rung signifying that Act Two was about to begin, and John had taken my elbow.

"Oh, golly, I was supposed to be fetching a drink," said MacPherson. "But listen, why don't you people come to a party at my place Saturday night. You will still be here, won't you?"

"Oh, yes," Edwina and I said in unison.

"Maybe," said John. "Thanks, though." John had been standing there frowning at MacPherson, and MacPherson had not looked at John. I could tell they didn't particularly care for each other, for some reason.

"I'm having a little gathering and it would be super if you all could come. About nine. Here," MacPherson said, taking a small notebook out of his pocket and scribbling something in it. He tore off the sheet and pressed it into my hand. "This is the address. There'll be people there who might interest you."

We parted then and, still feeling the pressure of MacPherson's fingers on my palm, I moved down the hall with Edwina and John. Like Elvira, I was completely out of my head, though it was important, I thought, to seem natural and sane.

"Why didn't you tell me you knew Robert MacPherson, Caroline? I swear," Edwina said fondly. "I can't believe he's actually invited us to his flat."

"He was just one of my teachers in college. I don't know him all that well."

I was thinking about Cheyne Row. Why, I had probably walked right past his flat the other night. He might have come out; we might have met that way, walked by the Thames! Immediately I started worrying about what I would wear out to Chelsea. An "arty party," as we used to call it at Whittaker, required something flowing, a long droopy skirt, a shawl perhaps, items of clothing that I had back at home but which naturally I had not brought.

"Don't frown, Miss Caroline," Mrs. O'Leary said by way of greeting as we entered the box. "You'll ruin your looks."

I attempted to concentrate on Acts Two and Three, where Elvira continued in her wilting, languorous "madness" until, by some means, she was reunited with Arturo. This settled, they planted their feet and sang, just as, near the end of a ballet, when the plot is all worked out, the principals take turns performing variations while the corps stands around to watch. So this is *bel canto*, I thought dreamily. Oh, no, there was more plot! Soldiers entered and took Arturo prisoner, and they all sang together sadly, as if Arturo were doomed. But then bugles sounded, and everyone sang the opening chorus again in high spirits (he was saved). Everyone had a turn to express his or her joy at the happy outcome, most notably the famous soprano.

∾ ∾ ∾

Afterwards, everybody streamed out of the opera house and across Floral Street to the underground station. We wanted a taxi, but so did everyone else since it was close to eleven o'clock, the hour the underground closed for the night. It was now quite cold, with a mist or fog that was not quite wet enough to justify an umbrella but made you feel clammy and chilled to the bone. There were simply no taxis to be had, and all we could do was pull our coats more closely around us and join the great throng of people trying to get on the last train.

Everything had changed in my life—I had just seen MacPherson, who might materialize again at any moment—but I had to try to appear unperturbed. "Was the performance good, John?" I asked. "Of course, I just loved it. The music was lovely."

"I liked that Tom Kelly! I wish we could meet him," Edwina put in.

"Well, why don't we? That looks like the stage door down there," said Mrs. O'Leary, who was lively now after her nap. "We're not going anywhere for the next few minutes anyway."

A small knot of enthusiasts was gathered at the stage door to see who came out.

First came some men in black tie, carrying instrument cases; one of the men was accompanied by that girl in the white jumpsuit. Then, as it happened, Tom Kelly came out.

I had no trouble recognizing him. He looked like an apostle with that beard and long hair, even in the modern dress of blue jeans and sweater. He seemed very normal as he came out of the door, waving to the crowd and smiling. Some people cheered and pressed up toward him for autographs.

"Let's go tell him hello," said Mrs. O'Leary, plunging through the crowd.

I was afraid Tom Kelly would not be glad to see Mrs. O'Leary (especially if she had taught him in school), but he did seem truly glad. "Mrs. O'Leary! Wonderful to see you! John, man, it's been a while!" exclaimed the young baritone, embracing the folks from home. "Wish we could get together. I have to fly back to Augsburg early tomorrow morning—I'm doing Rodrigo there tomorrow night."

"Rodrigo," said John, shaking his head. "You'll be fantastic. You were just fantastic tonight, Tom. Ye gads, those chest tones. Where did you get that chest?" John thumped his own powerful-looking chest several times.

Mrs. O'Leary took over. "Well, Tom, when are you coming home? I saw your mother in the library the other day, and she's going down."

"But I just talked to Mother Sunday. She sounded fine."

"She looks peaked, and I do believe she's starting to sink."

"Dora," said John firmly, putting a hand on her shoulder. "Don't worry poor Tom. Tom's got Rodrigo to worry about."

"I've got to face the firing squad," Tom said, apparently making some opera quip.

"May I have your autograph, do you think?" said Edwina, thrusting her program into his hands.

Tom Kelly started telling about Covent Garden, how cramped it was backstage, how you couldn't even take a shower, but my attention was deflected by another person coming out of the stage door: the conductor, Sir Harold. He was extremely famous, yet nobody stopped him for an autograph or even paid any particular attention to him, probably because nobody in the audience except the privileged ones in boxes near the stage had had more than the fleeting glimpse you get of a conductor when he peeps up over the rim of the pit to take his bows. He was smaller than I expected—no taller than I, in fact—and now he was striding briskly up Floral Street into the crowd, carrying an attaché case. Although he was still in his white tie and tails, he looked like a businessman. It was practically midnight, but he looked as bright-eyed and busy as if it were noon. He walked with clear purpose, not having to look around for transportation like everybody else. I knew there would be a car waiting for him, a long black limousine with (I imagined) a beautiful blond wife in it, waiting to take him to their elegant flat. It occurred to me that they might even live in that detached shingled house I had seen out in Chelsea, the one with the music stand.

"Just as nice . . . Doesn't put on airs at all!" Mrs. O'Leary was saying as we walked toward the Tube station. It would close in five minutes, which caused us some anxiety, but the crowd had resolved itself into a queue, and the queue moved fast of course, this being England. And before long we were inside the station and it was our turn to board the scary-looking elevator that descended to the trains. But the ride back to Holborn Station was swift and pleasant. You always have the feeling late in the evening in London that everybody else is still up and around, having a great time too.

Chapter 13

The next morning, I glanced perfunctorily at the letter rack. "Caroline Landry," I read on a small gray envelope. The address was written in a large, spidery handwriting I thought I recognized.

It's from home, I thought, my heart thumping. My grandmother had a stroke.

Dear Miss Landry,

I did not think there was anybody left alive who remembered my books! I hardly remember them myself, but if you are in the neighborhood, why don't you stop in for tea some day? I'm always here, tending my garden.

Very truly yours,
Emerald Glover
Rutland Cottage
Pelwichton, Northumberland

"A legacy, perhaps?" said the insinuating voice of Mr. Sparks.

"It's this writer I'm studying," I told him, too excited to banter. "She's still alive! She's asked me to come up and visit her."

"Not one of these romance novelists, I hope."

"Of course not!" I was scrutinizing the note and the envelope, which in my haste, I had torn.

Meanwhile, Edwina had come down the stairs. I showed her the note.

"Wow, Caroline! That's fabulous! You can meet her! You can talk to her! Jeepers, what I wouldn't give to know Lady Hermione."

"Where is Pelwichton, anyway?" I asked Mr. Sparks.

"I have no idea!" he said with a wince as if I'd asked him, say, where one bought snakes. "I never leave London!"

"Good man!" I said, looking at Mr. Sparks with new appreciation. I didn't want to leave London either. This was the day we were going to Greenwich, and I didn't want to go there, much less Northumberland. For a moment, I was even tempted to pocket this invitation, which was very casual, after all, and forget all about it. But of course, I could not do such a thing. The little note would turn everything topsy-turvy for a day or two—I knew that—but then I would be back. I had to tell Charles. And I had to tell Mrs. O'Leary and John. Why, this was their family!

Charles seemed genuinely excited by the note from Emerald Glover, and gradually it began to sink in that I was going to meet the woman who had lived in Red Lion Square and produced those books I had liked so much (I had never met a real author before, apart from MacPherson). Furthermore, it began to dawn on me that this was really a significant literary event, that, in a minor way, it was rather as if Virginia Woolf hadn't really walked into the River Ouse with stones in her pocket and now came forward as an old,

old lady from somewhere in the countryside. Emerald Glover was a living link with the twenties. I felt like a zoologist who looks up and sees a dinosaur wandering out of the woods.

And so it was that as the party bound for Greenwich gathered out on the sidewalk in front of St. Cuthbert's, I began to look forward to springing the news on the people from Jonesfield. The morning seemed particularly beautiful. It had rained overnight so that the terraces and trees looked freshly washed, and the air was damp and clean, almost dewy, like the air at dawn, although it was already after nine o'clock.

"You'll love Northumberland," said Mavis, who had been up there to a castle one time, and the others too were congratulating me on my impending exile when here came Mrs. O'Leary and John.

I went down to meet them. John received the news with glee. Mrs. O'Leary said "Hmmp" again. As she made this sharp sound, she lifted one eyebrow and pursed her thin lips. "Hmmp," the way she uttered it, could puncture a balloon.

"For tea, any day?" John said excitedly. "Well, are you going?"

"I believe I have to," I said as we walked toward the group waiting for us in front of St. Cuthbert's. "I hate to leave London for even one day, but I have this grant, you see, and I think I'm honor-bound to follow up any leads about Emerald Glover. And of course, the more I think about it, the more I want to meet her."

As I introduced the Jonesfield people to the Barston people, Mrs. O'Leary unsnapped her purse and took out a tiny leather-bound book. I thought it might be a pocket-sized Bible, but then I saw that it was called *England in Your Pocket*. It had thin, crackly pages like onionskin, and to turn them, Mrs. O'Leary had to lick her index finger, which she did slowly, with an air of luxury.

"Where is Pelwichton?" I asked urgently, hoping it wasn't too out of the way.

"I reckon we can get up there in five, six hours," said Mrs. O'Leary.

"We?" I said without thinking, wishing immediately I hadn't (it might seem rude), but good heavens! My thoughts this last half-hour about getting to Northumberland had been vague, but they had centered, I now realized, on myself all alone in Waterloo or another of the great stations of London, looking for signs to the North.

"Well, we're going up with you," Mrs. O'Leary said, in the sort of no-nonsense tone she would have used, say, to tell heathens they had to wear clothes. "And we need a car. We'll get a car and just drive you right up there."

John looked doubtful. "We can't just invite ourselves, Aunt Dora!"

"I don't know why not—we're family! She'll want to see us!"

"Aunt Dora," he said evenly, apparently going to try again. Discussing something with Mrs. O'Leary was a little like jousting. "Caroline might not want us along. She wants to interview Emerald Glover about her work. We don't want to horn in on Caroline's visit."

"We wouldn't interfere with a thing," Mrs. O'Leary said to her nephew with majestic blankness. "Miss Caroline knows that! The least we can do is go see Emerald, now that we know she's still in the land of the living. We'll just look in on her and see that she's all right. She may be in need, or sick. We have to find out! And we can give Miss Caroline a ride. We can't have her traipsin' off by herself on the train."

"Certainly I'd like to give Caroline a ride," John said in a tone which declared that this was quite beside the point, and I said, "That's very nice of you" in a tone which said clearly

that while I thanked him for his courtesy and thoughtful-
ness, nevertheless it was a preposterous idea, quite out of
the question. But at the same time, I was beginning to think
that it might not be such a bad thing to have a ride with
friends and compatriots, people who, back home as well as
here, were practically my neighbors, rather than have to find
my way all by myself to some village in Northumberland.
Northumberland, at this moment, seemed wild and remote.

"Perhaps we'd better be going, folks," said Sid Beckwith,
who had been sort of dancing around the group these last
few minutes.

We would leave the next day, we decided, as we made
our way to the Tube station; we would arrive in time for tea.
John would rent a car, and, as we would obviously have to stay
a couple of nights, he would make reservations for us at the
Percy, a hotel in Pelwichton that *England in Your Pocket* gave
four stars. I said I needed to be back in London on Saturday
afternoon. And so it was settled, or, rather, everything was
unsettled, for me. I felt terribly nervous about the expedition.
John said he felt nervous about driving on the left-hand side
of the road.

"Piffle," said Mrs. O'Leary. "If you're going to be lily-
livered about it, I'll drive."

〜 〜 〜

We were going to Greenwich by launch, the trip down the
Thames having been touted as a big part of the fun. The
boat departed from Westminster Pier, which is in the very
heart of London, right across the bridge from the Houses of
Parliament. Traffic was heavy on the bridge, and crowds of
people were going down the steps by the bridge to the pier,
but the atmosphere by the choppy gray water, where seven
or eight covered launches were anchored, was nevertheless

quite tranquil. This was probably due to the light. There was enough gold in the gray sky to suggest that the sun might come out, but then it was awfully damp, with some mist over the river, a combination of mist and light that made me think of Turner's late seascapes.

We were a little early for the next departure. Our party was milling around affably when suddenly we heard an ominous thundering sound. It was a group of schoolchildren hurtling down the steps, pounding over the wooden planks of the pier. I groaned quietly. We ran into these mobs of ill-mannered schoolchildren every time we went to a museum or gallery or any other edifying place in London. Apparently, in England, where the children went to school all year round, the schools tried to beguile the summer months with field trips. When I was growing up in Meridian, my little schoolmates and I had gone to the State Capitol in Jackson on field trips; here, schoolchildren had all the glories of London to visit, not that they seemed to appreciate it.

"Heavens, let's don't get in the same launch with them," murmured Allison, and we shuffled down the pier away from the little barbarians. Lucy, meanwhile, discovered a need to go back up the stairs and visit the "loo." (Even fastidious ladies like Mavis and Lucy could go to a public facility in London and be confident of its cleanliness due to the presence of some genial woman of the lower class to keep it tidy.) And now the other women in our party, even Mrs. O'Leary, wanted to go. I was pleased at how well Mrs. O'Leary seemed to fit into this group of nice Protestant ladies who taught English and traveled the world.

I lingered on the pier to talk with John, taking this opportunity to thank him again for the opera the night before.

"It's good you ran into your friend," he said.

"Mmm," I said noncommittally, trying not to blush. "It's exciting knowing somebody who lives here. Going to that party Saturday night should be an adventure," I said, not wanting to admit how much this party was on my mind. I foresaw it as a brilliant Bohemian gathering, peopled by residents of Chelsea's pastel houses. I realized that Cheyne Row was just down the river from here, on the other side of the Houses of Parliament, not far at all, I thought.

"Meanwhile, we meet Emerald Glover," John mused. "I started *Plantation Trace* last night. Read for hours. It's quite good."

"Do you think so? I'm so glad!" Sometimes I found myself wondering whether these novels I was trying to study really had any merit.

"Oh, yes, I think it's quite good—not that I'm any expert . . . "

But just then, Big Ben began to chime a quarter to ten. John held up a hand, indicating that he wanted to listen closely to the chimes.

"Aha! I thought so!" he said excitedly. "That third phrase—it's different from the Westminster chimes at LSU." He sang the London version and then the LSU version: the London version zigzagged a little, where the LSU came straight down the scale. "Of course LSU just uses a carillon."

By now, the Barston people were drifting back from the loo, and John returned to the subject of *Plantation Trace*. He was very familiar with the setting, of course, and interested in ascertaining whether the "Old Thunder Road" she used in the book was really the Woodville Road, that kind of thing. Meanwhile, we found a launch down the line from the launch the schoolchildren were clambering into and went down the aisle, finding seats on either side. The launch was covered, which gave some protection from the chilly wind, and, although it was quite low in the water, it was big and stable enough not to seem perilous as we eased away from the pier. But I was desolate, suddenly: we were leaving London! It was a kind of exile going down the river to Greenwich—there went the National Theatre, there, on the other side, the dome of St. Paul's. I gazed mournfully at the spires and office blocks of the fantastic skyline. Presently a guide appeared down in front of the thirty or forty people in the boat to begin a spiel about the view from the launch—the buildings we were passing, now mainly warehouses, also the river itself, which had undergone some kind of rebirth in recent years. He was very comical—he had a Cockney accent and the timing of a stand-up comedian—but even as I laughed with the others, I was yearning for the city that was slipping away. I even felt some alarm: the river was so broad, so blank, it seemed as if the little launch might go right on out to sea.

Actually, it was the trip to Northumberland that was bothering me. I was exaggerating its significance, I told myself. You could get up there in five or six hours, no time, and I would be back by four o'clock Saturday, but I hated to leave, nonetheless. I hated to miss *The Houseguest*, a play the Beckwiths had invited me to. Friday night they would be at the theatre, and I would be out in the wilderness. They had hotels up there, but, still, it had the sound of camping out. I tried to imagine "Northumberland." It was wild moorland with crags, great winds. I imagined trying to go to sleep up there with the howling of the wind.

Just then, the guide finished, and we all clapped enthusiastically. "I love London," I burst out to the person sitting next to me, who happened to be Allison Nicholson. "I hate to leave it."

"You do?" Allison said, sounding surprised, although to me, what I had said was a truism, no more controversial than "I love Christmas!"

"Well, yes!" I said. "I feel at home in London, far more so than I ever have in Meridian or any other place I've lived. I don't know why, I just feel at home."

"I love Paris," Allison said. "Charles and I had our honeymoon there." She sighed and said no more, and I regretted having confided in Allison. Usually, I was rather reserved with Charles's wife, never having completely made up my mind about whether she was a Yankee snob or not. Charles was not a snob, but Allison? I tried to imagine Charles and Allison as honeymooners in the City of Light. But Charles was so brisk! Allison must have been a pretty girl, but now her complexion was lined and leathery from too much sun—she played tennis—and her thick gray or frosted hair, chopped off chin-length, was swelled out and sort of frayed by the morning dampness.

"Paris is beautiful," I said, trying to be just, although I felt only antipathy toward Paris. "I guess it's because I had a tough time with the language. I studied French for years, but when I got there, it didn't seem to do any good. I could read the signs on the streets, even newspapers, but when I tried to speak French, people couldn't seem to understand me. They'd make me say things again and again. One time I asked a bus driver something, and he made me repeat it three or four times. Then he answered me in English."

"Why, that's extraordinary. I found the people in Paris perfectly lovely about the language," Allison said, looking at me in such a way as to suggest that the problem lay with me rather than the unpleasant people of France. I knew that Allison Nicholson had graduated from Vassar (although she never called her college by name when she referred to her undergraduate days, or even called "Poughkeepsie" by name, as if it might be indelicate to refer to such an insurmountable advantage); and now she seemed to be suggesting that the French

     A Prospect of London

you got at Vassar was simply more efficacious than the French you got at Whittaker. "Some people were helpful," I said, determined to be fair, recalling a particular ice cream vendor who sold me an ice cream cone ("une glace") after only one request. "It's just one or two that stick in your mind, I guess."

"I think Parisians are the snottiest people in the world," John Loganson said. He was leaning down over our seat for the purpose of handing us a hat (the guide was actually passing the hat, like some busker), and I beamed up at John, deciding, at that moment, that he was a person of great intelligence and perception, not to mention a vocal musician of the first class—his voice, I recalled at that moment, might not be an operatic voice but it was a strong, true voice with a unique plangent quality—while Allison was just an old Yankee snob. Allison, shrugging good-naturedly, took the hat and passed it on to me without putting anything in it. I groped in my purse for coins.

"They are rude, but I've always loved Paris," Lucy drawled as I passed her the hat. "My husband and I went to Paris on our second honeymoon. But the city I love is Bangkok. The river runs through the city, and there's nothing more romantic than floating down the Chaya Phraya in a little boat."

Several other people piped up over the noise of the launch to tell which city they liked the best—Edwina said New York, Mavis said Florence, Carol said New Orleans. Meanwhile, I looked out the window at the blank-looking warehouses across the water. "I think London is the best gosh-darned city in the world," I heard Sid Beckwith say. Sid was plain and simple, like a newspaperman or a sportscaster, but his heart was always in the right place, I thought warmly. This was an especially generous sentiment on his part in view of the fact that he had just been mugged.

"My theory is that the world can be divided into Anglophiles and Francophiles," Sid went on. "Have you ever noticed how people just love London or Paris, but never both equally?"

"I'm London, for sure!" I said, with a smile at Allison.

"London!" voted John.

"I'd have to go with London too," Lucy said.

"Me too," said Edwina. Mavis agreed, and murmurs of assent could be heard from the Beckwiths. Allison smiled and closed her eyes. I sat back and mused on Francophilia, which at that moment seemed an unpleasant condition I had just narrowly escaped. I was a Landry on one side, a De la Houssaye on the other. My love of New Orleans, a French city, also pointed me in that direction. I had studied French at my high school, also at Whittaker; I had gone to Paris in '72. You had to admire some things about France: it had produced such pretty pictures, such pretty music, and of course they had their language. The French always had the most precise term for everything, backed up by an academy, which made the French language seem absolute, like science or math, and this appealed to me. Yet I could not like the French. They were so aggressive about their precision and good taste. They took ordinary things like food and wine so seriously; they quarreled with you about them. I knew two Francophiles besides Allison: one a French teacher at NCLU named Mary Chase, the other, somebody named Susan Acree, the wife of a man in the history department. Both of them went to Paris nearly every year, brought back French things, cooked French meals. Perhaps it was just a coincidence, but they were both energetic and argumentative. They even carried themselves the same way—very erect, as if they were displaying their torsos. They had blank, positive expressions, and this, with their torsos, made them look like figureheads on

Mardi Gras floats. Their posture seemed to have something to do with France.

"Which city would you choose, Aunt Dora?" said John. He was sitting behind her, across the aisle, and now leaned forward, touching her shoulder. She had been asleep.

"What's that, son?" she said, looking around, blinking.

John repeated the interesting Paris/London proposition to his aunt. He was brave, I thought, like a boy hopping onto the spiny back of a dragon.

"My favorite city is Jerusalem," she announced promptly. "It's where the Lord did His work."

I wasn't sure where this fit into Sid's dichotomy, and I pondered this as Mrs. O'Leary answered questions from Mavis and Lucy about her recent trip to the Holy Land, where she had ridden a camel.

Chapter 14

As we approached Greenwich, a pretty place with brown brick buildings resembling a college, the guide described the various points of interest: the Cutty Sark, the National Maritime Museum, the Royal Observatory. Somehow they "measured time" here. You could also see the Prime Meridian, which was the official division between the east longitude of the world and the west longitude. I naively pictured the Prime Meridian as a chalk line in the grass, like the markings on a baseball field.

The Cutty Sark was up the hill in dry dock, looking much too delicate ever to have gone out to sea. (The Gypsy Moth was displayed to one side of the Cutty Sark. That this tiny, frail-looking craft had ever been to sea was completely incredible.) We boarded the Cutty Sark, descending into the hold, a dark and compact place where we enjoyed hearing Sid Beckwith tell about how uncomfortable the sailors were on long voyages, how bad their food was, and how many diseases they got. Then we moseyed along the narrow passageways and steep stairways to look at the tiny appurtenances of the ship. What little bunks the sailors slept in.

Some other Americans were touring the ship—you knew them by their Polo shirts and chino slacks, their colorful sweaters, also by their cameras, although tourists from Germany and of course Japan had very elaborate cameras too, each with a long, cumbersome lens attachment like a proboscis. There were also, as always on any sightseeing expedition in England, a surprising number of English people. I could always identify them by their mismatched clothes. English women wore flowered tops with striped skirts, or flowered tops with skirts in an entirely different floral print, the colors in the two clashing garments not even coordinating; English men were likely to dress in all sorts of plaids. They never had cameras. Or perhaps it was simply that they didn't need to take pictures. It might be that they lived right around the corner and could come back any time. The English people looked relaxed and happy in contrast to the other tourists. Whenever they caught my eye, they would smile, frequently revealing a missing tooth. Why, they were as dowdy as Russians!

Meanwhile, to our horror, the schoolchildren arrived. We had not realized that all the launches were going to the same place. The schoolchildren were as boisterous as ever. They ran up and down the ship, making a horrible racket. The boys were fighting, or pretending to fight, and the girls, most of whom were bigger than the boys, were giggling and encouraging their little admirers. They did have teachers with them—a couple of wan, listless young men who looked depressed and underpaid—but they seemed to have given up any efforts at discipline.

"Hold it, son!" somebody shouted, and I descended a staircase surely too steep and narrow for a grown sailor to negotiate to see Mrs. O'Leary standing in the hold. She had grasped the collar of some schoolboy, who was squirming like a worm. Like his classmates, who were clustering loosely around the scene, he was wearing a dark gray blazer with a crest on the pocket. I associated blazers with nice private schools, the kind the English so confusingly call "public," but somehow, I knew that Mrs. O'Leary had intervened in some rougher, state-supported institution. It was coed, for one thing, and a lot of these big, loud girls looked like the type that would smoke in the loo.

"I've never seen the like," Mrs. O'Leary said in her accusatory way, raking the crowd with a lazy gaze. "One thing you ought to learn from a ship like this is the importance of discipline. Do you think this vessel could a sailed with the sailors runnin' around like chickens with their heads cut off? They had discipline. They'd be flogged for behavior like this. We don't flog people in this day and age, but I declare, if I hear another peep out of any one of you, I'll snatch you baldheaded."

Everybody was quiet—even I felt chastened—and nobody moved until Mrs. O'Leary had released the little miscreant and climbed slowly up the stairs. Then the adult tourists began smiling at each other. The teachers, revivified, clapped their hands with authority and issued some order; the schoolchildren hastened to obey. Up on deck, people were taking their fellow travelers' pictures at the Captain's wheel. Everyone wanted a picture of Mrs. O'Leary at the helm, even some people not in our party. I did not have my camera—I could never remember to bring it—but most of the others in our group had cameras of varying sophistication, from Sid Beckwith's Nikon, which had an extra-long proboscis, to Lucy Maddox's Instamatic. Mrs. O'Leary's had an old box Brownie, which "took fabulous pictures," John told me proudly, and I believed it, having read about certain famous photographers who deliberately eschew complex equipment and achieve stunning results with something very simple. Sid and Allison had to focus and adjust the lenses of their cameras, worrying and fuming over them, while Mrs. O'Leary just pointed her Brownie and snapped.

Later in the maritime museum, I happened upon John studying a case devoted to Nelson's victory on the Nile. I took this opportunity to speak about something that had happened after lunch, which had been at a tearoom on the High Street of the town. Mrs. O'Leary snatched the check, according to her custom, and not even Sid Beckwith, who was a man's man (the kind who would take out after a mugger), could stop her. Even he had been reduced to just following along behind her, protesting feebly, while she unsnapped her purse and paid the bill. I was worried about this: nobody had expected Mrs. O'Leary to pay for all of us.

"Aunt Dora!" said John, shaking his head. "I guess I'd better tell you a little about Aunt Dora."

We sat down on a bench. Mrs. O'Leary was apparently a famous character, a law unto herself. For instance, John told me, when she was visiting with somebody and she was ready to go, she just got up and left. And her driving—she just went where she wanted to. She would pull out into a busy intersection or even run a red light, saying, "I've got to go too!" It was not exactly the cause of this behavior, John said, but the fact was, Mrs. O'Leary was inordinately rich. She was a Loganson, and that branch of the Logansons, it seemed, had timberland in Lincoln Parish where oil had been discovered a few years ago.

"Actually, Dora had money even before that," John said, lowering his voice and looking around to be sure we were still alone. "From the death of her husband."

"Did she kill him?" I asked, only half-joking.

John chuckled. "No, but he did die in a bizarre way. He had an accident. It was a long time ago, about 1930. He was a roustabout—an oilfield worker named Liam O'Leary. She met him in Texarkana when she was there teaching school. She was a good-looking girl in those days—you ought to see her pictures. He wasn't much to look at, in my opinion—just a little guy. But my mother used to say he was quite a lady killer. She talked about his blue eyes."

A magnetic one, I thought, immediately seeing this Liam O'Leary with the face and slight form of MacPherson.

"They'd only been married two or three years when Liam fell into a storage tank and drowned."

"Storage tank? Tank storing what?"

"Oil."

"You mean he fell in one of those things that looks like a giant aspirin?"

"Yep."

"How could that have happened?" I asked, feeling a pain in the back of my legs.

"I don't know exactly. He might have been drunk. He was a 'drinking Catholic,' as they say at home, but anyway, I have the impression this was part of the explanation. It's just one of those family stories you hear without ever getting any facts. All I know is that my uncle died when he fell in an oil storage tank. It's not something I feel I can ask her about."

"No, I guess not!"

"Anyway, the oil company paid her some big settlement, and she invested it. That, plus the money from the land. Also, she lives in *extreme* simplicity," John said weightily, as if to suggest no indoor plumbing. "She's paid for college for all her nieces and nephews—she paid for mine. Her only indulgence for herself is travel, and she usually takes one of us with her. Ever since she retired, she's been going all over the world, though she had a massive heart attack three or four years ago and is supposed to do all these things to take care of herself—watch her diet, rest. You know, for a while, she ate the things on her diet—brown rice and vegetables, then she'd eat whatever she wanted. When we fussed at her, she'd say, "Well, I eat the things I'm supposed to!"

We resumed our ramble after these stimulating revelations, presently rounding a corner into a small room where the others in our party were already gathered. Here were the relics of Admiral Nelson: his personal possessions, memorabilia of Lady Hamilton, but most importantly, the jacket in which he died at the Battle of Trafalgar, with bullet hole and bloodstains. I was not too clear on the details of the Battle of Trafalgar—in fact, at that moment, I could not have said just who it was that Nelson had defeated. Even so, I felt a strong emotion as I jostled with the others for the best vantage point from which to see these naval relics. Nelson's jacket was definitely the best thing we had seen all day. People were held before it as if hypnotized, and the schoolchildren coming in fell silent when they saw Mrs. O Leary bent over the case.

∾ ∾ ∾

By three o'clock, some members of the party, particularly Carol Beckwith, were inclined to want to "get on back." We stood in indecision at a rear door of the Maritime Museum, looking out across a vast greensward to a hill in the distance and, on top, a long irregular roofline with a white dome, white cupolas. This was the Royal Observatory. It looked as if it were about a mile away, and then there was the question of whether it was starting to rain. The weak light which, earlier on the river, had seemed to prefigure sunshine was gone now. Sid went outside and twirled around some, looking up at the sky.

Finally, we decided at least to take a look at the observatory. "It's just a drizzle!" some of us said, putting up our umbrellas. The stretch of grounds to the hill with the observatory was so broad it made you feel little, like an ant on a prairie, although in fact, it was nothing like an American prairie, having that delicate-looking English grass which is more like green fur than grass. Here and there were flower-beds with red poppies.

When at last we reached the hill, there was a trail to climb, and it was steep and winding, with much overhanging foliage. We could hear voices from somewhere up above. Otherwise, there was a remarkable quietness, the drizzle being too light to be heard on the leaves. We toiled upward, breathing hard (Mrs. O'Leary openly huffing and puffing, her hand on her heart). I thought we were never going to get to the top—it hadn't looked this high!—but at last, there was a guardhouse.

Usually, museum guards do not look at you: they stand in a corner of the room and show no more consciousness of your presence than the mummies in the British Museum. But these guards, perhaps because they were up here in the background and got so few visitors, actually noticed us.

"More Yanks," one of the guards remarked to the other. "You can tell by the twang."

"Yanks?" I exclaimed to Mavis when we were past the guards. "Twang?" I was a little offended to be taken for a Yankee, and as we entered the observatory, I said that the guards were almost as bad as those taxi drivers in '72 which I briefly described. And the guards hadn't even gotten the stereotype straight. "Twang" was a word usually applied to Midwesterners (Edwina!); Southerners were thought to "drawl." Mavis reminded me that "Yank" is a word the English use for Americans in general, not just people from the North.

Meanwhile, the focus of attention in the courtyard was the Prime Meridian, which was, in fact, a line on the ground made of metal strips rather than something ephemeral like chalk. People were having their pictures taken astride the line, one foot in each hemisphere, or touching hands with another person across the line, humorously enacting the notion of East meets West.

Sid was anxious for us to see the Royal Astronomer's house because it was the work of his hero Christopher Wren. No longer a residence, the house was now another museum. Just inside the door was a display of astrolabes and chronometers and other esoteric devices, but my eyes just slid over the intricate gears, past the explanatory placards. I was so tired by this time that I just stumbled through the polished and orderly little house, not taking the kind of interest in the furniture and the woodwork that the other women of the party did.

But I was able to appreciate the view. In the last room of the house was a desk by a window, and the view the Royal Astronomer would have had when he worked at his desk was the climax of the day. In the distance, beyond the park and the noble geometry of the Royal Naval College, I saw the bright little ribbon of the Thames winding away to the dense gray cluster that I knew at once to be the buildings of London. I could make out the dome of St. Paul's. It was like seeing London from an airplane. No, the view did not look real. It looked like one of those fantastical backgrounds in a painting by Leonardo or some other artist of the sixteenth century, not a landscape drawn from nature but an imaginary one designed to provoke wonder, like the topographically incoherent background in the *Mona Lisa*. Suddenly I remembered an old painting I had seen in a book, or was it an engraving, *A Prospect of London from the Royal Observatory at Greenwich,* or some such title, with ladies and gentlemen dressed in graceful seventeenth or eighteenth-century garb in the foreground and the wondrous city on the horizon.

"Come see this!" I called to whoever was handy. "Isn't this the most marvelous view you've ever seen?"

"Oh, my, that is gorgeous," said Carol Beckwith, with tears in her eyes. "And to think I wanted to go home. I'd have missed this!"

PART FOUR

THE TREE
IN JEREMIAH

Chapter 15

Leaving St. Cuthbert's for the trip up to Northumberland on Thursday morning, I felt like a little girl being packed off to camp—excited but frightened and already a little homesick. I told myself this was silly, that I was only going a short distance and would be back on Saturday—but the other people from Barston also seemed to have the idea that I was embarking on a great adventure. Wednesday evening they had offered me special clothing for the trip, also special equipment. Charles insisted I take his tape recorder. He wanted me to take his Nikon camera too, but I refused, declaring that I would never be able to work all its knobs and knockers. No, the trip to Northumberland was definitely an expedition into uncharted territory, and I left St. Cuthbert's that morning a little before eight with a heavy heart.

I felt better as soon as I saw John down in front of the Florence Hotel. He was awaiting the delivery of the rental car and already in a state of comical exasperation. His aunt, who was still inside having breakfast, had rented the car, an Austin Maxi, not from an Avis or Hertz agency in London but from some budget place in a suburb called Dorking, he explained. John fulminated about the arbitrary thriftiness of his aunt for a while. Then he decided to go inside and call.

"They say he's on the way," he came back to report in a skeptical manner reminiscent of Mr. Harold and the airline. "They had some trouble with the first car and had to make a substitution. But he'll be here shortly. They said."

John insisted that I go inside and sit with Mrs. O'Leary a while to get out of the biting wind. Ordinarily, I would have resisted such a tête-a-tête and just braved the cold, raw weather, but I hadn't had time for breakfast and really needed some tea. I was also interested in seeing the Florence. It seemed to me that the Florence had much more character than St. Cuthbert's. It was distinctly Italian. The lobby (long, like St. Cuthbert's) was decorated by prints or engravings of antiquities in Rome, and the man at the desk was also Italian. As he pointed me toward the breakfast room, I recalled other Italian places in this area I was pleased to think of as "our neighborhood." The day before, when I finally had to do laundry, Mr. Sparks had directed me to a washateria across Southampton Row on a street with the charming name of Lamb's Conduit, which proved to be in an Italian enclave of the city, with more *ristorantes* and shops, even a hospital with an Italian name.

The variety, the interest of our neighborhood was inexhaustible, I felt, tears welling up in my eyes. The breakfast room of the Florence was dim and quiet, the walls a robin's egg blue, with long tables such as might be found in the refectory of a monastery in the Tuscan hills. It was startling how different this austere breakfast room was from the jolly gold breakfast room at St. Cuthbert's, when they were part of the very same terrace, and I thought of a book I had liked when I was growing up about a community of bears who lived in a forest. Each bear had his own tree, and, while all the treehouses looked alike from the outside, each interior was decorated according to the bear's individual taste, which ranged from contemporary to medieval, the various decors having in common only a happy quality of snugness in the tree trunk. The terrace on Bedford Place was a similar collection of individual styles, and just as I was having to leave it, I felt an intense longing to stay and explore it, hotel by hotel. Even the guests sitting at the long monkish tables in the Florence looked different—more variegated than the university types at St. Cuthbert's—although I didn't have time to observe and differentiate. I was being driven away.

Mrs. O'Leary sat in a distant corner of the room in an alcove that extended to the back of the hotel and overlooked the garden. I heard an English bird. She looked up at me without surprise.

"Hello, Miss Caroline. Let me get you some breakfast."

∾ ∾ ∾

Half an hour later, I went back outside, where John was still pacing back and forth, waiting for the car.

"Why don't you show me where we're going?" I said.

We sat down on the cold stone steps, and John unfolded a map of the British Isles so big that it took both of us to hold it. London was the size of my fist. He showed me Dorking, which was many miles away but still at one edge of the fist. "London" comprised so many different places, I saw, catching sight of Greenwich, which was practically in the center of the city. John pointed to Pelwichton, which was way up the map in what might be called the neck of the island. Why, England looked huge, like Greenland! But when I remarked on this, John pointed out that England was only slightly larger than Louisiana—50,000 square miles, as opposed to 48,000. I could scarcely believe it.

Northumberland was right by the North Sea, I saw. I could envision the North Sea—wild, gray, and cold. I loved seas and oceans, I told John, although I had not seen very many, just the Atlantic Ocean a time or two and the Gulf of Mexico, if the Gulf even counted. John said that, unfortunately, we would not pass the North Sea, showing me the route we would have to follow if we had any hope of arriving for tea. It was one hundred ninety-three miles to York and seventy-seven more miles to Durham on the big red road—the M1—then about forty miles on smaller roads to Pelwichton, or three hundred and ten miles altogether, he said. Why, that was less than the distance between Barston and New Orleans, which was about three hundred thirty miles. On a good day without too much traffic, you could drive that in six, six and a half hours, I said, and John said yes, he hoped to make this trip in six or seven hours if the man from Dorking ever got here.

The phrase "the man from Dorking" struck me as funny, and I explained that it reminded me of "the man from Porlock," that faceless individual who woke Coleridge up from his dream of Kubla Khan.

"But the man from Porlock came," John said wryly, getting up. "That was the whole point of the man from Porlock."

Several cars came down Bedford Place, and I half-rose every time one passed, thinking this was the one. But when a little orange car pulled up and a man got out, we didn't even take any particular notice. We thought the beefy man climbing out of the comically small and battered car was a workman come to repair the hotel. He was dressed in the rough clothes of a workman, and the car, which had been in a wreck or two, was a little hump-backed thing with a spare tire fastened to its hood. He flexed a moment after getting out of the car as if he were stiff. Then he recognized us as his customers and touched his cap. "How do ye do. Ye moost be waitin' for me. Well, here she is," he said in some country accent, going on to apologize for the size and condition of the car with such courtesy that John could not possibly complain. He was so sorry, said the man, but on his way into the city this morning, the transmission of the Austin had fallen out, and this little Vauxhall Chevette was all that was available, much to his distress. But wasn't it good that such a defect had been discovered before we got out on the road? He presented a very positive view of the situation. The Vauxhall would certainly be adequate for our needs, he felt sure, since there were only the two of us.

"Actually, there's another person traveling with us," John said, and, as it happened, Mrs. O'Leary chose this moment to come out of the front door of the hotel. We all turned to look at her.

"Naturally, there's a reduction of the rates for the hire," the man from Dorking hastened to say. "There's more room in the back seat than ye think. Ye can move this passenger seat in the front up a ways, ye see." He opened the door of the car, showed us a lever.

"That's not our rental car, is it?" Mrs. O'Leary demanded as she came down the steps, glaring at this vehicle that was an odd orange color and looked as if it had been dredged up out of the Thames.

"That's the car," John said, scratching his ear and rolling his eyes. "It's a Vauxhall Chevette. Frankly, sir, I don't know if it'll do."

It looked so small, and the steering wheel looked extremely peculiar on the right.

"Is that a stick shift?" I asked, peering in the car.

"Good God," cried John, "we ordered an automatic."

"It's a simple little car," the man declared proudly. "I think ye'll find she serves ye well." With a determined sort of cheerfulness, he demonstrated its features. Of course, the nomenclature of the car was completely different: there was a lever for the "windscreen wipers," some trick to getting in the "boot," another for raising the "bonnet."

"Now the gearbox is a little dicey," the man said.

"Dicey?" said John, hunching over worriedly. "I've driven a stick shift, but oh, my God, you have to shift with your left hand!"

"Just be firm. It's back forward right reverse," the man said dismissively, climbing into the primitive-looking interior of the car and yanking the rusty gear shift around. "Just treat her firmly—she won't give you any trouble."

Mrs. O'Leary had her mouth pursed at him. "I guess we'll take it. I don't see that we have too much choice at this time of the day, do we, John?"

"We do need to get on the road now to be there by tea," John murmured.

I smiled politely, thinking longingly of fast, safe taxis and trains that ran on time.

"All right," Mrs. O'Leary said heavily, impaling the man with a stare. "If we have any trouble, you'll hear from me."

"Righty-o," said the man from Dorking, producing papers for her to sign.

"Can we give you a lift somewhere?" John asked.

"No, no, I'll take the Tube," called the man as he quick-stepped away. "Cheerio!"

☙ ☙ ☙

Getting out of London was harrowing, partly because I was in charge of the road atlas. I had objected to this responsibility—I'd never been able to make sense of a map—but Mrs.

O'Leary, planting herself in the back seat, had proclaimed that it made her sick to read in the car. So there I was, in the front seat, on the left, staring at the atlas, which imparted about as much information to me as a painting by Jackson Pollock. Since this is the driver's seat in a normal car, with a steering wheel in front of it, I felt strangely imperiled, as if I were on a roller coaster without a safety bar. When we got out on Great Russell Street and then into the thick swirl of Southampton Row, the Vauxhall seemed to be the littlest thing on the road, a kind of mechanized cart which was constantly being impinged upon by more powerful automobiles, particularly the aggressive taxis and buses coming at us from all sides.

The main problem, apart from the quantity of traffic, was that the streets never went in a straight line but meandered as if at random. And the names changed every few blocks, if you could even find a street sign to tell you the name. As John careened along—the traffic was so thick and fast, you could not go slowly—I looked desperately for street signs amid the welter of other signs. Only occasionally did I spot one, and then I felt the same jubilation I used to feel on car trips when Mike and I played Alphabet (where you try to find every letter in the alphabet, in sequence, on signs by the road), and I was able to find a "Q" or an "X."

Roundabouts caused a special problem because of the terrible rule of driving on the left. While I carried on this frantic search for signs, John, not being sure where he was going, naturally wanted to stay on the outer ring of these traffic circles so as to make the quickest possible exit, but this put him in the way of all the larger vehicles who knew what they were doing. Everybody blew horns at us on the roundabouts; occasionally, rough-looking men even leaned out of their windows and shouted. At one roundabout, we were crowded off the road by a truck and were left, as if beached, on a side street, trying to get back into the vortex of traffic. This took a while, with Mrs. O'Leary leaning up over the seat, saying, "Come on, John, pull out. We've got to go too!"

The situation was complicated by the fact that the gears of the little car jumped or slipped. John would put the thing in third or sometimes fourth on the rare uncomplicated stretch and suddenly we'd be in neutral. I had never known a car to do this—an old bicycle of mine had done it, requiring repeated repairs—which furthered my impression that the Vauxhall was not as sophisticated a piece of machinery as an automobile ought to be. John swore some, which his aunt probably didn't like, and it was a great relief when at last we attained the M1, which bore the picturesque name "dual carriageway" but which was, in fact, an ordinary-looking four-lane highway. John didn't have to shift now: he just sped along. We seemed to be going very fast, but everybody else on the road passed us. ("A one-legged man pushin' a wheelbarrow is lobble to pass us next," Mrs. O'Leary said scornfully.) There was no speed limit, apparently. Big cars would come out of nowhere and whoosh past, the worst offenders being Austin Rovers—"road cowboys," John called them. Rovers came by so fast he didn't dare try to change lanes.

Surprisingly, the motorway was not too different from Louisiana's I-20, except that in England you could see farther, there being no dense stands of pine trees crowding up to the highway, and the fields were neat-looking squares of various greens and golds rather than nubbly-looking cotton fields. Otherwise, the road was rather monotonous. Mrs. O'Leary instructed me to read aloud about it from *England in Your Pocket.* The M1 traced part of an old Roman road, it revealed, and we were passing places associated with famous people, like Dickens and Robin Hood. But after a time, she fell asleep, and even I nodded off for a while.

$$\backsim \quad \backsim \quad \backsim$$

We whizzed along this highway and that for hours and hours, stopping only once for lunch at some dreadful tea-shop that served sandwiches on gummy white bread spread thickly with butter and containing one paper-thin slice of ham. When at last we turned off the motorway at Durham and found the right two-lane road, I expected to be in the countryside everybody was always talking about, an "unspoilt" part of Britain. But in fact, that part of Durham County was not so beautiful. It was moorland with nothing notable about it but the vastness of the sky above, where enormous white clouds were being knocked across the sky by wind, changing shape before our eyes in the manner of time-lapse photography. The wind was blowing so hard here that it had actually broken up the cloud cover that seemed to lie permanently over England that summer like a goose-down comforter, and John had trouble keeping the car on the road. Sometimes there were hills, with the occasional industrial town that reminded me of the paper mill in Jonesfield. There wasn't even any traffic up here, at least on the road. Up above, two or three times, airplanes would come toward us, in pairs, flying low. They were olive green, obviously military, some kind of fighter planes that looked as if they were heading straight for our car. John dubbed them "batplanes," and we joked about them, pretending we were spies trying to avoid detection. But I really did feel uneasy about the planes, which came waggling through the sky at us, coming very close and looking as if they were about to open fire before they pulled up and flew away.

At the same time, I was beginning to worry about the impending visit to Emerald Glover. I had a clear picture of this. From my first reading of the little gray note, I envisioned Rutland Cottage as a small gray stone cottage surrounded by flowers. Inside sat Emerald Glover on a chair like a throne, and I approached her, my head bowed, anxious to perform my task of asking her intelligent questions about her life and work. I recalled other literary pilgrimages I had read about—that first time Henry James went to see Turgenev in Paris, or the time Virginia Woolf went to Box Hill to see Hardy—but I was no James, no Woolf. I was not worthy of such privilege. Then, too, we had Mrs. O'Leary to contend with. It seemed to me that Mrs. O'Leary was especially horsy and belligerent that day. I felt she was bent on going to Northumberland to seize Emerald Glover, by force if necessary. Granted, she had slept most of the way—she was asleep as we drove through Durham County—but that was all the more ominous. She seemed to be resting up to increase her strength for the fracas.

John was aware of this problem, however, and we developed a plan. John was going to let me off at Rutland Cottage; then he and his aunt were going on to the Percy Hotel, have tea, and check in. In an hour or so, they would come back and either come in or not come in, as I saw fit.

I shook my head again, thinking about my determination not to impose upon the old writer, who must want peace and quiet, who must, indeed, want complete solitude to live so far from civilization. John was shaking his head, too, chuckling.

"What?" I prompted.

"Oh, I was just thinking about a writer who used to live near New Orleans." This writer, he went on to say, had some admirers arrive at his place one day in a camper. He wouldn't receive them, but the admirers were not deterred. They simply camped there on the edge of the writer's property; they wouldn't leave and wouldn't leave. Finally, after about three days, the writer called the police. This story depressed me utterly.

"But those people weren't invited," John said reassuringly. "You're invited."

"Mmm," I murmured as I looked out at some gloomy crag off in the distance. "This is certainly unspoilt."

I was steeled for Northumberland to look as ordinary as Durham, but in fact, Northumberland was different from the very border. Where Durham was flat and colorless, Northumberland was hilly, and suddenly there were fields of yellow wheat waving in the wind and rich green forests. The wind blew the big clouds across the sky even faster than before, actually allowing the sun to shine through in patches on the lush fields and trees. You could see blue sky. The narrow road went up and down, up and down. There were signs along this road like "Blind Summit!" and even "!", humorous-seeming signs suggesting unique perils. It seemed, indeed, like a path through a bright virgin land in which we were the first outsiders to see.

I believed the vegetation in Northumberland to be different from that in any other place in the world. The trees seemed greener, the wheat more golden, and there were wonderful green pastures sprinkled with little yellow wildflowers that assuredly were unique. The very clouds scudding across Northumberland were different from the clouds over other parts of England. They were an especially pure white and seemed to possess great force and character, such as the clouds you fly over in a plane. There didn't seem to be any human beings in this part of England. We saw no villages, nor even any houses standing alone. The only signs we saw, apart from the comical ones alluding to the hazards of the road, were homemade-looking signboards with lists of villages or towns and the number of miles you had to go to reach them, none of which included Pelwichton. Finally, John turned off the two-lane road onto a road which, according to a hand-lettered sign, led to a town which I thought was somewhere near Pelwichton on the map, but we seemed to be getting farther away from civilization rather than closer to it. After trying one road and then another, John, as if completely out of ideas, pulled over to one side of a narrow road and stopped the car.

He took the atlas, without reproach, but then, instead of examining its tangly little lines, which made about as much sense to me as blood vessels in an eyeball, he opened his door and got out. So did I. The wind was cool, the sun was warm. "This wheat is gorgeous!" I said rapturously.

"They call this corn," Mrs. O'Leary corrected me from inside the car.

There was no sound anywhere apart from the wind undulating the wheat or corn, which stretched as far in every direction as we could see.

"Are we lost?" I said, not really caring as I breathed in the sweet cool air and felt, for the first time in so long, the sun on my face.

"I think so," said John, his face also lifted to the sun.

"There's got to be something on this road or they wouldn't a built it," Mrs. O'Leary said sensibly from the back seat. "Get a hold of yourself, John Loganson, and let's get goin.' I want some tea."

The car wouldn't start right at first, but finally, it did, and we bucked a few yards. Then the road ended, running into another road. Without any hints as to which way was the right way, left or right, John turned right, past more yellow fields. Just when I thought that we were completely lost, we came upon a small gray stone house. It was precisely the sort of house I had imagined for Emerald Glover. By some miracle, a human being was out in front of the house, looking under the bonnet of a car.

John jerked to a stop and called out, "Could you tell me the way to Pelwichton?"

The man straightened up and came forward in an obliging way, looking amused, as if we must be rather incompetent travelers not to be able to find so prominent a place as Pelwichton. "Ye can't miss it," he said in a roughly musical accent, which I thought I had heard on Public TV. He looked like a Viking—he was a statuesque blond—and, while repairing a car is ordinarily a very messy job (I thought of houses out in the country in Louisiana, the kind where people sweep the yard so that grass won't grow and where men or boys pull a car up in the yard and take it apart, how unsightly that is and how dirty they get), this man of the north was perfectly clean. Even his hand was clean when he reached in the car window to point at the atlas. Pelwichton was two or three turns down another road off the main road we had turned off back there.

"I don't suppose you'd know where Rutland Cottage is, by any chance?" Mrs. O'Leary inquired.

"Ah, Mrs. Glover now, she lives right up the road."

Chapter 16

We were surprised, as we chugged on down the road, to see a discreet white sign which said "Rutland Cottage, Bed and Breakfast." As we drove along a stone fence, slowly, looking for the place to turn off, I felt that one of my fears concerning Emerald Glover was about to be confirmed. She was poor; she needed to raise money. I pictured the bent old lady trying to sell her paintings, her eggs, trying by any honest means to supplement a meager old-age pension.

But presently, we came to the gate and turned down a gravel drive. We crossed slightly overgrown grounds of about an acre, and I saw that "Rutland Cottage" was one of those unduly modest names, not quite as incongruous as the use of "cottage" for the mansions at Newport, Rhode Island, but still an example of litotes. This cottage was actually a rambling, gabled house with a multitude of leaded windows and a steep, pitched roof. At first glance, it looked like a gingerbread house, but the exterior proved to be a mixture of brick, timber, and shingles. A casement window stood open, and I had the impression of a face, white hair.

"They expect people, anyway," I said, turning to look at John, feeling panicky, as if I were about to jump out of a plane.

"Okay, Caroline," John said, pressing my hand. "We'll be back in an hour."

The front door was under a little portico, which I entered to ring the bell. As I waited for the door to open, I turned away, waving to the Vauxhall, which was paused there to be sure I got in. The lawn was like a little park. There was a gravel path through the rosebushes and billowing oak trees. The wind was not blowing so hard right now, and, apart from the chugging of the car, it was very silent here. Suddenly I was startled by an eerie cry, like the howl of a cat. I jumped, bracing myself for something to leap out at me, but then I saw a peacock coming down the gravel path. It paused, undertaking a display of its tail.

The door opened then, and I was further startled to see a dark-haired, dark-eyed youth of seventeen or eighteen in the loose white cotton clothes of India. He bowed without smiling.

"Hello!" I said brightly. "My name is Caroline Landry. I've come to see Emerald Glover, if I may. This is Rutland Cottage, I trust. I do hope she's home."

The Indian boy bowed again and murmured something I did not catch. He stepped back to usher me in, and as I stepped over the threshold, there she was: a bent little woman materializing out of the background, wearing a smock and an old straw hat, carrying a basket of roses.

"Accommodation, for one?" Emerald Glover asked in a high, quavering voice, smiling a crooked little smile as she flung off the hat.

"I'm Caroline Landry," I said, smiling hectically. "I wrote you about your books."

"Miss Landry? But you're an American girl!" she said, coming closer, twisting around so that she could look up into my face. I am not particularly tall (five feet five), but Emerald Glover did not even come up to my shoulder. And something was definitely wrong with her back: she had a hump on one shoulder-blade and seemed unable to turn her head. I have compared Mrs. O'Leary to a turtle on a rock, but Emerald Glover really did look like a turtle the way her neck extended forward rather than straight up and down. The hump even resembled a shell. She had the bright dark eyes I knew from the pictures, but she had aged since the *Our England* picture in 1965. Now her face was extremely wrinkled, like an ancient apricot, a comparison I am compelled to make by the peculiar yellow tinge to her complexion. Her hair had been long and red once, according to Mrs. O'Leary, but now it was short and pure white, also a little wild, like cotton just pulled from the boll. "I didn't dream you'd really come," she went on, staring at me, "but I'm so glad you did. It's been years since I've seen an American girl.

"And who are these people?" Emerald Glover said pleasantly.

"These people?" I echoed, turning to see Mrs. O'Leary coming through the door, John following behind. I wanted to say something light and dismissive, such as, "Mrs. O'Leary? She's just a relative of yours who, when she heard I was coming, wanted to look in too," but my heart sank. It was no more possible to minimize the arrival of Mrs. O'Leary than, say, to downplay the approach of a navy destroyer into some private cove.

"Emerald, I'm your cousin Dora," she announced. "Your mother was sister to my mother."

Emerald took a step backward, looking perfectly blank. For one terrible moment, I thought she was going to faint.

"Emerald?" shouted Mrs. O'Leary.

"Do I know you?" Emerald Glover said warily.

"I don't 'spect you do, but you ought to—we're family."

John, meanwhile, was miming utter helplessness.

"This is my nephew, John Abbott Loganson. Your first cousin once removed, I suppose."

"Well, well, do come in and sit down," Emerald Glover chirped vacantly, gesturing us into a sitting room or parlor and ordering the Indian youth, "Rajiv," to make tea.

"It's all right," I murmured to John, who was extremely apologetic as we took our seats in oversized armchairs, and although I had the uncomfortable feeling of being part of an invasion, I could not help but look eagerly around. In the back of my mind, I now realized, I had been afraid not only that Emerald Glover was poor and barely able to make ends meet, but also that she was odd—one of those bizarre old people that collect newspapers and keep a hundred cats, drink wine all day. But the house, at any rate, was not at all odd. This was a lovely room we were ushered into, darkly paneled and full of comfortable old furniture with fine, faded rugs. The curtains were made of a dark green fabric in what appeared to be a William Morris pattern. There was an inglenook fireplace and a telly. She did have one cat, which was hunched on a chair. It was large and brownish, with such a broad tail that if you saw it outside, you might take it for a beaver.

But Emerald Glover was the focus of my attention. She had gone away to take off her gardening smock. Now she was back in a little forest-green suit (a skirt and blouse and buttonless vest) that might be homemade. I noticed anew how crooked she was and saw now that she was tremendously bowlegged, so much so, in fact, that she toddled from side to side when she walked. She was wearing shiny slip-on shoes with square toes, heavy buckles that could belong to a gnome.

"Where did you say you were from?" she asked disconcertingly in that high voice.

"Louisiana," Mrs. O'Leary said in a patient, hortatory tone. "Jonesfield, Louisiana."

"Mrs. Glover, did you get my letter?" I asked intensely.

"Of course I got your letter, dear," she said with a smile. "Otherwise, I wouldn't have written you!"

"No, I mean a second letter I posted yesterday morning, saying we were coming today, and that Mrs. O'Leary and John were coming too," I pursued, it being very important to me to establish that I had tried to be courteous. Emerald Glover shook her head, smiling. I embarked upon a complete explanation of who I was and what my errand was, also how by astounding coincidence I had run into her kinswoman in London.

"We thought you were dead, Emerald," Mrs. O'Leary inserted. "All your sisters are—Ruby, Pearl. It near about broke Aunt Jewel's heart that you never came home."

Mrs. Glover looked startled at these remarks, as who would not? And, I thought, this is a catastrophe.

But John stepped in, saying gently, "Mrs. Glover, I hope you can forgive our bursting in on you like this. We didn't mean to. My aunt and I just tagged along with Caroline, who's studying your books . . . "

Mrs. Glover gave me an alert, blazing look.

" . . . and you'd probably appreciate it if we just went on right now and left Caroline with you for a little while. We have to check into our hotel before it gets too late."

"Yes, yes," I said, anxious to reassure Mrs. Glover that we had no wish to impose. "We have reservations at the Percy Hotel."

"Well, I do wish you would stay with me," said Mrs. Glover, looking a little put out. "We take guests, you know."

She smiled, cocking her head to one side. She had been smiling continuously. In fact, she smiled so steadily I was afraid she was a little dotty. "I'm delighted to have visitors," she said. "I have so few, and none from Louisiana all these years, not one."

"I knew you wouldn't mind seeing your own kinfolks," Mrs. O'Leary said, looking solid and settled in her green velvet chair.

"You must tell me all about yourselves," said Mrs. Glover, looking brightly at each of us in turn.

"I teach in Barston," I said promptly to forestall Mrs. O'Leary from saying anything else unsettling. "But I grew up in Meridian, Mississippi."

"And you, John? I never thought I had such a handsome young relation."

John blushed to the roots of his moss-colored hair. "I'm from Jonesfield. I teach music at Louisiana State University in Baton Rouge."

"My brother James's son," Mrs. O'Leary specified.

"Well, well, Jonesfield," Mrs. Glover said, smiling a little crazily at John. She turned back to me. "So you're studying my books, my dear. You actually find things to study in them?"

"Yes, certainly. Yes, of course!" I said, though in truth, I had not exactly formulated a scholarly topic.

"Do they . . . " Mrs. Glover hesitated. "Do they read my books at your university?"

"They should," I declared warmly. "I can't say for sure that they do," I had to add, thinking of the quartet packed dustily in the stacks in what seemed, in retrospect, the most distant corner of the old wing of the NCLU library, knowing quite well that they didn't. "I've certainly read them, and Mrs. O'Leary has read them—and John is reading one now," I said, trying to suggest a wide, diverse readership, hearing as I spoke the unnerving cry of the peacock. "I discovered them last year after seeing your picture in a biography I was reading."

Mrs. Glover's eyes flared. "Biography?"

I mentioned Ralph Strachey.

"I don't remember knowing a Ralph Strachey. Did I know him?"

"I don't know whether you knew him or not," I said, beginning to relax. "I'm afraid the book didn't give much information about you, but I was so impressed by that photo. It showed a whole group at a house party at Garsington. I wonder if you'd remember that weekend?" I probed, without much hope that Mrs. Glover would remember one house party out of all the multitudinous events of her long, eventful life.

"Certainly, I remember," she said. "That awful weekend! I couldn't go to sleep either night! I felt like the devil. Do I look bad in the picture?"

"You had on a hat . . . I wish I had the picture to show you."

"Of course, somebody was always taking a picture in that crowd," Mrs. Glover said.

"Did you spend a lot of time with them?"

"Heavens, no! I never got on with those people. All they did was talk, talk, talk."

"Such brilliance," I murmured.

"They just knew how to talk," Emerald Glover said. "They were educated to it! I wasn't. I couldn't go to sleep after one of those talky evenings. I had such trouble sleeping all those years. Now I've just given up—I never sleep now. But I understand that's often the case with us older people. Isn't that true, Sarah?"

This last remark was directed at Mrs. O'Leary, who was looking around the room as if she were an appraiser from an insurance company. John cleared his throat, glaring at his aunt meaningfully.

The remark was repeated to Mrs. O'Leary, who said, "I sleep like a log."

"I visited Red Lion Square last week," I told Mrs. Glover, hoping to provoke more memories, but just then, the good-looking Indian boy came in with a large tea tray, which presented the usual distractions.

"Your old building is an insurance company now, I'm afraid. The other buildings in the square are nice—some flats, some offices," I remarked over tea.

"Did you notice an architect's office? When I lived there, I was a typist for an architect."

"Really!" I said, very surprised, as none of the four heroines was a typist. "I thought you were a nurse."

"Oh, I was never a nurse myself," she said, smiling. "I made all that up!"

"How on earth did you get way up here, Emerald?" Mrs. O'Leary demanded. "Miss Caroline said the last time anybody heard tell of you, you were in Africa."

"Africa," Mrs. Glover said, smiling. "I only went down a time or two, for my health, you see. I went with Alan when he had some business down there. Alan was my husband, you know. I lost Alan in 1968. We came to Northumberland in, let me think, 1944. I've been here nearly forty years."

"Thirty-six years," computed Mrs. O'Leary decisively. "It's 1980."

"Ah," said Emerald Glover. "Almost half my life. Is that correct, Sarah? I am eighty-six."

"Name's Dora, Emerald, your Aunt Mary's daughter. I was the one with the dog."

"I beg your pardon, Dora. In any case, I've been here more than half my life now. Of course, I'm still a newcomer to Northumberland. You're a newcomer here if your ancestors didn't fight on Flodden Field. This place was a ruin when we bought it. We had to rebuild the house and clear the land ourselves and plant it. It was completely overgrown."

It seemed impossible that only two people could do the work Mrs. Glover went on to describe in her rambling fashion: replacing the roof, knocking out walls, replacing the shingles, an architectural element more common in the south of England than in the north. I had an image of the young Emerald Glover scaling the walls like a fly, complicating the surface of these picturesque walls.

"What happened to your husband?" grilled Mrs. O'Leary.

"He died," Mrs. Glover said vaguely. "He was ill a long time. And I've not been well. That's the main reason I didn't write any more stories," she said to me. "I fell ill. After that, I didn't have much strength. People don't realize how much physical strength it takes to write."

"Well, I do," Mrs. O'Leary said indignantly. "For years, I did the church bulletin, and it liked to kill me every week!"

"But you painted," I said quickly to Mrs. Glover to prevent any blunt questions from Mrs. O'Leary relating to the old writer's spine. Also, I didn't want Mrs. Glover to think she appeared to have failed in her life or that she had disappointed us in any way by abandoning the noble vocation of novel-writing for landscaping and house remodeling, although, in fact, I did feel disappointed. Why, Emerald Glover's life in its later years was not too different from that of my own mother and grandmother, who also gardened and redid rooms, whose lives were bound by house and garden. I had run across a French term that applied to my mother and grandmother—*femme d'intérieur*, which had pleasant connotations of comfort and coziness, although the term also made me feel vaguely anxious and restless. At least Mrs. Glover had an English husband, an English house. She even had traces of an English accent. It came out every few minutes in a word ("plänt") or in certain debonair elisions ("architec-ch'rly").

"I'd love to see your paintings," I said.

"I don't paint much anymore," Mrs. Glover said dismissively, pouring more tea. "I'm too old!"

I wanted to ask Mrs. Glover more questions about the time when she wrote—the time she lived in London—but over our second cup of tea, Mrs. O'Leary changed the subject to Jonesfield, filling her old cousin in on what had happened to every member of their family back home, her account consisting mostly of what they had died of. Mrs. O'Leary also expounded on the changes that had come about in the town. Up to this point, John had been very helpful in trying to corral his aunt Dora, but now even he took part in this Jonesfield talk, asking Mrs. Glover about which streets she remembered, which houses, telling her what was there now. It seemed to interest Mrs. Glover that the house she grew up in had recently been bought and remodeled by a young doctor. She even seemed interested in the fact that the house Mrs. O'Leary grew up in was the same house she lived in now, and she was almost positive she knew John's family home on Woodville Road. The disappointing truth was that we spent most of the time over tea talking about Jonesfield. Mrs. Glover didn't know about a high school that had been there since 1940, for instance, or the new Baptist church. We had to tell her what a "mall" was.

Presently the beaver-like cat got down from its chair and went over to Mrs. O'Leary's chair, jumping gracefully into her lap.

"Oh, glory," she said, tugging fruitlessly on the cat, which, while purring loudly, had inserted its claws into the tough-looking fabric of her dress.

"Rajiv!" Mrs. Glover called gaily, wagging her head at the cat. "Jarvis is being bad!"

Rajiv darted in and took hold of the animal, extracting its claws one by one from the bombazine. Then he took it away, stroking it and seeming to cajole it in some Hindu tongue. The conversation turned to cats. I commented that the cats in England seemed larger than those at home, recalling certain examples of the species I had seen around Bloomsbury that were so huge they could hardly fit on windowsills. What I wondered was whether England had developed its own ultra-large species of cat as a result of the strict quarantine laws requiring you to leave dogs and cats six months in isolation before you bring them into the country, laws which meant, I figured, that very few cats made it in from the outside. But Mrs. Glover said she didn't know—it had been so long since she had seen an American cat. A little earlier, I had been thinking nervously about the tape recorder, wondering whether I ought to set it up, or at least take my Cambridge Reporters notebook out of my purse and write down what Mrs. Glover was saying about her job as a typist and the trip to Africa, her husband Alan, redoing the house. I had the feeling I should do this (I could just see Charles up here, his clipboard on his knee), but it would have been indelicate, I thought. In any case, Mrs. Glover wasn't giving out much information, certainly nothing of literary significance. Here we were having tea and chatting about the size of the British cat. Meanwhile, I just gazed at our hostess, trying, without much success, to connect this little old lady with the dashing young girls of the books.

CHAPTER 17

Mrs. Glover would not hear of our going to a hotel; consequently, we ended up staying the night at Rutland Cottage. There was some hemming and hawing and embarrassing insistence on the part of Mrs. O'Leary that we would pay, but even stronger insistence on the part of the deceptively feeble-looking Mrs. Glover that we would not. I was delighted to stay. Not only did this give me more exposure to Mrs. Glover and her habitat, but, I realized, it was actually the first time I'd been in a private house in England. (Of course, as a bed and breakfast establishment, it was open to the public, in a sense, but weren't just about all the houses in England, even the great ones, reduced to this fund-raising expediency?) Mrs. Glover asked us to sign her guest register, where I saw with interest that Rutland Cottage had had hundreds of guests. The first entry in the register (a couple from Cheshire) was dated June 3, 1969, and this was followed by page after page of the names of people from all over the world whom I took to be renters of cars who had the good luck to find such nice lodgings in this remote corner of the countryside.

Rajiv took us upstairs to our rooms. Mrs. Glover had told us that Rutland Cottage had been built in the sixteenth century as a farmhouse and that, although the house had been expanded considerably and remodeled time and time again, parts of it were the original house. We followed her up a winding staircase of wood quite worn by centuries of use, and, while Mrs. Glover wouldn't have had to stoop to walk through a door upstairs, I had to watch my head, and Mrs. O'Leary, of course, had to stoop way down. The bathroom, in contrast, was modern, a fairly large room with a blue carpet and the unexpected luxury of a shower stall in one corner. My room was to the rear of the house. It had a sloping ceiling and another inglenook fireplace with an armchair. Bookcases lined two walls, and the bed, with a filigree iron bedframe, was covered with a golden coverlet and a pile of plump pillows—a perfect bedroom, I thought.

I looked down on the gravel drive, which extended around to the back of the house. Apparently, Mrs. Glover liked animals: an English setter was sunning himself on the gravel and several more cats prowled about. Occasionally a peacock strutted into view, and later when we took a turn around the grounds, a line of ducks marched across our path. It was charming. Rutland Cottage seemed more like a playhouse, or a dollhouse, than a residence for grownups. But there was a vegetable garden out back, and some chicken coops, also a barn with some heavy farm machinery parked in front—a tractor, a tiller—which betokened real work. But honestly, when I raised the window and breathed in the air, heard the cry of a peacock ("mew!"), the place did not seem real.

I took a few minutes to write down what I had gleaned about Emerald Glover's life: that she had been married since 1921 to one Alan Glover, an officer in a "Building Estates" institution; that she had worked as a typist during the 20s and 30s; that she and her husband had moved to Northumberland in 1944, buying some overgrown old property, clearing the land and completely remodeling the house; that Emerald Glover had suffered an illness of some undisclosed nature and that she continued to suffer ill effects from that illness; that at some point she stopped writing, turning her attention to painting and gardening; that since the death of her husband in 1968 she had maintained their house in beautiful fashion, taking in overnight guests. This information fit on one sheet of my Cambridge Reporters notebook. I was going to have to get more information than this. Naturally, I could not take the tape recorder down to dinner, but I determined to ask Mrs. Glover if we might get together the next morning for an hour or so after breakfast and really talk. "Really talk," in my mind, consisted of my asking Emerald Glover questions and Emerald Glover answering them, into the machine, with Mrs. O'Leary in a totally different part of the house, or better still, out of the house completely. (John would help me with this.)

Feeling better, I examined my room more closely. The one picture on the wall was a watercolor entitled *From Filey Brigg*—a nice seascape in grays and purples with the initials "EG" in the lower righthand corner. The nightstand had a selection of books—not the quartet, by the way (as far as I could see, the guests at Rutland Cottage would never know their hostess had been a writer), but a selection of novels by English authors. I saw A. E. Coppard and A. J. Cronin, authors I recognized from *Masterpiece Theatre,* and other writers who were not necessarily first-rate by my graduate school standards but who could be counted on for "scenes," evocations of the gentle charm of England whose books were the kind of thing you'd like to read in a hammock on a long summer's day. Rutland Cottage was the kind of place where you'd like to come and rest for two weeks—just sleep late and read. The Harolds would like it here, I thought, vowing to tell them about it. I had never stayed in a place I could recommend to the Harolds!

Dinner was served in a small dining room dominated by a sideboard that displayed a collection of china plates. One window overlooked a rose garden. I could hear the cry of the peacocks.

"Flannery O'Connor raised peacocks too," I commented to Mrs. Glover as we were sitting down at a long, glossy table elaborately set with blue and white china. Someone (Mrs. Glover?) had folded white napkins into stiff little towers.

"Did she?" Mrs. Glover said absently, seeming not to recognize the name. I did not mind: I was resigned to the fact that conversation at dinner was not going to be literary. This was like a family dinner in a formal home, and, like John, I seemed to be paying a visit to some ancient old aunt. Mrs. Glover appeared to be enjoying the visit. She seemed to have had no part in the preparation of dinner, and now she took no part in serving it. Rajiv did all the work, scurrying between kitchen and table, while Mrs. Glover presided at the head of the table like a queen of the gnomes.

"How'd you come to hire this Indian, Emerald?" Mrs. O'Leary said in a loud voice which implied a sensible distrust of foreigners.

He was the grandson of a friend of a friend, Mrs. Glover said vaguely, a brilliant boy preparing for exams that would get him into Oxford. I gathered he was an aristocrat—Mrs. Glover named his grandfather, someone with a long Indian name who sounded noble—but an aristocrat who had fallen on hard times and had to hire himself out. Apparently, it was a common practice these days for aristocrats from the colonies or former colonies to work their way up in England. And Rajiv was only the latest in a series of students who had spent time working at Rutland Cottage, according to Mrs. Glover. I thought of all those brown scholars in the tearoom of the British Museum fanning out into the countryside, when suddenly I was struck by the fear that this Rajiv was an Emerald Glover scholar who had moved in and cornered the market, the way, say, Robert Craft had done with Stravinsky. But he was studying chemistry, I learned with relief.

The food was local—I mean literally local, grown on the place (we were having one of the chickens that laid the eggs). Our dinner was superb: roast chicken, crispy new potatoes, and tiny peas. There was also a crisp lettuce salad. I ate with gusto. It occurred to me that I hadn't had a fresh vegetable in two weeks. The food at the *ristorante*, which I had thought so satisfactory at the time, seemed canned in retrospect. You could get pale and sick, eating at the *ristorante*!

Over a dessert of strawberries and cream, Emerald Glover brought up the subject of New Orleans, where she had gone as a girl, the only place she had ever been before she ran away to Europe. She remembered buying pralines attached to a miniature bale of cotton. "Do you ever go to New Orleans?" she inquired.

"Not too often," I said. "The city has a lot of problems. A lot of crime. High prices."

"A lot of the American cities are like that now, I understand," Emerald Glover said. "I watch the telly news sometimes. But they have riots in this country too, you know."

"It's the immigrants," Mrs. O'Leary said, looking straight at Rajiv.

"It is often the immigrants, I believe," said Mrs. Glover sociably. "Unemployment is a problem just now, with Mrs. Thatcher and her reforms."

Mrs. O'Leary said, "A smart woman. Just what this country needs."

"Have you ever been to Mardi Gras?" Mrs. Glover asked John, who had been absorbed in his strawberries. "I've read about Mardi Gras. Is it really wonderful?"

John had gone to New Orleans several times for Mardi Gras, and he began describing the marching bands and the floats with people throwing beads, and how you got in the spirit of trying to catch beads at all costs, the noise, the euphoria. I chimed in with a couple of stories about going to Mardi Gras. I grew excited talking to Emerald Glover—I was used to trying to talk to older people like my mother and grandmother, the Harolds, Mrs. O'Leary—people who had their minds made up about life and who might give you the floor for a moment but who would yank it back without notice. But Mrs. Glover sat rapt, drinking in what you said.

Meanwhile, Mrs. O'Leary was pursing her lips, appearing to have about as much empathy with enthusiasts of Mardi Gras as with headhunters in New Guinea. But she, too, had been to New Orleans one time.

"I went down there on the bus for a Methodist Conference," she said. "Somebody was supposed to meet me, but I got to the bus station and nobody was there. So I went out in front to look for a taxi, and the first thing I saw comin' down the sidewalk was a man with a monkey. A *monkey*, in a red suit! Then I saw a woman just talkin' to herself and wavin' her arms, like a crazy person. I just turned around and went back inside the station and bought a ticket for Jonesfield."

Mrs. O'Leary set her mouth and looked indignant, but then she seemed to be clearing her nasal passages or snorting, and suddenly she let out a big laugh. It was a distinct "he-he-he" from the great buttress of her diaphragm. She continued to laugh until tears ran down her face, with

John and me joining in. We rose from the table, Mrs. Glover laughing a tinkly little laugh that sounded like wind chimes.

∾ ∾ ∾

In Louisiana, it is clear and cold and really dry about three days out of every year, and the air is never as thin and pure as the air of Northumberland, which seems light blue at dusk. I thought the vegetation of Northumberland was unique, as I've said. Well, the air seemed unique, too, and that evening when we went outside after dinner, I even entertained the idea that it might be superior to that "English air" in London of which I've made so much. John and I trailed along behind Mrs. Glover and Mrs. O'Leary as Mrs. Glover pointed out each variety of plant, and flowers I had never heard of, such as fritillaries and martagon lilies. Mrs. Glover and Mrs. O'Leary were as different as the rose and the cactus, but they had a strong mutual interest in gardening. Mrs. Glover had a large and varied garden, and Mrs. O'Leary, John informed me, raised vegetables and flowers; she even mowed her own yard. Mrs. Glover had a night-blooming cereus, which bloomed only every four or five years, on which occasions she would sit and watch it all night long. I admired this devotion to growing things, which seemed to take so much time. The final stages of gardening—the cutting of flowers, their artful arrangement in some pretty vase—appealed to me greatly. But the early stages (the wet, clinging dirt, the possibility of worms) appealed not at all. I did have three or four potted plants, however, and as we walked around the grounds of Rutland Cottage, I thought about them for the first time since the night before leaving for London. I had bought some watering devices which promised to dole out just the right amount of water for them until I got back, but I fully expected them to be dead.

"Do you like gardening?" I asked John.

"Hell, no," he said cheerfully.

Finally, the sky darkened a little and we went inside, lightheaded with the cold. A fire was going in the sitting room, and cordial glasses were set out on a table before it. Mrs. Glover graciously offered us cherry cordial. Mrs. O'Leary assumed that hooded temperance look.

"It's medicinal, Dora. It'll do that rheumatism of yours more good than anything in the world," Mrs. Glover said, and to my surprise, Mrs. O'Leary accepted a glass. We sat close to the fire, which gave the room a pleasant rosy glow. I admired the fabric of the curtains, now drawn closed. William Morris's Blackthorne pattern, Mrs. Glover confirmed.

"It's cold as a wedge up here, Emerald, and it's July," Mrs. O'Leary said. "How far is this from the North Pole?"

"The doctors told me it would kill me," Mrs. Glover replied. "They advised me to move to Italy or the south of France."

"Doctors!" Mrs. O'Leary said with scorn. "Hmmp! I prefer your medicine, Emerald," she added, holding her glass up to the firelight. "Reminds me of cough syrup." She took a stiff dose.

"It's excellent!" I hastened to say, and John said, "Hear! Hear!" The cherry cordial was intensifying the little glow produced by the air. I was here, by the hearth of Emerald Glover! I laughed at the person I had been that morning, the nervous traveler filled with foreboding about the wilds to the north. I mustn't dread the unknown. I mustn't get old!

"Northumberland is simply wonderful," I said boldly to Mrs. Glover, "but it seems as though you'd want to live in London. That's where I would live, if I could live anywhere I wanted to."

"Ah, London!" Mrs. Glover said, wagging her head back and forth. "I used to love it, when London was London. But I could never live there again."

"Really? Why?"

"Alan always hated London. He hated pavement, you see. He needed the green. I remember Alan saying, 'come on, my love, let's go for a tromp.' That's what he'd say on a beautiful morning: 'come on, my love, let's go for a tromp.'"

"I married an Irishman, Emerald," Mrs. O'Leary announced.

"I married a Jew!" retorted Mrs. Glover, and the two old ladies stared at each other.

"Glover, Glover," Mrs. O'Leary murmured as if trying to sound out the name's ethnic overtones.

"He was born in London—Dulwich, to be precise. He rose to great prominence in the city."

"Jews!" Mrs. O'Leary exclaimed, embarking on this favorite topic. "They do have a gift for money! They're God's Chosen People, but I've never understood why—"

"Aunt Emerald," John said divertingly, leaning forward to change the subject, although, in fact, Mrs. Glover was looking at her cousin Dora with tender interest and did not appear to be offended. By the way, in saying "Aunt Emerald," John was using a form of address that had been decided upon at the dinner table. Even Mrs. O'Leary, who took a strong interest in the genealogy of the Loganson family and who had identified her nephew John Loganson as "first cousin once-removed," thought it seemed more appropriate that he call her "aunt" than "cousin" in view of her advanced age. "Aunt Emerald," he said, "what do you know about Hadrian's Wall? We thought we'd go see it tomorrow."

"The wall! I've not been there in ten or twelve years!" she said, closing her eyes for a moment. "But there are several good places to see it. Do you know that most of the houses in this county are built with stones from the wall? The Percy Hotel has stones from the wall. For the best view of what's left, I suggest you go to Housesteads. And Chesters. Chesters is a fort, you know. And you must see Brocolitia."

"You must come with us, Emerald," said Mrs. O'Leary.

"Oh, could I?"

"You too, Miss Caroline."

"Well, I suppose," I said, finding myself wanting to go to these places which interested Mrs. Glover but torn, anxious to get on with the business of talking about her books.

John mentioned *Norma,* which, I gathered, was an opera having to do with the Romans, and the talk turned to singers. Emerald Glover, it now came to light, was as ardent about opera as John. She and her husband used to go to the opera at Covent Garden, and after they moved north, away from any opera houses, they sustained themselves by collecting recordings of operas. They would sit by the fire on evenings like this, Mrs. Glover recalled, listening to their records. With John's enthusiastic encouragement Mrs. Glover toddled off to fetch some of her favorites. These were ancient 78s. John was asked to operate the record player, an old high-fidelity set that required much fiddling and adjustment. Both John and Mrs. Glover went into raptures over the crackly recordings, though it sounded as if the singers were down in a well, and even Mrs. O'Leary, who sat back with her eyes closed, appeared to tolerate them fairly well. They particularly liked one famous old soprano of the past, Kirsten Flagstad, whom even I knew about because she was the inspiration for Willa Cather's heroine in *Song of the Lark,* though I was amazed at how hooty and terrible her voice sounded on the ancient recording. But I was objecting to more than just the quality of the recording, I believe: to me, the soprano sounded like a woman who went to my church in Barston. I called this woman, who dominated the soprano section of the choir and sometimes even inflicted solos on the congregation, "the terrible gray-headed warbler."

"Does the train still come through Jonesfield?" Mrs. Glover asked suddenly as some shrill song died away. "I remember being out on the screen porch and hearing the whistle as the train came through. I never saw the train—it was beyond some woods across the street. You know, I never knew where it came from or where it was going."

"It was just going to the paper mill," Mrs. O'Leary said matter-of-factly. "That was the log train."

"It still runs," John said. "I love that whistle too. What timbre!"

John realized he had made a pun of a sort and was pleased with it, though the pronunciation ("tam- ber") made his joke rather oblique, and only Mrs. Glover got it before it was explained. Then they began to reminisce about Jonesfield again, but I didn't even mind now, it was so pleasant by the fire. It was so English here, I thought, reveling in the fact that I was in an actual Tudor house. It was completely dark outside, at last, but still, I was conscious of the lawn and the roses and the English bricks and shingles. The peacocks emitted their shrill cry—a pleasantly lonely sound which resembled a train whistle as well as a cat—and Mrs. O'Leary remarked, "It's a wonder you can sleep with all those birds, Emerald. Sakes alive!"

Mrs. O'Leary accepted a refill of cordial. "Emerald," she said confidentially, "you ought not to take in lodgers in this out-of-the-way place. You can't tell what kind of people they'll be. You might get murdered! Mrs. Hicks took in lodgers for years in Jonesfield, and last year one of 'em killed her with a rake."

"Aunt Dora! Aunt Dora!" John chided with his eyes closed, shaking his head slowly from side to side, but he was smiling peacefully. Such a warning seemed so preposterous in this beautiful place.

Mrs. Glover looked benign.

"Mrs. Hicks," she repeated, smiling, and I stared at her face in the firelight, impressed with how many knobs and wens it had, like one of those rubber masks for Halloween. And yet, she was not ugly. Indeed, she was actually pretty in the firelight with her aureole of white hair.

"You ought not to live alone. You're gettin' too old," Mrs. O'Leary continued instructively as we got up to go to bed. John looked after the fire, and I took the cordial glasses to the kitchen, which looked old-fashioned and behind the times, something like I remember my grandmother's kitchen looking when I was a child. As I returned, I heard Mrs. O'Leary's strong, heavy voice.

"I want you to consider goin' home with us, Emerald, back to Jonesfield. It's high time you went home. It's not safe. You're not strong. You ought to be with your family. You've got nieces and nephews, cousins—people to take care of you. Good people, like John here. Miss Caroline is just down the road in Barston."

But Mrs. Glover didn't answer, and I remember thinking, she can't leave this place—take her out of this rarefied air of Northumberland and this house she built up brick by brick, shingle by shingle, and she'd crumble into dust.

Chapter 18

Mrs. Glover and I didn't "really talk" the next morning—there was too much to do, with breakfast and such. The fact is, Mrs. O'Leary was a champion of the early start, and it was only about eight o'clock as we set out on our sightseeing expedition. Both Mrs. O'Leary and Mrs. Glover insisted on sitting in the back seat of the Vauxhall, and we were off in a fierce grind of gears. I read aloud from *England in Your Pocket* about our first stop, Chesters, where we would see well-preserved remnants of Roman barracks, stables, and baths. Remnants of the Roman bridge over the River North Tyne were supposed to be particularly well preserved.

I looked around and saw Mrs. Glover leaning forward into the wind. She was wearing an elaborate traveling costume this morning—a tweed suit with a long skirt and a vest and a jacket, and over this, a long black cape. The rather artistic effect was heightened by a red velvet beret in her cottony hair. But the way she was smiling reminded me of something that had nothing to do with art; rather, it reminded me of Mitzi, a cocker spaniel I had when I was growing up, and the way Mitzi looked when she rode in the car, her ears blowing back in the wind. I felt a surge of hope. We hadn't really talked, but we were going out in Emerald Glover's country now—perhaps I could learn something after all.

At first sight, Chesters, the place with the fort, did not seem to be anything very extraordinary. You went down a country lane to a stone building that looked like a Boy Scout hut, out beyond which were fields of long green grass. Beyond the fields were some wooded hills, and you could hear the wind and the sound of rushing water. The stone building turned out to be an excellent museum, with archaeological finds and scale models that told the story of the Roman occupation of Britain. "It must be ten years since I've been here," Mrs. Glover said, beaming as she toddled reminiscently around the cases, followed by John and Mrs. O'Leary, who also attended the exhibits attentively. I tried to learn something about the Romans, but it was no use. I was too distracted to read. I had to get out in the air.

At the door of the hut, I encountered another visitor as he came in, a backpacker in big boots. You would think that no one else would be here in this hidden pocket of Northumberland except the guards, yet this backpacker was here; and a mystifying quantity of other people were on the path, which was bordered by fenced fields. In one stood two fine horses in the high, waving grass. More people were at the ruins taking photographs. Some were actually climbing on the ruins, despite the several signs prohibiting such liberties. I expected actual barracks and baths, but in fact, the ruins were just the outlines of these structures in gray stones. Other people seemed fascinated by these remnants, studying them closely with reference to a guidebook, but they did nothing for my imagination. Well, they did remind me of Block City, this building set I had as a child consisting of interlocking white plastic "bricks" about the size of the first digit of your finger. The set, which came in a tall can, included windows and doors and gables and other building accessories, even sections of roof, which were red. Theoretically, you could construct any kind of building (the can pictured a great variety of buildings that went to make up Block City). But, perhaps because there was only the one kind of red roof, one kind of door, the set seemed to lend itself exclusively to the ranch house or something really plain, like a jail. I started thousands of buildings, intent on creating a uniquely interesting block house, but they all turned out much the same, and I was reminded of this as I looked at the rim of gray stones which was supposed to represent the barracks and, on down the way, the baths.

A field or two away from the ruins was a real house, a handsome residence in (this was curious) the style of a chateau, but I lost interest in it once I caught sight of another house in the opposite direction, way up on a hill in the distance. I immediately fell in love with this house. It was gray stone, just a small house nestled among some oak trees. It was not the only house on the hill—once you got out to the ruins, you could see several gray stone houses. Even so, I still thought of Northumberland as basically unpopulated. Each of these houses seemed to be isolated, complete in itself, unknown to the other houses or indeed to anybody but me.

Keeping an eye on my house, I went down to the river, which was shaded by thick, fluffy trees. It was a wonderful river, clear and fast-moving, noisy as a waterfall, and the wind was blowing so hard that the trees moaned and groaned. You had to work hard to get near the water—there was a steep bank with a drop of four or five feet, then a stretch of slippery round rocks—but I braved these obstacles (treading carefully in my Famolares, slipping once, but staying upright), in order to dip my hand in the river, which was freezing cold. The bottom of the river was covered with thousands of rounded rocks—it was paved, this river, as if the Romans had managed to install a subaqueous mosaic. The water was as clear as a goblet of ice water (amazing to a person whose main experience of rivers was the brown old Mississippi).

I was conscious of somebody up on the bank and turned with a smile, expecting to see John looking over, but it was that backpacker I had seen entering the museum. He jumped down the bank and began striding easily toward the water in his heavy hiking boots, which seemed to grip the slippery rocks like the suckers of an octopus. I opened my mouth to pass some pleasantry about this—he looked like a student—but he would not catch my eye, being German, I suppose, or some other unfriendly nationality, and for a moment, I felt oddly forlorn.

❧ ❧ ❧

We drove on to Brocolitia through open country. Fields stretched out as far as you could see—velvety yellow fields, green fields with little yellow flowers—and the sky was splendid, with white, fast-moving clouds. The wind buffeted the little car around so much that John had to wrestle with the steering wheel to keep it on the road. All the roads looked alike. Even Mrs. Glover, who had lived here forty-four years, had trouble finding the next point of interest. It was eleven o'clock when we reached Brocolitia and the next ruin, the Temple of Mithras. This one was just off the side of the road, beyond a gate or two. You knew you were going on somebody's private property this time, and it frightened me, momentarily, when I saw the owner's cows sort of hustle toward us, but they quieted down and resumed eating grass. After several fields, we went down a hill to a rectangle of stones that was supposed to be the ruin of a temple to the sun. I could understand worshiping the sun in England, I thought, waiting for it to come out from behind a cloud. I couldn't see much of interest in the ruin, but the country was grand out here. I loved the little yellow flowers, which Mrs. Glover told me were poppies. I had thought all poppies were red; these were special Northumbrian poppies.

It was almost noon when we got to Housesteads. This domestic-sounding name was given to another fort, this one right on Hadrian's Wall. It was still out in that open country, and as we pulled into the parking lot at Housesteads, where again I was struck by the large number of cars, and saw the fort way up on a hill in the distance, John expressed doubt that we should try to see it. The wind was blowing very hard now, and in the last few minutes, the white clouds had been replaced with bulging dark gray masses. The people walking up a winding path toward the ridge looked awfully small, and the sheep on the hill were like wool toys. You knew, then, that it was quite a trek and that the people who undertook it were likely to get soaked. In fact, it looked as if you would be walking right up into the worst of the storm clouds.

John was looking up through the "windscreen" as if out of a burrow. "Um, ladies, I wonder if maybe we ought to skip Housesteads."

"Oh, I hope not!" piped Mrs. Glover. "This is the best part! I can't have you miss Housesteads!"

"We have our scarves and raincoats," Mrs. O'Leary said in a tone suggesting that John was a pantywaist.

"What do *you* think, Caroline?" John turned to ask in his mild, probing way, as if we were the parents of headstrong children.

"It's hard to say," I replied, looking out at the dramatic clouds. I heard the not-so-distant rumble of thunder. "Is that a museum up there?"

Another Boy Scout hut was visible part of the way up the hill, and after a vigorous discussion, in which Mrs. O'Leary took the lead, we decided to start out and seek shelter there if the storm broke. It was slow going with Mrs. Glover, and Mrs. O'Leary did not help by charging on ahead, turning periodically to chastise us for dawdling. The path was very rough. In some places it looked as though it had just been dynamited out of the hill to provide footholds for the sheep, and I was sure a storm would break at any second. I even felt a drop or two in the wind that whipped around us. The path did not go straight up, as it had seemed to from the car; rather, it made a very gradual ascent. The higher we went, the wider the vista behind us, and after a while, it seemed as if you could see the whole county. And the sky! I was sure I had never seen so much of the sky or been so completely exposed to the elements, as they say. I felt dizzy from the wind, which actually whipped the sense out of you, like a ride in a fast convertible. As we approached the museum, I wanted to go in, just for some relief from the wind, but Mrs. Glover and Mrs. O'Leary sighted some ruins, the same kind of stone rectangles we had seen at Chesters and at Brocolitia, another Roman Block City. Shouting to each other, they charged off that way.

Hadrian's Wall runs along the crest of this hill, which, as we had learned from *England in Your Pocket*, is part of the Pennine Mountains, a long mountain chain often called the Backbone of England. Why, this was Whin Sill, I realized, the very place where Emerald Glover had been photographed holding on to her painting for *Our England*. Once you got up here, you saw that it was possible to mount the wall, which was only five or six feet high, and walk along it, but I didn't want to—what I wanted to do was go back down to the car and brush my hair, go somewhere for lunch. I was hearing more thunder and recalling the oft-repeated folk wisdom about lightning striking the highest thing in the landscape. This had always been a comfort when I was down on the ground in regular circumstances, but it was hardly comforting now.

"Don't you think we'd better go back?" I shouted to John.

"They want to walk the wall," he shouted back with a pained expression, and, preposterous though it seemed in these frightful conditions, people were walking the wall. It looked about as safe as walking on the wing of an airborne airplane. Just then, a family with two little girls was descending some steps from it. They were laughing, and—this was astonishing—they hardly looked windblown at all!

John, who apparently was willing to go to any length to accommodate his old relatives, helped them up the steps to the wall, then held a hand out to me. I was indignant—Mrs. O'Leary had a weak heart, and Mrs. Glover was so old and fragile she looked as if she were made out of matchsticks, neither having any business being on this dangerous rampart. But once we were up on the wall, I saw that it was not so perilous after all. It was actually as wide as a sidewalk. And to the other side of the wall, conditions were completely different. The side we had just come up was wind-whipped and under threat of a deluge, but on the other side was the steep incline to a peaceful-looking valley. There was a little lake down there, so far away it looked about the size of a dish of water for the cat. You saw some minuscule sheep, with the sun shining on them. I could see that the Romans had found an excellent defensive position here at Housesteads, and I followed along as we began to go down the wall.

In any case, we were soon in a wooded area that didn't have such a sharp drop to the right, where you couldn't even feel the wind, though you could hear the trees creak and groan from it, calling to mind the phrase "shiver me timbers." There was something else strange about this place among the trees: to our left was a thick carpet of tropical-looking ferns, which would look perfectly normal in Louisiana, but which were very surprising up here.

I commented on the odd flora.

"Oh, you can see all sorts of wonders on the trails," said Mrs. Glover up ahead. The Pennine Way, she went on to say, was a hiking path renowned as the roughest, bleakest path in the nation. This was an easy part! Elsewhere it was rugged peat and gritstone. There was one especially difficult portion of fissured limestone where Alan once broke his leg. It sounded ghastly to me, did the Pennine Way, but Mrs. Glover seemed quite nostalgic for it, and John said he definitely planned to come back next summer and hike the whole thing.

"Get good boots," quavered Mrs. Glover, toddling down the wall, and I thought what a remarkable old person she was. Frankly, I was not even thinking of Emerald Glover as a writer by that time. It seemed to me that her life had been very long, like this mountain range, with those novels of hers just one outcropping way back in the past. A more recent outcropping was her painting ("Her greatest problem is the wind!"), but elsewhere along the chain was secretarial work and bad health and marriage and household renovation and now, I learned, serious walking. She disclosed that she and Alan had once walked the entire length of the Pennine Mountains, from their beginning down in Lancashire all the way up to their end in Scotland. Mrs. Glover extolled the footpaths of Britain. Did we know that you could get from almost any town or village in England to the next by means of public paths? That was the way to see England, she said, and I stored that away to tell the rental-car enthusiasts.

Presently we were out in the open again where you could scarcely talk for the wind. But at least the sun was shining on us now, the threat of the storm removed. Mrs. Glover drew our attention to some trees down the slope that were knotted and gnarled, completely bare of leaves. Clearly, fierce winds were the norm in these parts. When I took out my notebook to write "ferns" and "wind!" the wind was so strong I thought the notebook might be swept out of my hands and down to the valley below. This really might be too much for Mrs. O'Leary, I thought, and it occurred to me that Mrs. Glover might well be blown off this crest. Both John and I were actually in the act of reaching out to Mrs. Glover to save her from this catastrophe when she wavered and swayed, then sank gracefully to the path.

"Emerald!" Mrs. O'Leary said sharply, leaning over her. "Speak to me!"

John was hunkered down, taking her pulse. In a moment, he looked up and nodded, his eyes going blankly from me to his aunt in indication that she lived; at the same time, he stroked her white hair. Farther on, some people appeared over a rise and came toward us. John found it necessary to move her to one side, hefting her gently. Her body looked alarmingly limp.

"She's gone, oh Lord, she's gone!" Mrs. O'Leary groaned, looking stricken, flapping her purse over her old cousin—as if she needed more air!

"I think she's just fainted, but we've got to get her down from here," John said, rising to his feet with his little burden.

"We've got to get a doctor," I said in desperation, suffused with the fear that all was lost, that it was all our fault. "I wonder if they have a phone in the museum?"

John was already heading back down the trail with Mrs. Glover, and Mrs. O'Leary and I followed along behind, our attention riveted to the back of John's beige windbreaker, Mrs. Glover's cottony head sticking out to one side, her gnome shoes to the other. We had to go up and down on the path, up and down and left and right (the backbone of England not being very straight here); we had to pass into the woods and out of them. Then, with some anxiety, we had to negotiate the steps from the wall. Thank heaven the weather was less violent on the hillside now, though there were still gusts of wind. Just as we started down the long, rugged path, two bat planes came out of the sky and headed straight for our exposed position, as if they were piloted by kamikazes with plans to crash on the hill, though at the very last second, they veered away and tore off in some other direction. The path seemed interminable, and during the long progress down, our party met several other parties of visitors to Housesteads whose expressions, on seeing us, indicated a new respect for the rigors of this trail.

❧ ❧ ❧

What happened next is something of a blur. At one point, I cut away from the group and ran over to the museum, where the guards, disavowing any knowledge of first aid, gave me directions to a clinic in Pelwichton. With shaking hand, I attempted to transcribe these directions in my notebook, then ran down the hill. By this time, Mrs. Glover was lying with her head in Mrs. O'Leary's lap in the back seat of the Vauxhall, with Mrs. O'Leary continuing the fruitless fanning with her purse.

"Start, dammit," John said, and the car, which had been going yih-yih-yih in this anemic way, finally kicked over.

"Hallelujah!" shouted Mrs. O'Leary. "She's comin'

around, y'all. Her pulse is strong, and I think her color's comin' back."

With this hope, we embarked upon the maze of roads. I tried to tell John the right way to go, based on the guards' directions, but there were no road signs of any kind. One time we took a road we thought would take us to Pelwichton, and it turned out to be the drive for some country hotel. Mrs. Glover seemed to slip in and out of consciousness. "Take me home," she quavered during one period of lucidity. "I want to go home!"

"We're just going to stop by a clinic in Pelwichton, Aunt Emerald," John said soothingly. We were emerging from the hotel drive, with John looking first one way and then the other, trying to decide (as he put it later) "which the hell way Pelwichton was."

"Take me home," Mrs. Glover repeated more aggressively, and Mrs. O'Leary leaned up and said, "Well, take her home, John!" as if John had her out here on the road as some kind of prank.

"I think we ought to stop at that clinic," John said courageously, looking into the rearview mirror. "It won't take long."

"If you're talking about that clinic in Pelwichton, I won't go. The doctor there is a beast," said Mrs. Glover.

"A beast," said John with a sigh, deciding to turn left, scowling at the road, suddenly realizing that he had naturally positioned the car in the righthand lane, which was, however, occupied by a lorry hurtling toward us at a high rate of speed. "Oh, shit!" he said, yanking to the left.

"We could call a doctor from Rutland Cottage," I said nervously.

John nodded, concentrating on his driving and the seemingly hopeless task of finding Mrs. Glover's house. But at last, we did find it. Once there, Mrs. Glover would not go to bed but, rather, insisted on sitting by the fire. "Lunch," she commanded in that weak, eerie voice, and Rajiv, who appeared quite shaken by the condition in which his bene-factress had returned home, ran to comply. First, he brought tea, with the first sip of which Mrs. Glover seemed to revive. John and I looked at each other with profound relief. She was going to be all right. Of course, we were not sure of Mrs. Glover's true state of health. It was possible that this was the beginning of the end, as when an old person breaks a hip; it might mark the change from Mrs. Glover's being an active old lady who works in the garden to a frail old lady who sits by the fire, wrapped in an afghan. But at least she was going to survive the misbegotten expedition; she was going to live over our visit!

Mrs. Glover minimized the collapse on the wall, blam-ing the whole incident on not having lunch. She had always had to eat right on schedule, she said.

All the Logansons were like that, Mrs. O'Leary said. They had to eat right, or they got what she called "the weak trembles."

"But you shouldn't live alone, Emerald. You're going to fall out like that some time, and nobody'll be here to help you."

"Rajiv is here!"

Mrs. O'Leary pursed her lips in a way to suggest he might just wield a mean rake. "I think we ought to take you home. There's a place for you in Jonesfield," she said high-handedly, as if to say, "Admit it! You're feeble! Enough of these foreign shenanigans!"

John took in breath to object, but Mrs. Glover said, "Thank you, Dora. I'll think it over. Things will be changing soon. Meanwhile, I'd like to ask you a favor."

"Name it," Mrs. O'Leary replied with that stare of hers that was so direct it seemed insolent, and we all looked at

Mrs. Glover attentively. Mrs. Glover paused, seeming to make some calculation.

"I'd like to go somewhere else today. I'd like to go to the sea."

"All right," Mrs. O'Leary said instantaneously, without even asking which sea she wanted to go to or how long it would take to get there. I believe she would have replied with exactly the same promptitude had Mrs. Glover named some-place requiring a heroic journey, "Aqaba," for example.

"This won't interfere with what you want to do, will it, Dora?" Mrs. Glover said, looking at Mrs. O'Leary with her bright brown eyes. "Now tell me honestly."

"Of course not. We don't have any definite plans, do we, John?"

"Plans? No, no!" said John, who was walking away to fetch his big map, waving his arms rather comically at the idea of "plans."

"The North Sea?" I ventured.

"Yes," Mrs. Glover said, looking at me alertly. "It's rather special, I think. You *are* staying, aren't you? Dora, when shall we go? This afternoon or tomorrow morning?"

John returned with his maps, saying, "We'd better wait till tomorrow. It's at least a two-hour drive."

❧ ❧ ❧

"I think I'm drunk on this air," I told John, trying to push back the thought of MacPherson's party in London the next night out of my mind. I knew now that I would not be able to leave the next day in time to make it back. I had called the hotel from Mrs. Glover's phone. "Give Edwina Warren a message, please. Tell her to go on to the party without me Saturday night. She'll know what that means," I told Mr. Sparks. "I won't be back until Sunday or Monday."

The old ladies sat by the fire that afternoon, but John and I had taken a turn in the garden, and after dinner, encouraged by Mrs. Glover and even Mrs. O'Leary, we took off for Pelwichton. It was Friday night, and later we would stop in a pub and drink lager, listen to the jukebox (recover from the strain of the day), but first, we took a long walk. At dinner, Mrs. Glover had said more about the network of public footpaths in England, speaking in particular of a path right outside Pelwichton. It started right across the road from the Percy Hotel and offered "a nice little potter to the Roman bridge." I had never seen such an excellent place for a post-prandial walk: a black cinder path through the fields wide enough for three or four people to walk side by side.

I felt quite worn out by the events of the day—the wind, Emerald Glover's near-death. Yet at the same time, it seemed to me that we had been to the outer limits of England, and you could hardly expect to return unscathed. Now the tumult was over, and there was an extraordinary twilight—cold, clear, with the sun gone but the sky still bright, and air that was very, very still. The wind had swept the sky clean, it would seem, and gone home for the night. I had on every garment in my suitcase as well as my coat, but it wasn't enough. The evening had that chill, still feeling you get with a fresh snowfall—it was cold enough to see your breath—and as we turned onto the footpath, the cinders crunched like snow.

We walked in silence, seeing nothing but fields of grass or wheat and, above, the wonderful sky. There was a full moon, though it was still white this time of evening, and flat-looking, perhaps because we were so far north. We began to feel warmer as we tromped along. Presently I caught sight of a house. It was beyond the fields on a tree-studded hill, against the luminous sky, a dark gray house, the windows glowing gold, a thin trail of smoke rising out of the chimney.

"Why, that's *my* house," I said incredulously, continuing to watch it as we walked, the house seeming to stay right with us, like the moon. Was it, in fact, the house that I had seen earlier that day?

"Are we near Chesters?" I cried, twirling around, seeing fences, fields, trees, and, ever and always, the sky. It was growing darker, though the sky was still luminous, the moon getting silvery, starting to glow.

"I don't know where the hell we are," said John jovially. We had been walking so long!

But we didn't come to anything, we just kept on walking, farther and farther, getting warmer and warmer (the house staying with us), John remarking how the English would send you off on a path, calling it a "good little potter," and it would turn out to be fifteen miles long. I thought I heard the river, then decided I did not. Finally, we reached a stile. I had never seen a stile before, but I had read about them in fairy tales and so could identify this set of double steps that permitted you to climb over the fence and get over to where the river was. Was this my river, from earlier in the day, the River North Tyne? Was that Chesters over there? The Roman bridge Mrs. Glover had been talking about looked exactly like that bridgehead right across from where I had gone down to the river and dipped my hand in the water. It was under a thick stand of trees—the fluffy trees that had been whipping and waving in the wind earlier that day but which now stood thick and still. It was completely dark under the trees, and cool, but I knew from that morning that the grass around the bridgehead was a green of unusual darkness, as if it had received extraordinary nourishment from this most perfect of rivers. It smelled so sweet in the dark that evening! We sat on the chill grass a while, resting for the long trek back, talking about our lives back home.

"Is there someone waiting for you at home?" John asked at one point.

"No. How about you?"

"No."

How pleasant it was, how filled with promise. I would return to this place many times in my mind. I would think of it the next time Jeremiah 17 was the reading in church: "A blessing on the man who puts his trust in Yahweh," the reading went, "with Yahweh for his hope. He is like a tree by the waterside that thrusts its roots to the stream: when the heat comes it feels no alarm, its foliage stays green; it has no worries in a year of drought, and never ceases to bear fruit."

Chapter 19

"Bamburgh is my favorite view of the sea. When I die, I hope I go to Bamburgh," Mrs. Glover had said that afternoon when we were studying the maps. (John and I exchanged anxious glances, the idea of Mrs. Glover's dying on our next sightseeing expedition seeming all too possible.) Nevertheless, Bamburgh was chosen for the view of the sea. It had the additional advantage, beyond being Mrs. Glover's favorite "scene," of being close to Lindisfarne, the Holy Isle, a place where Mrs. Glover believed some of their forebears might be buried. I was interested in the Holy Isle, the place where the *Lindisfarne Gospels* had been produced and where St. Cuthbert had lived. I reminded Mrs. Glover that I was staying at St. Cuthbert's Hotel, which seemed to make St. Cuthbert my personal saint.

The Holy Isle had an interesting geographical position. It was actually an island in the North Sea, but you could drive to it when the tide was out as there was a causeway going across what they called "the wash." Every day the newspaper gave the times of the tides. The next day, according to the newspaper, you could drive out there after nine am but would have to be off the island by three pm unless you wanted to spend the night. For centuries it had been a monastic community, Mrs. Glover said, but now it was just an ordinary secular community. They produced a world-famous mead.

Our preparations for the trip to the sea were elaborate. We took a large hamper of fortifying food and several blankets; we had a supply of aspirin and smelling salts, even a flask of cherry cordial for emergencies. The one doctor Mrs. Glover could tolerate had come by the night before and pronounced her fit, and John was armed with the doctor's phone number in case this should prove not to be true. Saturday was a cold, cloudy day, and before starting out, we tucked Mrs. Glover, who seemed eager and happy despite all the rough solicitude she had had to endure from her cousin Dora, under a plaid lap blanket. It seemed a very great journey. We had to drive about an hour just to get to the coast, and it was not easy driving. The roads were narrow, mostly one-lane, bounded on one side by stone walls, on the other by hedgerows. We kept meeting larger cars coming around the bends. John would have to jump on the brakes, causing the Vauxhall to veer to the right or the left, then inch slowly forward past the other car, with Mrs. O'Leary leaning up from the back to say, "Well, go on, John, you've got *worlds* of room!"

But finally, we reached the coast. My first view of the sea was its empty bed. The word "causeway" had naturally made me think of the long elevated highway over Lake Pontchartrain north of New Orleans, but this causeway was just a narrow macadam road winding across a wide stretch of wet-looking sand littered with dead fish and seaweed and other marine detritus. We drove almost a mile on this damp little road. Here was the Holy Isle—just a small island, but large enough not to have a view of the sea as you drove into a gray stone village, with a church, a hotel, some shops, and a few buildings now in ruins where the monks once lived. The highest point, atop a hill, was Lindisfarne Castle.

The Church of St. Mary the Virgin was a modest Gothic structure of multi-colored stone with a patchwork effect. The interior smelled musty, like a basement, but the monumental arches bordering the aisles and the tall, narrow stained-glass windows gave it a sense of grandeur. I made an important discovery in the church: Emerald Glover was religious. Instead of walking around the aisles to see the statues and paintings, she headed for a pew near the front, the slant to her head making her look particularly dogged and purposeful. There she dropped to her knees and seemed to be instantly absorbed in prayer. This surprised me a good deal—none of the heroines, those cigar-smoking adventuresses, had been religious, but there she was, looking perfectly at home on her knees. John followed along behind her, entering a pew two or three rows back and hunching down thoughtfully. Mrs. O'Leary acted the part of the inspector, as was her wont, beginning to read the history of the island as presented by the wall plaques and exhibit cases. Only two other people were in the church at the time: a photographer, probably on assignment from *National Geographic*, stationed in the center aisle fiddling with his camera, and a stout-looking priest, threading his way through the pews, picking up paper and putting away books.

I busied myself taking notes. There had been two completely different sets of monks on the Holy Island: the first had been Celts, who had come about 635 A.D. from Iona, another holy isle to the west of Scotland. Saints Aidan and Cuthbert had been Celts. But the Celtic community, which apparently built only simple wooden huts, had been driven away by the Vikings and Danes. The second set of monks were Benedictines, who came in the eleventh century and stayed until the sixteenth, at which time they were run off by Henry VIII. The Benedictine way of life was much more humane than the usual monastic practice. It allowed the monks enough food and rest to live a healthy life, and their work was varied, with time to read and study as well as perform hard manual labor. Poor St. Cuthbert should have been a Benedictine.

I delved into the life of St. Cuthbert, finding that he was indeed a saintly man. A plaque stated matter-of-factly that his body did not decay during those two centuries of peregrination. But even before Cuthbert died and did not decay, events took place that were clearly out of the course of nature. At seventeen, he had a celestial vision. One night he was out on a hillside when he literally saw angels in the process of escorting a soul up to heaven. The next morning, he received the astounding news that Aidan, the famous abbot of Lindisfarne, had died in the night. Cuthbert enlisted as a monk at once, and in time he succeeded Aidan as abbot.

But before coming to Lindisfarne, he was at a monastery at Ripon, where he had another famous experience. All these monasteries operated according to the great principle of hospitality that each guest should be treated as if he were Christ. One winter night, a visitor came to Ripon, and Cuthbert received him in the required hospitable manner, making him comfortable, then getting him some food. But when he came back, the visitor was gone. In his room were three loaves of freshly baked bread, and, even more miraculously, no footprints could be found in the snow. Clearly, an angel had visited Cuthbert, if not Jesus Himself. Cuthbert became known far and wide as a holy person and healer so that even at Lindisfarne, which was way out across the wash, people flocked to him for spiritual help. But because he simply wanted to study and pray, he left Lindisfarne and went to an even more remote island down the coast, Inner Farne. But even there, he was besieged by visitors. At the King's special request, Cuthbert returned to civilization to serve as Bishop, but after a couple of years, he returned to Inner Farne, where he died. Such was his holiness that the monks started the process of canonization right away. The *Lindisfarne Gospels* were made as part of these preparations.

Presently I became aware that Mrs. O'Leary had collared the priest and was ruthlessly grilling him on some of the more implausible points of the saint's biography, but he stuck to his story ("Yes, madam, several independent accounts confirmed it—absolutely no footprints"). I managed to insert myself in the conversation to say how moving I found the story, allowing the priest to scurry away. As we left the church, I pondered Mrs. Glover's apparent piety, which seemed to put her simplicity and what I had come to think of as her "dottiness" on an entirely new basis. I also saw that Mrs. O'Leary paused to stuff a number of English bills into the donation box.

∾ ∾ ∾

The wind was much too cold on the island for a picnic, so we took our hamper into the hotel and found seats at a table in the dining room. A pot of hot coffee was ordered. Mrs. O'Leary sat as proudly erect at the head of our table as a wooden Indian, seeming to dare the young waitress to object to our having brought in our own food. Afterward, we inspected the priory, which was just a ruin now. Within its walls was a cemetery, where Mrs. Glover pointed out two or three tombstones that bore the name "Loganson," a matter of great interest to Mrs. O'Leary and John. Mrs. O'Leary gave a little speech about how the Logansons were a Scottish clan, tartan and all, that had resettled in Northumberland. (Northumberland was Border country, which was sometimes part of Scotland, sometimes part of England, depending on who was ascendant in the long-running Border wars.) On this note, with a jolly sense of belonging to this place, we went to the shop, where John and I bought bottles of mead.

We drove on to Bamburgh. The castle was beyond the quaint little town, a huge citadel on a great promontory that required the Vauxhall to climb a steep hill. It was from the castle battlements that you first saw the beach. I leaned over the parapet, looking in the distance below to a broad sandy beach where long soft waves with whitecaps were lapping gently. Why, this beach looked like Florida or Greece! To the north, you could see the little green hump of Lindisfarne; farther out to sea were a couple of smaller humps, which must be the Farne Islands. The sun was shining now; the water was blue. Behind me, Mrs. O'Leary and John were urging us to go inside the castle, famous for its immense collections of pictures and armor and plate. But I couldn't go in. Somehow this beach seemed to be the real object of my journey. I clung to the parapet, and Mrs. Glover came up beside me to smile out at the water.

Later the four of us went down to the beach, descending what seemed like miles of stone steps, going very slowly in the fear that either Mrs. Glover or Mrs. O'Leary would fall and break a hip. But at last, we reached the sand, thick, white, and loose, and I went slowly, thinking, this is it, this is *it*. Then you reached the hard-packed sand, which got wetter and wetter, more and more carved and curved by the force of the tides, with little inlets of water. I stopped and took off my Famolares, experiencing the cool wavy sand, approaching the outer edge of the beach, and finally stepping into the advancing wave, finding myself in the sea. The water was so cold it took my breath away, and I turned around, my arms shooting up. John answered with a lift of the arms, then immediately bent down to take off his shoes and come out, and I believe Mrs. Glover was making some move to remove her little shoes for the purpose of wading, but Mrs. O'Leary put a stop to this. John and I sloshed in the sea just a minute; then we had to come in out of the icy water, our feet a bright red. We couldn't put on our socks and shoes right away—our feet were too wet and we had nothing to dry them with. John took off his windbreaker, and with jocular comparisons to Sir Walter Raleigh, spread it on a dry portion of the beach for his old aunts to sit on. We left them circling around it and settling themselves, still spatting slightly like two cats.

We practically had the beach to ourselves, which was amazing, considering how beautiful a beach it was and how many people were up at the castle looking at the armor. But down here, there were only a few people in sight. A man walked by with a prancing brown Poodle. Back in the direction of Lindisfarne was a small knot of people. Two of the tiny people, wearing bathing suits, kept walking toward the sea, putting one foot in and then running back, like sandpipers. It was our idea to walk to a point parallel to Inner Farne before turning back. I was mesmerized by the sun and the waves. Only once were we startled by someone else on the beach: a horse galloping up behind us—no, not galloping, but cantering (tha-da-rump, tha-da-rump), leaving sidewise prints in the sand. The horse was ridden by a woman in black riding clothes and helmet-like hat.

After walking a very long way, we did come almost parallel to Inner Farne, a white-cliffed island that seemed much smaller than Lindisfarne, with just one or two buildings. I remembered reading that one of the reasons St. Cuthbert retreated to this particular island was that it was supposed to be infested with demons (his fondest ambition being to wrestle prayerfully with the demons of evil), but how could demons live in this heavenly place?

"That's St. Cuthbert's Hotel," John remarked, slipping an arm around my shoulder to turn me around, happening to leave it there.

The drive back was hilarious. It was late—oh, it must have been five-thirty or six when we finally left Bamburgh. We sang songs in the car, and it seemed amusing when we met aggressive cars on the roads. We understood now that we weren't going to suffer a horrible accident. John had had trouble driving at first, but now he had gotten the hang of it. My feet were cold—they had just *stayed* cold, after that dip in the water—but this wasn't unpleasant; it was simply a constant reminder of having been to the sea. This was the source of such joy that I was very silly in the car, singing songs, telling stories, being quite uncharacteristically boisterous.

We were all in high spirits when we reached Rutland Cottage.

"Company's here," John sang out as he drove down the drive, for in the parking area opposite the front door was a nice-looking car, much larger than the homely Vauxhall. As we parked, we saw that it was a black Austin Rover. "Road cowboy," he added, permitting himself a little kick at a tire.

"Maybe a paying customer for you, Emerald," Mrs. O'Leary said enterprisingly.

"Well, let's go in and see," said Mrs. Glover, heading for the door, and as I followed her, the way she walked reminded me, oddly, of a young girl sashaying down a garden path. She entered the front door, which was unlocked, and as Mrs. O'Leary commented on this lack of security, pointing out that anybody could just "waltz in," we pressed on into the foyer, beginning to take off hats and coats, the top layer of sweaters.

I heard a voice in there. No, I thought, it can't be, but I went on in, extremely conscious of my feet at that moment, like great blocks of ice. The new arrival was none other than MacPherson.

Chapter 20

We went around the doorjamb into the parlor, and there was MacPherson, rising from a chair. He had been sitting by the fire, reading a book, which he still had in his hand with his finger marking the place.

"Hello, Caroline," he said as if this meeting were nothing remarkable. Then he looked back and forth between Mrs. Glover and Mrs. O'Leary, trying, I realized, to decide which one of them was Mrs. Glover.

"Hey!" I said lamely, feeling windblown, windburned, maybe even a little bit sunburned, but definitely disheveled and discombobulated. "Mrs. Glover, this is Robert MacPherson," I managed, touching her shoulder, and he went up to the old writer without a word, gazing at her adoringly, kissing her hand.

I think I said something fatuous like, "This is Robert MacPherson, the famous writer," so that Mrs. Glover wouldn't make the mistake of thinking he was just an ordinary person. Actually, MacPherson didn't even look like an ordinary person. He looked more like one of the unemployed, or even, since his eyes were so red, like one of the derelicts in the squares. He was wearing his pipestem pants and an old wrinkled shirt with the sleeves rolled up. Yet he had arrived in that Rover, which connoted a post in Mrs. Thatcher's Cabinet, not a place on a park bench.

"And this," I said, turning toward John and Mrs. O'Leary, "is John Loganson—you remember John from the opera—and his aunt, Dora O'Leary. They're related to Mrs. Glover."

"I take it you're the author of the *Teasdale Saga*," Mrs. O'Leary said to MacPherson, flooring me. She towered over MacPherson as she pumped his hand. I sank down in a chair, my heart thumping.

"Guilty as charged," MacPherson said with a laugh, moving Mrs. Glover toward a chair before he sat down again. We all gathered around the fire. I myself was developing a serious chill, which caused my teeth to knock against each other.

"My nephew told me he met you. Your books are mighty popular at the Lincoln Parish Library," Mrs. O'Leary went on in her heavy way, which might be sarcastic but which seemed sincere enough now. "We keep three copies of each."

"Super!" he said.

"I don't believe I've had the pleasure of reading your *Teasdale Saga*, but I will certainly look for it now," Mrs. Glover quavered in a sociable way. "Perhaps it's in the village library."

"I hope you don't mind my barging in you like this," he said tenderly to Mrs. Glover. "Especially since you're having a family gathering. I had no idea. I took the liberty because I was told you offer bed and breakfast. I was just asking your man about accommodation."

"Of course you can stay. Of course," said Mrs. Glover.

And then we all looked at each other, wondering (I at least was dazedly wondering) what had brought MacPherson all the way up here. Now would have been the perfect moment for MacPherson to explain this unnerving advent, but he did not explain. Rather he just smiled at Mrs. Glover adoringly and looked around the dark-paneled room.

"I shall see about dinner," Mrs. Glover said, getting up. "We've had quite a day, Mr. MacPherson, as I'm sure you have too. I expect we could all use a drink."

"Scotch, if I may," MacPherson said promptly, not at all like someone who had "dried out."

"Yes, Scotch," John chimed in. He had been looking at MacPherson in a not-altogether-friendly way.

"Scotch," I said also. I never drank Scotch, but this seemed the kind of emergency where one needed whiskey.

Mrs. O'Leary fixed her mouth in a line and asked for a cup of tea.

"Yes, dear," said Mrs. Glover, toddling out.

"What were you reading?" I asked MacPherson, trying to speak casually.

He seemed surprised to find he was holding a book and looked inquisitively at the spine. "Oh, a lovely book, *Sunset on the Savana*," he said.

"Where did you get that? I've been looking for it every-where, " I exclaimed, and we talked about bookstores in London.

Mrs. Glover toddled back with a tray holding three glasses of Scotch. She served it English-style, with no water or ice, just bare in the glass, like mouthwash. "Super!" said MacPherson, taking his, and I recalled how he always used that boyish exclamation even in the most serious contexts, in the Lawrence seminar, for instance. "Now this," he would say, in reference to some turgid Lawrentian climax, "is a super scene."

"I've been reading your work, Mrs. Glover," MacPherson said, showing her the book. He was studying her closely, I observed, not missing a thing about her crooked back or her bowed legs. "When Caroline first mentioned your name, I thought I had seen it somewhere. Well, it was right on my dining room table." And now MacPherson held up a second volume he had with him, a small, dun-colored pamphlet.

"Is it that *Hedgehog*?" quavered Mrs. Glover.

"The *Hedgerow*," said MacPherson.

"What's the *Hedgerow*?" demanded Mrs. O'Leary, getting up and taking possession of it, peering at it critically.

"Yes, what is it?" I cried, and MacPherson explained that the *Hedgerow* was a literary quarterly, just one of the many British journals and quarterlies to which he subscribed. ("One tries to keep up," he murmured.) This issue happened to have an article on Mrs. Glover's old crowd written by one Nigel Carter at the University of Manchester.

"Have you read it?" MacPherson asked Mrs. Glover.

"No, but they sent it, I believe."

"Do you *know* Nigel Carter?" I asked her.

"He was here to talk to me. Last winter, I believe. It snowed that day."

"Oh," I said, abashed. I had thought I was the first literary pilgrim to Rutland Cottage. I was also indignant at MacPherson for having this article. I had been going to the British Museum every single day for the past two weeks— well, almost every day—and MacPherson had possession of what seemed to be the only interesting piece of material on Emerald Glover in Britain, hot off the press, apparently too new to have been cataloged yet in the British Library.

"Look, John, Emerald's been written up," Mrs. O'Leary said, waving the *Hedgerow*.

"It's a nice piece, Mrs. Glover," said MacPherson. "It's going to stir up interest."

"Do you think so?" Mrs. Glover said, smiling her vague, dotty smile.

"Reputations are like that. Gone today, here tomorrow." MacPherson sipped Scotch, looking sage.

Presently I got a look at the *Hedgerow*. A quick scan relieved my mind. The article was called "The Red Lion Square Circle: Missing in Action," and it dealt with seven or eight different people who had lived in Red Lion Square during the 30s, writing books and painting pictures (making tapestries, in the case of Jane Winkler), but who were scattered by the war. Emerald Glover was the only person still alive, and this Nigel Carter quoted her. She mainly reminisced about other people.

At dinner, MacPherson slipped easily into what had come to seem our domestic circle. He sat on Mrs. Glover's right, and both he and Mrs. Glover ate continental-style, holding the fork in the left hand, tines down, the knife in the right, cutting meat and then not shifting the fork to the right hand but poking it into the mouth upside down with the left, slipping it slowly out, upside-down and empty. Ordinarily, it rather irritated me to see people eating that backward way, but MacPherson still ignited my attention, no matter what style of eating he employed, no matter how dried out he was or was not. Yet, he did not monopolize the conversation. In fact, he said practically nothing at first, just ate (cut, poke) and looked with interest at whoever else spoke, smiling quizzically as if ready to be entertained. Nevertheless, he was the focal point of the conversation, perhaps because he was a newcomer to our circle and had to be brought up to date, perhaps simply because he was magnetic.

We had wine with the meal, and MacPherson had several glasses. I would have expected Mrs. O'Leary to show strong disapproval of this, but her mien was friendly. She seemed to look on MacPherson with respect and did not grill him the way she did her relatives or clerics. Perhaps this unwonted gentleness on her part could be accounted for by a resemblance between MacPherson and her late husband.

Mrs. O'Leary asked when the next volume in his Teasdale series was coming out. MacPherson confessed that he wasn't doing much writing at the moment: he had "gotten involved in television work, even doing a little producing."

"What are you producing, Mr. MacPherson?" I asked, that still being the only thing I felt comfortable calling him. Characters in English novels always make a big thing over whether to use somebody's "Christian name" or not, and I've always thought this issue overblown. But this really was a problem with regard to MacPherson, whose first name still seemed entirely too intimate.

"Please, please, call me Robert," MacPherson implored. "Please, all of you, call me Robert."

"Well, Robert," I said, blushing, "what are you producing?"

"Well, now," said MacPherson, leaning back in his chair. "That's why I stopped in."

At last. Why indeed! It was Saturday, and he was supposed to be hosting a party in London. But then I knew that MacPherson was a person who was wont to disappear without warning. He now revealed that he had become a kind of "producer" (he used the word deprecatingly) for BBC4. Lately, he had been doing a series of interviews called *Lives of the Novelists*. He mentioned V. S. Naipaul and Anthony Powell. Then, when he learned from the *Hedgerow* that

Emerald Glover lived in Northumberland, he decided to just come on up and see if she would consent to an interview. ("I would have called you, Caroline, but I didn't know where you were staying," he said in an aside.) It would be so interesting to have her on film, not to mention her wonderful house, he went on to say.

We all turned to Mrs. Glover, who looked stunned.

"She's not been well for years, and she's practically a recluse. I don't know that she's up to it," I would have said to MacPherson had he done me the honor of asking my opinion before springing this on her.

"Sure would be good for business," Mrs. O'Leary said with her usual insensitivity, smiling like an alligator, and I glared at Mrs. O'Leary, and John, for good measure. John raised his eyebrows.

"You'd enjoy it," MacPherson said in a jolly way to Mrs. Glover, who responded, "Yes, I think I would!"

"Super!" said MacPherson. "The crew will be here tomorrow afternoon, and we'll take it slow and easy. I like to get a lot of film. Do you think you could find a place to stash me and the crew for a couple of days? They can sleep anywhere. Do you have a barn?"

"I'm going to be on the telly," Mrs. Glover said gaily to Mrs. O'Leary. "Don't you love the telly, in spite of everything?"

"How did you get into producing?" I asked MacPherson, hardly believing that he was actually here, much less that he could summon the resources of the BBC and put Mrs. Glover on telly screens across the world.

"Well, all it takes is a little capital and then knowing a few people," MacPherson said modestly. "Truth is, I've been making a pile of money from this soap opera I've been writing for British television, little thing called *This Other Eden*. Pure trash, of course."

There was an immediate clamor. Why, *This Other Eden* was just about the most popular soap opera in Britain— even I knew that. Some of the Barston people watched it at St. Cuthbert's—Carol Beckwith, of course, but also Allison and Edwina. Even Mrs. Glover watched it. John did not participate in the admiring hubbub but watched, eyebrows still raised.

"The title—it's from *Richard II*, right? That famous speech about England?" I put in. (Of course, MacPherson's "soap" would have literary allusions: the whole thing would be fiendishly clever!) I had memorized this speech in high school and now felt compelled to chant such portions of it as I could remember:

> This scepter'd isle,
> This earth of majesty, this seat of Mars,
> This other Eden, demi-paradise . . .
> This blessed plot, this earth, this realm, this England,
> This nurse, this teeming womb of royal kings . . .

"I suppose I could have called it *This Teeming Womb*," MacPherson said.

"Yes, when is Angela going to have that baby?" Mrs. Glover asked. "She went into labor week before last."

"Let me see, Wednesday, maybe," said MacPherson, leaning back on the back two legs of his chair, looking sly.

"Who killed David?" Mrs. Glover inquired darkly.

MacPherson laughed. "I can't give away all my secrets, dear lady. That's my 'blessed plot.'"

"Do people ask you questions like this all the time?" I asked, imagining the haggard MacPherson going into a pub down in London for some much-needed refreshment, being jumped on by a curious populace.

MacPherson looked horrified. "Oh, but nobody knows! I don't tell people in London!"

"I can understand that," murmured John, looking searchingly at his silverware.

"No, I write *Eden* at night," MacPherson said, taking no notice of John. "I was up all last night, finishing the episodes for next week. We don't work very far ahead on the show. Sometimes I'm writing an episode the night before."

"Brave man," Mrs. Glover said. "I'd be a nervous wreck."

"I can't believe you're doing all this . . . " I said, still non-plused by his presence, "dramatizing your book, producing documentaries, writing a so—, a daytime drama. That's really amazing."

MacPherson shrugged and asked for more wine.

∾ ∾ ∾

After dinner, MacPherson asked me to take a turn in the garden, and presently I found myself out in the blue twilight of Northumberland nervously pointing out the features of Mrs. Glover's domain. MacPherson seemed much older than he had in 1972, a mere eight years before. The age difference between us seemed to be widening rather than narrowing, the way it usually does the older you get. MacPherson was still attractive, but he seemed wizened, also preternaturally focused, like an old Chinese monk. He was still Lawrentian, though, he still had that air of romance. He did not ask any personal questions, so neither did I. But he did ask, as we passed by the flowers, whether I would stay and appear on the program.

"*Me?*" I said. "Don't you do the interviews?"

"Yes, but you can provide some background. You're *the* Glover scholar. You'll be great."

"Yikes!" I said with a shudder. What would I wear? How would I sound? But it occurred to me how ecstatic the progressive and ambitious Charles Nicholson would be at the involvement of one of his faculty with the prestigious BBC. "Yes, okay. . . . Of course."

"Besides, you have to catch me up on Emerald. Ninety-nine percent of viewers won't have heard of her. Help me bone up."

"This crew," I mused. MacPherson had made no telephone calls, to my knowledge. "You scheduled them to come before asking Mrs. Glover?"

MacPherson laughed. "No one says no. Unless they're ultra-famous. Graham Greene said no, but I have some people working on Greene's people. Of course, I could always have told them to drive on to Manchester. That's our next stop. Might as well get a snippet or two from Nigel Carter."

Back inside, John, Mrs. Glover, and Mrs. O'Leary were sitting *en famille* by the fire, discussing the Logansons. Having had the idea of looking for Logansons in the local telephone directory, John was now reading the entries aloud. The directory served the whole county but was no bigger than a pamphlet, about the same size as the little phone book for Barston and its rural environs, and it followed the old-fashioned practice of listing the subscriber's occupation along with his or her name. There were some forty-five Logansons, most of whom seemed to be farmers and teachers. Mrs. O'Leary could barely be restrained from putting on her church hat that very minute and going out to pay calls.

"Mind if I smoke?" MacPherson asked, taking out a pack of thin cigars. He offered the package around. Everyone declined, except Mrs. Glover.

"Are you a Loganson, Mrs. Glover?" MacPherson asked as he lit her cigarillo.

"They tell me I am!" she said with a jaunty exhale.

"A Lowlander then!" he said.

"What's a Lowlander?" I asked.

"A variety of Scots," he said. "You've noticed that some Scottish names begin with Mac- and some end with -son? Well, that's a difference between Highlanders and Lowlanders." The people of Scotland were divided into two groups, he went on to explain: the Highlanders, who lived north of Stirling and west of Aberdeen, and the Lowlanders, who lived in the southern part of the country. They seemed to have completely different natures. The Highlanders were a fierce, warlike people. They wore the kilt and played the bagpipes. The Lowlanders had little to do with kilts and bagpipes, and instead of being warriors, were usually farmers and clerks and sometimes, if they could manage to get the education, teachers or lawyers. It was education they prized the most, along with prudence and thrift, whereas Highlanders valued hospitality and valor. It was the Lowlanders that people were speaking of when they said Scots were tight.

"What are you, Robert?" John asked. "Judging by your name, you seem to be both."

"Oh, I'm descended from Highlanders," he said, going on to speak offhandedly of 'an old wreck of a castle' in Perth. He had been to a couple of gatherings of the clan near Ullapool, he said, mentioning a laird or two who was particularly eccentric or amusing.

"I think we'll go up to Edinburgh," Mrs. O'Leary announced. "We're close now. A couple of our ancestors were hanged in Edinburgh for supporting the King against Cromwell's army. Covenanters, don't you know. John should see Edinburgh."

"You haven't seen Britain till you've seen the Highlands," MacPherson said with that obnoxious insistence with which one traveler lectures another about what he is not going to see. He spoke of lochs and misty mountains, which provided much greater scenery, he implied, than anything to be seen in the Lowlands around Edinburgh.

"John, you'd better make some phone calls," said Mrs. O'Leary. "Emerald, we'll get out of your way, with people coming. You'll need all your rooms."

It was one o'clock, past time to go to bed. On the stairs going up to our rooms, I said to John, "I'm sorry everything is so turned upside down. That you and your aunt are leaving. Today was so perfect."

"It was, it was. But Caroline, I have to tell you one thing."

"Yes?"

"He's an ass."

"John!" I said, a little shocked. "That's not true."

"Just take care."

I had the *Hedgerow* with me, and, since I knew I was too stimulated from the day to go to sleep, I started to read. Most of the article was about the other people in the Red Lion Circle, no one I'd ever heard of (Elvira Morgan, a printmaker, Henry Forest, a composer, and so forth), people who were toiling away back at the very same time as the people in the Bloomsbury Group were writing *their* books and painting *their* pictures, giving *their* parties. Only nobody in the Red Lion Circle ever became famous. The article was dry and pedantic, but it succeeded in transferring the yearning I felt for the day we had had back to the past. I could just see Red Lion Square in the dusk some cool London night, all the windows open, people visible in each of the windows busily creating in one form or another—fiddling at a piano, shaping a lump of clay. It reminded me of *Rear Window*, where Jimmy Stewart could see the lonely songwriter across the way, and the dancer; but it reminded me even more strongly of an Advent calendar I had had as a girl. It represented a Swiss chalet, curiously, with twenty-five windows. Each window had a flap, and every day you lifted a flap to see some special picture or message. And now I seemed to see Red Lion Square with flaps over its lighted windows. Under one of those flaps was the young Emerald Glover, bent over her desk.

Chapter 21

Things moved very fast the next morning. When I woke up, Mrs. O'Leary was already up, with her bag—she called it a "grip"—in the front hall. She was in the kitchen, instructing the help, a local woman named Mrs. Nesbit, who had come in to help with the extra visitors, on how to cook her eggs. "And no tomatoes, Miz Nesbit. Tomatoes belong in salads, in my opinion."

MacPherson was already in the dining room with a pot of coffee, and after a quick breakfast, we split into two groups: MacPherson, who desired to be briefed, took me off into the drawing room, which was much larger than the parlor where we had been gathering. Mrs. Glover, Mrs. O'Leary, and John stayed in the dining room, talking. I was dying to hear their conversation, but MacPherson was in high working mode, and I had to be professional.

My Glover notes and Xerox copies were spread out around us, and MacPherson began to take in this material, absorb it like one of those people who can learn a foreign language in just a day or two. Later he was able to quote from my research; I believe he could have written an article or even a book-length publishable manuscript off the top of his head. Not only that, but he had finished *Sunset on the Savana* the night before, and that morning he began perusing my copy of *Café of Sorrows*. But we did not have copies of *Guns at Noon* or *Plantation Trace*. MacPherson sent me to get them from Mrs. Glover, who directed me to go up to what she called the "lumber room" to find a particular trunk.

Down passageways and up several flights of stairs, I made my way to the attic, which was cramped (I had to stoop) and crowded with furniture, pictures, books, bottles, jars, and assorted boxes, old "grips." I spotted a black leather-covered humpback trunk with brass hardware. It wasn't locked, and the hinges creaked. From the outside it looked so much like the trunk owned by Miss Flora McFlimpsey, the eponymous heroine of another book from my childhood, that I expected to find tiny old muffs and capes in there, kid gloves—yet inside were indeed copies of Mrs. Glover's quartet. They were in their original dust jackets, illustrated with watercolor scenes from the stories—an antebellum house with a girl running across the lawn clutching her breast on *Plantation Trace*, a stern-looking soldier embracing a slender girl on *Guns at Noon*. I wondered how Mrs. Glover could have packed them away as I looked at the charming street scene on *Café of Sorrows*. I selected one copy of each book, a complete set, then closed the trunk, looking yearningly at the other trunks and boxes but knowing I must hurry back down.

Just as I got to the first floor, Mrs. O'Leary called out, "Bye, Miss Caroline! We're going now," and I arrived just in time to see Mrs. O'Leary and John down at the door saying goodbye to Mrs. Glover, John standing next to his ancient little relative with his arm around her, gently jostling her back and forth. "Look pretty on the telly, Aunt Emerald. Don't let them wear you out."

"I'm going to send you some quilts, Emerald. You need 'em up here," Mrs. O'Leary said.

"Caroline," John said, holding out his hand, which was big and squashy like a baseball mitt. "I wish we weren't leaving you. Can you get back to London okay?"

"Of *course*. Don't worry about me. I'll see you in London." Suddenly he released my hand and pulled me against him for a heart-stopping moment.

"Thursday afternoon. Aunt Dora mentioned a church service y'all are supposed to go to. Take good care, my dear."

And then they were in the Vauxhall, and it was lurching away.

∾ ∾ ∾

MacPherson had insisted that Mrs. Glover not make any special preparations for the interview. *Lives of the Novelists* was supposed to be *cinema verité*, as if Emerald Glover were just sitting around home, talking about herself, a camera just happening to be on. But while MacPherson and I boned up, much energetic housekeeping was being done. We could hear Mrs. Nesbit going from room to room upstairs with a noisy vacuum cleaner. I saw great moils of used sheets and towels brought by Rajiv through the hall, neat stacks of linens carried back the other way. Presently Mrs. Nesbit moved her tidying operations downstairs, but when she appeared at the door of the drawing room with her vacuum cleaner, MacPherson put his foot down. "Turn that thing off, woman. We're trying to work."

As MacPherson read and wrote ideas onto a legal pad, I picked up *Sunset on the Savana*, which at the time was the novel in the quartet I'd read the least (only twice). The jacket depicted a lissome girl on a horse looking out over a field dotted with flowers. The house was quiet. I began to read—not at the beginning but in that part where Rachel is stranded for the night with the native Oginga, the part with the tiger. Some time must have passed. That afternoon a voice was raised, a voice which seemed to be the noble Oginga but which was, in fact, Rajiv at the door. Ordinarily, Rajiv was so quiet and self-effacing you hardly knew he was there, but now he was shouting, "Miss Glover, Miss Glover!" We all ran to the door to see a vehicle racketing up the driveway. It was a blue van with BBC4 written on the side, turning with a spume of gravel, halting next to MacPherson's black Rover.

A series of people started jumping out of the van, reminding me of those films you see of the troops hitting the beach at Normandy. But these people all had long hair and wore blue jeans and black T-shirts from some rock concert, toting cumbersome equipment—cameras and soundboards and lights.

Their shoes were noisy, Doc Martens boots or the like that tracked in gravel from the driveway. Rajiv hovered, asking them to take off their shoes, but they just came on in. They began to set up equipment in the drawing room, which, I now realized, was filled with fragile and precious objects— lamps, vases, a terra cotta bust (Emerald Glover?). Jarvis the cat had been asleep on a needlepoint chair but woke up in a state of alarm, and as he attempted to slink away, one of the crew in hiking boots stepped on his tail, evoking a cry that outdid the peacocks. It was an onslaught into Rutland Cottage. Actually, the television people weren't like the soldiers at Normandy, who were forces of liberation; they were more like the Vikings, storming the Holy Isle.

At first, the crew was just an undifferentiated crowd of rough, slangy kids or people who continued to dress like kids and chew gum, but presently MacPherson stopped one long-haired young man and, even though this youth was shouldering a cumbersome camera, embraced him ardently. It turned out that this was William, MacPherson's son. I tried to remember MacPherson's children, whom I had last seen my junior year of college. It had been at that party at MacPherson's house. I believe William was the elder of the two children the MacPhersons had had together. He was now about nineteen or twenty, a student in some film program at NYU and, as I learned later, just here for the summer.

William did not say much. In fact, the crew would spend most of the time they weren't actually filming either in their rooms or out back smoking. The principal interest in William's presence was not William himself—he had his father's eyes, but they were pretty glazed most of the time. Rather, his main interest for me was something he said to his father when he came in that led me to understand that MacPherson and his wife were still very much married: "I talked to Mom last night, and she said to tell you she got her paper done," or something like that indicating a continuing connection. MacPherson listened to William's news attentively and said he would call "Mom" that night.

"Beryl's in law school," MacPherson said to me.

I hastily closed my mouth and nodded.

"She's at Seton Hall. She wanted something to do. I'm keeping out of her way."

"Right," I said, understanding that MacPherson was still a husband; he still had a home. He might have mentioned it. I might have asked. I should have known. It was his "essential matrix," which was even more diffuse than I had imagined. The fact that MacPherson had no detectable connection with his wife seemed to make their marriage even stronger, even more indissoluble. They were so bound, it seemed, they didn't even have to live on the same continent.

Another important member of the crew was Alexandra Chauncy, MacPherson's production assistant, whom he called "Chauncy." Actually, the crew had been there about fifteen minutes before I noticed that she was a woman, the only real indication of this being her rather wide hips. Like the others, she wore jeans that were thin with age, like an old prospector's. She also wore an Iron Maiden T-shirt and a man's buffalo-plaid overshirt. She was about my age or a little younger, with strong, manly features and a particularly strong jaw. Of course, she wore no makeup. Nor did she take any trouble with her hair, which looked slept-on and uncombed. She was American, from New York City, and while she was very friendly toward me, even deferential, seeming to take seriously MacPherson's introductory remarks that I was a "super scholar" and "*the* expert on Emerald Glover," I found her thoroughly intimidating. First of all, she was a graduate of Radcliffe. Not only that, but I recognized her immediately as the kind of person who, at school, would not only have aced physics but would also have achieved important things beyond the walls of the school, such as working in some Kennedy's campaign. She was the sort of person who would publish a book of poetry while she was still an undergraduate, or, after graduating, do this—somehow land a job in England with the BBC and rattle around the countryside interviewing famous people. To top it all, she had a flat in Finsbury Park, a completely unfashionable part of London where her neighbors were all from Pakistan and Zimbabwe. I could almost see her flat. It would have little furniture, just a mattress on the floor with rumpled bedclothes, some pillows scattered around, no food in the refrigerator except some moldy cheese and a half-empty bottle of wine. She would be far too busy with her work for the BBC4 to clean or cook. What she was, I thought, was a *femme d'extérieur.*

I wanted her to tell me that living in London was not as great as it seemed, that the traffic was intolerable or the weather unendurable, but Chauncy said it was "fabulous." She had been living there for four years. In fact, she was the reason MacPherson had gotten work in British television in the first place. He had been her teacher at Radcliffe one year, and later, when she was working in London, she managed to bring him over to dramatize one of his books.

"She even put me up," MacPherson said, darting a smile at Chauncy, adding "on the couch, of course," in such a way as to imply that he had not slept on the couch.

MacPherson and Chauncy worked well together, setting up the TV equipment in Rutland Cottage. I was reminded of a surgeon and his nurse. Like a surgeon, MacPherson concentrated totally when he worked. He was also like a terrier the way he went after things, taking notes or overseeing the crew. If Chauncy interrupted him with a question or request, he would bark like one of those aggressive little dogs. But Chauncy, who knew her job, was unfazed by a barking boss.

∾ ∾ ∾

Monday morning Emerald Glover entered the drawing room, negotiating around the equipment, essaying not to trip over all the electric cords running across the floor. She was dressed English-style in a collection of incongruous woolen garments which, taken together, constituted a "suit." She was also wearing a shy but radiant smile, like a bride's, and, also like a bride, she had altered her appearance a good deal from the everyday. To my dismay, she had applied black eyeliner, two spots of rouge, and bright red lipstick in an exaggerated bow shape last fashionable about 1925. A thick foundation, which made her wrinkles less yellowish, was also visible in the bright lights the crew had positioned facing the fireplace.

Mrs. Glover sat down, looking skittish and frail, and MacPherson took his place in the armchair opposite. Suddenly Chauncy was holding one of those black and white-striped clapperboards near Mrs. Glover's face, saying, "Emerald Glover, Take One," going *snap*.

"Mrs. Glover, why don't you tell us something about your background. Where were you born?" MacPherson said.

"I was born in Jonesfield, Louisiana. That's in the southern part of the United States," Mrs. Glover began, but with the first words in her high-pitched trilling voice, the member of the crew responsible for the sound, a hirsute young man, dove for his control panel, and Chauncy yelled "Cut!" Readjustments were made for Mrs. Glover's voice, and we began again. I had worried about whether the interview would be too great an ordeal for Mrs. Glover, like walking Hadrian's Wall, but I saw that she was enjoying it. She looked quite voguish under the lights, like Isak Dinesen. You were supposed to add extra make-up for the camera, and the camera, I had heard, would add ten pounds. MacPherson smiled encouragingly at Mrs. Glover as she answered his questions about Jonesfield, her family ("very ordin'ry, really"). There she sat in the spotlights, her head jutting forward as if she were peeping out from under something.

I thought she might be different under the pressure of microphone and camera, but Mrs. Glover was much the same as the day we arrived for tea (how long ago that seemed!)—vague, smiling, a little dotty. MacPherson elicited the familiar information about her youth in Jonesfield ("uneventful"), her running away at eighteen, her brief time in New York, where she met a young Englishman, a "sweet boy," married him, and went with him to England. The war started soon thereafter, and he went off to France. There he died. She spent the war years in Norfolk with his family and afterwards went to London. She worked as a typist and married again. One new thing did emerge: it was this second husband, Alan Glover, who encouraged her to write, even pushed her (not quite like Willy pushed Colette but still, quite insistent). MacPherson asked her about her books. Looking misty, Mrs. Glover referred to them as her "children" but then, in attempting to discuss her favorite, was unable to remember its name. Chauncy yelled, "Cut!" and we took a break. Mrs. Glover toddled off to her room.

We took a lot of breaks. MacPherson, who paced back and forth on the periphery of the set, required a number of re-takes for reasons which he did not explain, and Mrs. Glover requested an even greater number, either because she drew a blank on important items like the names of her books or the name of somebody who was supposed to be her best friend, or because she thought of a way she could express herself more clearly. During breaks, she would disappear into her room and, after the passage of fifteen minutes or so, have to be fetched.

Actually, the best segment we got that first day was when MacPherson asked her about the Red Lion Circle. Did they know they were "the Red Lion Square Circle" in those days?

"No, dear," Mrs. Glover chirped. They were just friends and neighbors. They lived in Red Lion Square because the rent was low. It seemed "very ordin'ry" at the time. It just happened that everybody wrote, or painted, or composed. Mrs. Glover spoke generously of several people's work. She also spoke as if making things, or writing, were just normal activities. Everybody had to do some other kind of work to make a living, then work on their "real work" at night. They all had trouble getting recognition. She thought she would never get published, she said. Everybody rejected *Plantation Trace*, including the Hogarth Press, which pronounced it "too conventional." Perhaps that was everybody's problem at Red Lion Square, she speculated: doing traditional work at a time that valued only the new. Finally, however, this little firm named—"Cockerham and Gatehill," MacPherson murmured—Cockerham and Gatehill took *Plantation Trace*, then the others, and she even got an American publisher, but publishing her books was "like dropping a stone in the water—plop, a few circles, then nothing."

"Alan always said to our friends in Red Lion Square, 'Your time will come, your time will come.' Alan was an immensely comforting sort of person," Mrs. Glover said.

At Chauncy's request, Mrs. Glover had unearthed some old photographs from somewhere upstairs. I recalled the photo of Alan, a large man with protruding eyes wearing a Norfolk jacket and holding a gun. Mrs. Glover spoke of the Second World War, telling what I already knew from the *Hedgerow* article about Red Lion Square being bombed in May of 1941, how Jane Winkler was killed by a buzz bomb, and how several of the men no one had ever heard of—John Morse, the sculptor, and George Dabson, a man who made stained glass—went off to fight and were killed in France. She lost the diaries she had kept for years, her manuscripts, a few letters, she almost lost her life. Had she kept diaries since the war? Occasionally, but she had burned them. Letters from friends? No, no one knew where she was. She wasn't one to keep up with people. Alan was involved in some war work on the home front, but after the war, or perhaps while the war was still going on, he needed to move to Northumberland.

"Needed to move?" MacPherson prompted.

"To get some fresh air," Mrs. Glover replied lightly. "And I wanted to leave too. To make a new start. Give up the struggle."

MacPherson had been interested in Mrs. Glover as a "living link" with the literary life of the 20s and 30s, and many of his questions were designed to bring this out. He brought up the Bloomsbury Group. Mrs. Glover said she had met Virginia Woolf and Vanessa Bell and the others "on one or two occasions" but "never felt comfortable with them." I hoped Mrs. Glover would mention the house party at Garsington, but she didn't. Did she know Lawrence, he asked? No, they never met. Bertrand Russell? "No!" She had met Augustus John. The ill-fated Jane Winkler had studied at the Slade; Jane had also done some modeling for Augustus John, who had dropped into a party at Red Lion Square one time and was "terribly handsome." Mrs. Glover had met Aldous Huxley once but couldn't remember much about him. The main thing that interested her about those days was what was on at the opera, and she kept getting sidetracked that afternoon on ancient opera stars like "Martinelli" or "Schumann-Heinck."

I could tell that MacPherson was disappointed with the interview; it didn't have much meat. It was borne in upon me once again that although Emerald Glover had been a fine writer in her youth, she was completely unintellectual, quite innocent of movements or schools. In any case, I was afraid she was just too old for such inquiries, just too long removed from the world. It occurred to me, as she digressed about Nellie Melba or some such famous singer, that there were hardly any books in the house, apart from the ones in my bedside table, and those probably belonged to her husband. She had some magazines, but those were not even vaguely literary.

"Is there any one particular writer whom you admired?" MacPherson now asked Mrs. Glover, trying to bring her back to the subject of literature. Mrs. Glover cocked her head and looked blank. "Cut!" snapped Chauncy. MacPherson got up from his chair and paced back and forth, rubbing his eyes.

"No, we just have to let her talk," MacPherson said at the next break when I asked if he thought he could get anything more. So the interview wasn't going to be over that afternoon or even the next morning. MacPherson intended to get hours and hours of film and then edit it down to one or two. (This was a man, after all, who wrote seven hundred-page novels, not to mention a soap opera where the birth of a baby takes weeks.) "I must say, though," he added, "so far, I find it a little dull."

In the end, there were some twenty hours of film. I didn't see all of it. I would get too restless and have to go outside and take a walk. The crew also filed throughout the house and gardens, with Mrs. Glover telling how she and Alan had redone the house and reclaimed the grounds from nature. All the animals had their turn before the camera—Jarvis the cat, the English setter (Basil), and I remember William toting his camera in pursuit of a peacock who refused to spread his tail. At one point, the attention was focused on Mrs. Glover's painting with her posing at her easel in the garden, wearing her straw hat. For a while early Tuesday afternoon Mrs. Glover rested, and the crew, MacPherson, and I hurtled around the neighborhood in the van to get scenic views of Northumberland. We even mounted the hill at Housesteads to get some footage of Hadrian's Wall.

During breaks, the crew played cards. They seemed to lead an intense life of their own that had nothing to do with their surroundings. But one thing did get their attention. Monday afternoon, in the middle of filming, somebody shouted, "*Eden's* on!" and Chauncy yelled "Cut!" although we were right in the middle of some reminiscence about Rosa Ponselle. Just as if a fire alarm had sounded, filming shut down and everybody, including Mrs. Glover, repaired to the TV in the sitting room to watch *This Other Eden*. I was particularly struck by how the sound man sat cross-legged on the floor close to the screen, like a small child watching *Sesame Street*. Everybody knew all the characters in the story and seemed to participate in it with them, making frequent comments on the action and ripostes to the dialogue. Like their counterparts in American soaps, the characters in *This Other Eden* were each incredibly beautiful or handsome, like models, and the music was the stereotypical organ music, the heavy vibrato swelling and fading with the drama. I thought the crew might view *This Other Eden* with some irony or amusement—it seemed like all live soap operas to me, raw somehow in its production values, with constant close-ups— but their interest seemed serious, particularly Chauncy's. MacPherson was not in the audience—he went outside to walk around the garden, and from time to time, I would catch a glimpse of him passing slowly by a window, looking moody. I gathered that there was a particular problem that day: "Elizabeth," one of the Barbie-like actresses, had threatened not to appear, but she was appearing. She played a villainous character and was frequently hissed by the crew.

Thus passed two days, with sessions of filming interspersed with catch-as-catch-can meals and junkets around the countryside and the daily screening of *This Other Eden*. Finally, on Tuesday afternoon, MacPherson said to me, "Why don't you ask some questions, Caroline? Maybe she'll open up a little more, say something interesting."

Emerald Glover took her seat by the fireplace one last time, and I took mine. I was clammy with nerves. The plan was for me to ask Mrs. Glover about another list of prominent literary figures MacPherson had thought of, but as Chauncy snapped the clapperboard and yelled, "Emerald Glover, take one hundred forty-three," I couldn't put my hands on the list and just asked the first thing that came into my mind.

"When did you first realize you were a writer?"

"Oh, heavens, I never believed I was a writer. That would be like calling myself a saint," Mrs. Glover declared, and I sighed, relieved that Emerald Glover wasn't one of those artistic children who had started writing poems and stories at age five and never looked back.

"It was Alan who thought I was the writer," she added, wagging her white head back and forth just slightly, tortoise-like.

"What was London like, in those days?"

Mrs. Glover looked away. "Homely. Grand. Not so pretty as Paris. But I worked so hard in those days, my dear, I might as well have been in the Aleutian Islands. I didn't know where I was. You work too hard, I daresay, Caroline. You're so very intense."

I laughed a little in embarrassment, but Chauncy didn't yell "Cut!"

"Did you have trouble with your books, or did they just come?" I asked, thinking of the time I tried to write a story in my Barston townhouse. I sat at the desk in my office upstairs, feeling horribly alone. I felt panicky. The subject of the story I wanted to write was London. I intended to write from my own experience, just as they say you should do. I was going to fictionalize the trip in '72. I would begin with the taxi ride from Victoria Station. With tremulous hand, I put down a sentence descriptive of this ride, complete with fictional heroine—"Jane peered out of the window at the grand stone buildings," I believe was my sentence—but that is all that would come; I couldn't imagine what would come next. I tried to imagine somebody sitting across from Jane in the taxi, but no one was there. I believed that novelists wrote the first sentence of their novels, then the second and third, that the novel simply unrolled for the author as it does when you read it. And when nothing "unrolled," I believed I had no talent and got up from the desk, fled from my apartment, sweating, and drove to Middleton, where I shopped for the rest of the day.

Mrs. Glover was laughing her tinkly little laugh. Then she collected herself and said she wrote slowly and revised ceaselessly, indeed that writing was so difficult for her that she was glad she had stopped ("like Rossini"). If she had any advice for the young writer, or the beginning writer at any age, it was, "Don't, if you can help it."

"But didn't you miss London, after you moved?" I asked, imagining Emerald Glover under the little flap of her window at Red Lion Square, engaged in her work. (Of course, I did not take seriously what she had said about writing being so hard for her. *She* hadn't fled after one sentence—she had produced a quartet of novels, which, for the purpose of impressing the viewers, was stacked on a table at her elbow.)

"Of course I did, of course I did," Mrs. Glover declared, "especially the theatre and the opera. But my life was *here*. Let me tell you about the last time I was in London," she said, and I sat back. The cameras were whirring, but Mrs. Glover seemed to have forgotten about them, the way they say you do. She had completely lost the coy, actress-like quality she had exhibited at first, and we seemed to be alone in the room.

"It had been home to me, before the war. I felt completely at home. But after the war. . . . Late in 1946, I was invited down to a party for Daphne Taylor. You know Daphne Taylor's work, don't you? *The Spinet*? And what is her other novel? Oh, I forget. It isn't important. Anyway, Daphne had come out with her second or third novel, and I was invited to a party for her. Alan didn't want to go—didn't care for Daphne or something of the sort, didn't want to leave the house, probably some work being done. Anyway, I yearned to go. I had a new cape, black, with scarlet lining, beautiful thing, first new coat I'd had since before the war.

"I took a train down to London. It was delayed somewhere, I forget why, but finally, I got to King's Cross and took a taxi to Bloomsbury—Mecklenburgh Square. I was an hour or two late, and as I got out and paid the driver, I could hear the party going on. It was up on the first floor, and the windows of the flat were open, though it was November and a very cool day. You could look up and see people's legs in the windows—men's legs, and women's legs—and hear them talk. You could even hear ice. Or that's how I remember it—I distinctly remember the clatter of ice. I went up the steps, thinking 'I'm so horribly late, people will be leaving now,' but nobody came down the steps as I went up, and when I got inside the hall, a servant met me and offered to take my cape, and somebody at the party saw me and came toward me to greet me and I thought, 'I can't go in'! It was so crowded in there it looked like a solid mass of people. And they were all talking to each other—talking, talking, talking, and brilliantly, you understand. It wasn't just party chatter but brilliant talk they would go home afterwards and write down, bring out in a book.

"Rebecca West might have been in that room, or Bertrand Russell, any of those people you've been asking me about. But they belonged, don't you see, and I didn't. I was just an American who had contrived to stay here a while. London was theirs, don't you see."

"But it's ours too, isn't it? At least, I feel that it's mine, in a way," I said unguardedly.

"Oh, it's everybody's now," Mrs. Glover said, a wild look in her eye. Then she returned to the past. "I couldn't go in. I felt desolate; I felt *wounded* in some way. I turned my back on that acquaintance of mine and ran down the steps and away from the flat. It was several hours before another train to the north, and so I went and sat in a square, Russell Square, I think it was. I could not think at all. I felt cold, then hot. Before long, I realized I wasn't well. Every time I breathed in, I felt a knife-like pain in my chest. I don't know how I got home—I hardly remember the train. I was terribly ill. I was in bed three months. They never decided what I had, nor did I ever fully recover. One doctor said I had pleurisy, another said tuberculosis. Another said it was all in my mind. Alan nursed me all that time, like an angel."

"You and Alan must have been very happy," I said. I had forgotten about the camera too.

"Alan and I didn't have an ordin'ry marriage, though it was a very good marriage."

"Is your illness the reason you never went back to Louisiana?"

"Well, I always meant to go. I never deliberately decided not to go back home. But there was always something. I was working so hard between the wars; then, of course, I fell ill. And Alan was a Jew, don't you know, and my family was hopelessly prejudiced against Jews. Then, too, ours wasn't a normal marriage such as people understand in Jonesfield, Louisiana. Alan had his own friends, don't you see. The carpenter who helped with the house was a dear special friend of Alan's."

"Oh!" I said, looking around for Chauncy to yell "Cut!" but Chauncy, along with the rest of the crew, was standing transfixed much as they did when *Eden* was on.

"Alan fell ill the last years of his life. He had Addison's Disease," Mrs. Glover went on. "Wasn't it ironic? I married

Alan in 1921 so that I could stay in England. Then, in the 50s and 60s, he was the reason I couldn't leave."

❧ ❧ ❧

"Super! We finally got something!" MacPherson exclaimed after that final session.

"Thought we had a dud for a while," remarked Chauncy in passing.

I said, "It seems awfully personal, all that about her husband."

"It's history, literary history," MacPherson said. "You really got on her wavelength that last hour!"

"Robert! Come on, let's go!" Chauncy called. Chauncy and the crew were in the front hall, putting on their coats.

MacPherson did not appear to have heard Chauncy. "You've done such a fine job with the interview, Caroline. Why don't you stick around and help with the edit?"

"'Stick around.' You mean stay in England?" I said, incredulous. "That's not possible, I have to get back! I have a job, you know."

"Quit it!" said MacPherson with a shrug.

"Wish I could," I said to this outlandish idea. Other outlandish suggestions were being bruited about. John, the sound man, wanted to drive to Manchester that night, and Chauncy agreed. But MacPherson, who was apparently more stable than he'd been in '72, nixed these wild plans and said they would spend the night. They were going to a pub in Pelwichton. MacPherson asked me to come.

"Thanks, but I'd better stay with Mrs. Glover," I said, thinking how drained she had looked after that last part of the interview. What I wanted was not an evening with MacPherson and the crew. I wanted to help Rajiv put the house to rights, take a few photographs of my own, perhaps sit a while with Mrs. Glover. Feeling dazed, I went around the house, picking up glasses and ashtrays, restoring pillows and bibelots to their original places, while Rajiv prepared a simple supper. I finally thought to get my little camera, and I wandered around the house, trying to document everything so that I could try to create the same effect in my own apartment. Nothing *matched,* I observed. Colors and patterns of fabrics and carpets might be wildly discordant, but that didn't matter in this palimpsest of old and new. For the first time, I found myself wanting a house, wanting a garden. Would fritillaries grow in Louisiana?

When dinner was ready, I fetched Mrs. Glover, who was in her room writing a letter or perhaps even a diary entry, I remember thinking at the time. The three of us ate together in the kitchen, talking of anything but literature or television. We drank the bottle of mead, which brought on a pleasant glow. Rajiv chatted about his family, his studies. As I listened, I found myself thinking about John and Mrs. O'Leary, in the Lowlands by now.

By the time we went to bed, MacPherson and the crew had not come back. Mrs. O'Leary would have deplored how Mrs. Glover left the front door unlocked for them. Much later, when I was already sound asleep, I was awakened by a noise. It was a soft knock on my door. I awoke with a jump. I had been dreaming I was in a Tube station, part of a huge crowd attempting to mount a steep escalator, only it was broken and we had to walk up it—tramp, tramp, tramp, all packed together in a phalanx. I suppose I was really hearing the crew come up the stairs, but, as I say, what actually woke me was the knock on the door. It was a very soft knock—bump, bump, bump—the back of somebody's hand, not knuckles. At first, I doubted that it was a knock at all, attributing the bumps to the settling of the old house. But then I heard it again—bump,

bump, bump. I sat up in bed, suddenly hot under the thick duvet. MacPherson, I thought, blushing in the darkness; then I thought of all the other people it could be. It could be a member of the crew seeking to visit another member of the crew but mistaking the room. It could be Rajiv, coming to tell me that Mrs. Glover was dead. I did actually think it was Rajiv for a moment, but I knew that even so polite a person as Rajiv would not announce death so discreetly. I chose to lie still, pretending even to myself that I was really asleep.

PART FIVE

A PROSPECT OF LONDON

Chapter 22

When I woke up the next morning I had been dreaming about Franklin Harold. We were exploring some house together. It seemed to be in London, though it was a crazy kind of house, with distorted perspectives—crooked floors and crooked walls—and we kept falling down and laughing, getting lost. When I woke up, I was thinking about Franklin, and London; the word "flailing" was also in my mind. It occurred to me, as I lay under the heavy duvet, trying to wake up, that you could just sink into Northumberland and never be able to pull yourself out. "Northumberland" rhymed with "slumber-land." A day or two before, I had been thinking how much Franklin would like it up here. It was so beautiful and remote, offering none of the distractions that London did to the person who wanted to write, but then maybe it wouldn't be good for Franklin after all. Emerald Glover had not written anything up here. She had turned to easier forms of artistic expression—the remodeling of houses, the painting of landscapes.

As I showered, I felt a tremendous urgency to get back to London. I seemed to have awakened from a larger dream than that specific dream of Franklin and the crooked house. Suddenly I realized that it was Wednesday morning, and I was flying home on Saturday, that my time in London was countable not only in days (three) but hours (seventy-two), several of which would be used up just getting back to the city. I felt very isolated in this country place as I went down to the kitchen to dry my hair. It was still early, and I seemed to be the only one up. For a moment, I thought MacPherson's crew might have left Rutland Cottage, but no—the van and the black Rover were still parked out front, and presently MacPherson himself appeared, looking worn out and dissipated.

"I must go," I told Mrs. Glover when she appeared, looking tired and a little bewildered. "We're all leaving. You must get some rest. Robert has offered to drive me to the train in Durham."

At we left, Mrs. Glover presented me with copies of each of her four books with personal inscriptions, and as we were leaving, embraced me emotionally, pressing her cottony head against my chest.

"Come to Louisiana—we all want you to," I urged as the Rover revved up. "I'll write."

"We must write," she called back.

We were off, and I looked back at the rambling house with little Mrs. Glover out front, waving a handkerchief.

The sun was shining on Northumberland, the wind ruffling it, though I made only a pretense of admiring the landscape. I was waiting in a virtual rigor of attentiveness for whatever MacPherson might say.

"So tell me," he said after a few minutes of high-speed driving. "You're a scholar now?"

I took a deep breath and plumbed my mind for the most completely truthful answer to this question. MacPherson stimulated you to think what seemed like brand-new thoughts. "No, I'm not a scholar," I said finally. "I've been trying to be a Lady in a Seersucker Suit."

"Explain," he said, grinning (this was just the kind of thing MacPherson liked you to say).

I didn't know if I could, I said, the idea had just occurred to me. But it had to do with Mrs. Cannon, a woman I had worked for one summer in college. I had worked at Selbin's, the largest department store in Meridian, in Better Sportswear. I had always been interested in clothes but had thought this was a frivolous, even reprehensible side to my character until I worked for Mrs. Cannon. She was the kind of stylish, efficient-looking person who looks good in glasses, the type who used to be called a "career woman." Mrs. Cannon took a professional interest in clothes. I saw that she studied them with the same diligence as you study a book. New stock would arrive, but before we could put it "out on the floor," she would hang representative pieces up in her office to examine. She would have a lot to say about the width of the seam allowance and the depth of the hems and the presence or absence of esoteric features like "gussets." She was interested in how clothes looked on people, too. She would have me try on things and then say, shrewdly, whether they "did" or not (I always bought the things that "did") But the interesting thing about Mrs. Cannon, I told MacPherson, was that despite this vocational interest in clothes, not to mention her excellent opportunities for buying them, she herself wore the same thing to work almost every day, a blue-striped seersucker suit. She changed it up, of course, I went on. She would wear it with different blouses, or wear the jacket without a blouse, adding a chunky piece of jewelry or some other deft accessory. But still, it was the same suit every day, and it came to me that it functioned as a kind of uniform for Mrs. Cannon. I concluded that you could work better if you had a uniform. You would never feel drowsy during working hours if you had your uniform on, you would never feel bored; you would not feel any awful doubts about the value of what you were doing. You would just experience your block of work, then go home and take off your uniform, satisfied with a good day's work, ready to live your life. And this was a very attractive idea to me, as the eight-hour shifts I worked at Selbin's seemed complex and interminable, and afterward I felt like a wet dishrag, unable to do anything more than just go home and collapse in front of the tube.

Yet now, even though I had my own career at NCLU, teaching freshmen and sophomores about British and American literature, I still felt like a dishrag at the end of the day, and each day, far from being a satisfying block of time, was still fragmented and interminable. But I kept hoping that if I got on the right track, if I found the right subject for research, I'd be more like Mrs. Cannon.

"And you came up here for that?" MacPherson asked.

Well, yes, I went on, but Mrs. Glover was different from what I expected, nothing like a sage or writer, more the *femme d'intérieure*. Meanwhile, we had passed out of the green and gold of Northumberland and into the flat, dun-colored county of Durham, but I scarcely noticed, by this time being worked up to a confessional pitch such as is usually reached only by college freshmen about two in the morning. I sought to describe my mother and grandmother to MacPherson. Both were college graduates, but neither had ever "worked" like Mrs. Cannon. As a matter of fact, both my mother and her mother had been married only a day or two after they graduated from college.

My mother had followed the example set by her own mother—remained *intérieure,* so to speak—though my father was not so well-off as his father, and our house in Meridian was not nearly so handsome as the house on Palmer Avenue. Her family was also on a smaller scale, just Mike and I. Yet, she cared for her home and brought up her children with an assiduity equal to her mother-in-law's. Perhaps my mother cultivated her garden with an even greater assiduity. Our yard was perhaps three-quarters of an acre, and Mother cultivated every square inch of that yard. Inside the house, she maintained baker's racks of difficult, temperamental plants like African violets. I pictured my paternal grandmother in her gardening things—loose old shirt and slacks, beige Keds, a limp straw hat that one of the dogs had chewed on. Like Mrs. Glover, Grandmother was very thin, although she had been more fortunate with regard to her health and had a straight back. Her white hair was long, and she always wore it pulled back in a bun. It did not seem coincidental now that I had first seen Mrs. Glover in her gardening things.

"Look for signs for the station, will you?" he said, swiveling around continuously as he jockeyed for position in the rapid flow of traffic.

"Are we in Durham already?"

"We better be," said MacPherson.

We found a parking place, and MacPherson maneuvered into it. Crossing a busy street, we entered the railway station. Carrying my bag, MacPherson found the ticket window, bought my ticket on a train leaving in two minutes, and hustled me toward the right platform.

"You're in luck," he said.

"Please let me pay you back."

"Forget it!"

"I'm sorry I talked the whole way."

"Nonsense. That's important stuff. Put it in your fiction notebook."

At the train, people kept pushing past us and struggling up the steep steps. A porter stood in the door, looking down at us, extending his hand to take my bag. The train was making those lumbering, clanking noises preparatory to sliding away.

MacPherson had hold of my arm. "We get back on Friday. May I see you?"

"I'm at St. Cuthbert's Hotel," I said as he leaned in, to kiss me? Turning my head, I felt a warm kiss on my cheek. The train had actually begun to move as I scampered up the steps and swayed down the aisle, my mind a white blank. By the time I had the presence of mind to look out the window to wave good-bye, we were already thundering through the countryside.

❧ ❧ ❧

All the way back to London, I felt low, wondering what on earth to do with my life, wondering whether I would ever find a place in this world. I stared at the sheep in the fields. They had all been shorn, but they must have wanted their wool coats in the wet, windy fields. And London, as we approached it from the north, looked gray and grim. Passing through the dismal boroughs of north London, I supposed I could see what people meant when they said London was poor and overcrowded or used phrases like "sprawling urban blight."

No matter what was happening in Northumberland, they were definitely still having that cold, wet summer in London, and whizzing through the crowded streets from King's Cross to Bloomsbury, I foresaw getting back to St. Cuthbert's Hotel in the middle of the afternoon and finding it completely empty, then being at loose ends until dinner time with nothing to do but walk gloomily through the streets. In fact, however, a number of Barston people—Carol, Edwina, Allison—were in the telly room when I arrived, watching *This Other Eden*. "Caroline!" they cried, and I greeted them gladly, feeling as though I'd been away for a month. They had just gotten back from Harrods and were collapsed in the easy chairs, near the fire, surrounded by green plastic shopping bags. They had their shoes kicked off, and their coats spread over them like cover.

"How was it?" Edwina said excitedly, whispering so as not to disrupt the drama. It was a scene in a hospital room. Angela had just had her baby.

"It was just great," I whispered. "You will never believe it, but MacPherson writes that!"

"Writes what?" said Edwina, with glowing eyes.

"*This Other Eden*."

"No!" cried Edwina out loud. Carol Beckwith said, "Shhh!" But just then, the organ swelled into a crescendo, and a commercial for some quaint British product came on.

"He knows that actress. She's been threatening to quit," I said, realizing that I was betraying a secret but simply unable to resist exciting Edwina and Carol and even Allison, who was taking an interest, asking who this "MacPherson" was.

"You know, I had noticed that it had good dramatic tension," Edwina said appraisingly.

Allison said, "I told Charlie there was some intelligence behind it!"

"Is that the same Robert MacPherson who wrote the *Teasdale Saga*?" asked Carol Beckwith. "I loved the *Teasdale Saga*."

Angela's baby was revealed to have a heart defect during the final segment of this episode, but when it was over—during

the vibrato-filled theme music and then during the next program, another daytime drama which the women from Barston
agreed was "much less literate" than *This Other Eden*—I
answered questions about my sojourn in Northumberland.
I displayed the quartet, pointing out the autograph on the
flyleaf of each volume ("With love to Caroline, who found
me—Emerald Glover, July 16, 1980"). They took an enthusiastic interest in Emerald Glover, her house, and the countryside. I described the arrival of MacPherson, and the BBC
interview seemed, in the telling, a great achievement. Edwina
pressed for details about Emerald Glover and what it was like
to meet her. (As I described going up to the "lumber room"
and finding the quartet, Edwina clenched her teeth and sort
of panted in scholarly excitement.) Presently Mavis Adams
and Lucy Maddox came in the telly room and, after being
brought up to date, evinced a particular interest in Rutland
Cottage, declaring that they would go stay there on their next
trip. When Sid Beckwith came in, I showed him the books
and tried to answer his questions about Rutland Cottage's
vernacular architecture.

But the climax of my return was, of course, when Charles
came in. Shaking out his umbrella and removing his raincoat,
he came toward me, his eyes alight, his hand outstretched,
to receive the word from my own lips that Emerald Glover
was alive and well, that I had not only spoken with her but
stayed with her for five days and nights, practically lived with
her, all the while gathering no telling how much scholarly
material. He and Allison had spent the weekend in Essex
with Sir Dudley Cranmer, a poet and collector of eighteenth-
century memorabilia, from whom Charles had succeeded
in buying a first edition of Pope's "Essay on Man" for the
Rare Book Room at NCLU, but my expedition completely
overshadowed Charles's expedition, as he, a gentleman as

well as a scholar, was the first to admit. Charles fingered my first edition of Emerald Glover, wondering if I might donate them to the Rare Book Room, meanwhile questioning me eagerly about Emerald Glover and the state of her health. He was also avid for details about the BBC interview, and I realized that he had never been directly involved in the exciting medium of television (the possibility of interviewing Smollett never having arisen, of course). Charles had never heard of MacPherson, by the way, and Allison seemed to enjoy being the one to educate him.

I was no more sure now of how I could write two scholarly articles or a book-length publishable manuscript than I had been before, but I had two battered Cambridge Reporters notebooks completely filled with notes. I also had Charles's tape recorder, which I had sometimes remembered to turn on during the filming until I ran out of tape. Now I took it out of my bag, rewound a tape, and turned it on. There was Emerald Glover's high, quivery voice, right there in the telly room, saying, "I loved the underground, in the beginning. I used to get on the underground just anywhere and ride to the end of the line and back." Charles sat there listening, stroking his mustache. He looked enthralled, much as I imagine the British had looked in the early days of the wireless, listening to far-off news of the world.

Chapter 23

Wednesday night, after dinner with the Barston people at the Lamb on Lamb's Conduit, Edwina and I talked a while before going to sleep. The windows were open, and we lay in our beds under the orange bedspreads in the darkness, occasionally feeling the gusts of cold, damp wind on our faces.

At Edwina's urging, I told about Northumberland, going into more detail about that first hectic tea, and Chesters and Hadrian's Wall (*that* frightful day), and Lindisfarne, my beach, then the arrival of MacPherson, the turmoil of the filming.

Edwina, in turn, told me about Saturday night and the party I had missed, describing the funny arty people who were there, their outlandish clothes, the colors of their hair. A famous artist had been at the party, somebody who had just made one of those notorious sales to the Tate involving the exchange of millions of pounds for paintings consisting solely of stripes or something. Edwina had been much taken with the flat on Cheyne Walk. It belonged to some actress we had never heard of, and it was decorated entirely in chintz. Edwina really meant entirely: chintz was everywhere, not only in normal places like curtains and upholstery but even on the walls. Someone had quipped that the inside of the refrigerator was chintz, and she wasn't entirely sure it was a joke! It was a different world, Edwina said, meaning more than the omnipresence of chintz, recounting how she had walked into the kitchen and encountered people sniffing and snorting in a telltale manner, commenting, too, on MacPherson's friend who had served as hostess. Her name was Victoria.

"She works at the BBC. She started telling me how much she missed having sex. Can you believe it? It seems that she and Robert had been having an affair, but he broke it off when he moved to London and took the flat. She said his move 'cost her a perfectly good lover.'"

"*God*," I said, not terribly surprised, remembering Chauncy. I couldn't visualize MacPherson's face now. I could see his slight frame, dressed in a wrinkled white shirt with the sleeves rolled up, black pipestem pants, but this body had no head, just some sort of agitating aura. Then suddenly, I could see his boyish, withered face and his very blue eyes with brilliant clarity. I saw that playful, penetrating expression, and I knew for certain then that the knock on my door the night before ("bump-bump-bump") had been the work of MacPherson. I was equally certain, at that moment, that he had, in fact, been making a pass of some sort back in the V & A all those years ago because that is what he would do, given the opportunity, given such an adoring girl.

"MacPherson was Victoria's lover?" I summarized tentatively. Perhaps, after all, Edwina was referring to some other "Robert" at the party.

"That's what she said. She said he used to come to

London on short visits and stay at her flat, but when he moved here, he broke it off."

"*God*, what a jerk." I wasn't "in love" with MacPherson—never had been, in any real sense—but he had had some power over me that seemed to be gone.

The subject of men having been raised, Edwina ventured to ask me about Jerry Braswell. Apparently, Edwina had been laboring under the idea that Jerry had "left me" and I was suffering from a broken heart, but I assured her that this was not true. Jerry had proposed before he left, I confided, but I had turned him down. I tried to think of Jerry, but Jerry had no head either, and I said, quite sincerely, that I had forgotten all about him.

I asked Edwina whether she missed Ernest, and she said, "not really." Then Edwina actually said that she found Ernest dull sometimes, going on to reveal that even though she was about to be married, she continued to be powerfully attracted to other men. I found this extremely surprising, as I believed at that time that married people, and even people engaged to be married, were incapable of feeling sexual attraction for anyone but their mates unless they were wild, lawless individuals such as MacPherson. I found it even more surprising in Edwina, who looked too stocky and sensible for such rogue sensations. She told me she had felt a surprisingly strong attraction to MacPherson.

"I know the feeling," I said. "I used to think I was in love with him at school," I said, seeing myself in that distant time at Whittaker as a callow schoolgirl, wearing pigtails and pinafores, as it were. I told Edwina what had happened that day in the V & A.

"I think he's a Don Juan, Caroline," she said, using the pronunciation we had learned for Byron ("Don Jew-an") as if to heap Byron's libertinism on top of the Spanish seducer's.

"No doubt."

"John, now," Edwina mused. "I'm thinking you might fall in love with John."

"He's great," I said, "I like him a lot." I wondered how he felt about *me*. I thought of the postcard he had sent to the hotel for me from Edinburgh. "Having a great time. Vauxhall behaving better than Aunt Dora. Scotland enchants. Back Thursday aft. Aff, John." Was that a love note?

I dozed a moment, but suddenly I was wide awake, saying, "You know, Edwina, sometimes I think about staying in London. Just throwing everything over and staying here."

Edwina didn't answer, and I thought she was asleep, but then she said, "I do too, Caroline. Last year I applied for a position as a tutor at Oxford."

"Heavens, Edwina. I didn't know that!" Despite the fact that she was a Midwesterner rather than a bona fide Southerner, Edwina was very gung-ho about the English Department back home and even NCLU itself. She actually went to the football games.

"I didn't tell anybody, including Ernie. But I didn't get it."

"I would have thought, in view of your tenure . . . "

"I know, you'd think so. But I loved Oxford my junior year. That was the happiest time of my life. I was crushed when I didn't get the job."

"So this was before you got engaged."

"Yes. We got engaged Christmas."

"Gee, Edwina."

"What would you do over here, Caroline?"

"Well, I don't know," I said in the vague light, not willing to say that my only hopes in this direction rested on a vague offer from Don Juan. "I suppose I could work at Wimpy's."

ॐ ॐ ॐ

The next day John and his aunt were supposed to be back in London for the Vespers service at four o'clock, and at 4:10, as I approached St. George's Bloomsbury in the rain (late due to the vagaries of Number 14s), I hoped they were there. I hoped this for Father Davenport's sake, I told myself, and for his little band of regulars, whose faint voices I could hear as I trudged up the steps. I had intended to bring some Barston people with me to help constitute a crowd, but everybody had plans of their own that day—the Nicholsons, Mavis and Lucy having gone down to Rye, the Beckwiths having gone out to Hampstead, and Edwina, who I believe was feeling guilty about some of the feelings she had expressed the night before, having planned to spend the afternoon shopping for a special present for Ernest and some things for their house. But as I reached the great gloomy portico of the church and pulled open the door, I saw that the church was packed! A great volume of voices, like all the nine orders of angels, was backed by powerful blasts of the organ. The church was ablaze with light, and priests in white robes, the Benedictine monks, were processing down the side aisles and up the center aisle, carrying crosses and waving censers. An usher, a nice gentleman I had never seen before, came over and escorted me to an empty folding chair in the rear. Then, at last, the procession was over, and everyone sat down with a tremendous rustling shuffle.

The Vespers service was in Latin. Because of the astonishing quantity of people, it was actually warm inside the church, and as I sat in my folding chair, trying to appreciate the occasion, it was so warm and stuffy, the Latin chants of the Benedictines so soporific, that I kept dropping off to sleep, dreaming confusedly of my beach and the view of Farne Island, the little white house. St. Cuthbert wasn't a Benedictine, but Benedictines seemed to be looming large in my experience. I had spent most of the day at the British Museum seeing the *Benedictines in Britain* exhibition—manuscripts, archaeological objects, and so forth—and I had carried away a souvenir, a trophy, a handsome poster with an image from an illuminated manuscript. I would get it framed as soon as I got home. The poster, encased in a handy tube to keep it safe, was balanced between my knees to avoid poking the people on either side of me.

The service seemed interminable, but finally, the last chant was sung, the monks processed in reverse, and we were released into the gray afternoon. I was one of the first ones out into the refreshingly chill air. Father Davenport was under the portico to greet the departing people. Surely, he was happy today, I thought, pausing to speak with him and to wait for John and Mrs. O'Leary, should they be back in the crowd somewhere. "Ah, Caroline, there's someone I should like you to meet," Father Davenport said, greeting me familiarly, without fuss, as if I were just one of his parishioners. He indicated a man in a dark suit, a beaming, silver-haired personage with a large gold medallion around his neck. "This is the Lord Mayor of Holborn," he said. The medallion, which was in the shape of a starburst, seemed to be encrusted with precious jewels. It made you think of the royal carriage rolling through the streets and "Pomp and Circumstance" sung by fervent students in the Albert Hall. I wanted to curtsy.

"How do you do?" I said to the Lord Mayor, who was genial and unassuming, much like Queen Beatrix of the Netherlands, who was said to ride a bicycle through the streets of The Hague.

"Turn this way. Smile!" somebody commanded, and I

turned to see the large woman who worked at the Cumberland Club, the giant man-woman, in her black satin motorcycle jacket, aiming a serious-looking camera with an extra-long proboscis at us.

I chatted with Father Davenport as the people continued to stream past, expecting any moment for Mrs. O'Leary to appear and mount an objection to the popish proceedings, with John behind her, looking wry. But this didn't happen as we chatted about Northumberland and the sacred places of the North. Presently, as the crowd was beginning to thin and I was about to say my goodbyes, I became aware of a commotion somewhere below. Looking down the wet steps, I saw a confluence of people, heard someone moan. A woman had fallen; another woman was trying to manage the gaggle of Good Samaritans. I caught a glimpse of white hair. But Father Davenport continued to tell me something about Durham Cathedral, not taking any notice of the accident, just persisting with his pleasant talk. His face wore a gentle, weary expression.

"I think I may know that injured person," I said to Father Davenport, unable to bear it any longer, conscious of how easy it would be for Mrs. Glover to come down to London with the brave object of going home, coming first to this service, which we had definitely talked about in her presence, then having this happen. I took my leave of Father Davenport and made my way down the steps. If Mrs. Glover had broken her hip, which is invariably what happened when old ladies fell down the steps, she would need full-time nursing. I would simply stay and be her nurse, I decided by the time I reached the place where the wounded woman was lying.

But it wasn't Mrs. Glover. It was no one even like her but rather a portly white-haired woman in a thin flowered dress. She had a gash on her leg, and the chief Samaritan was applying a tourniquet fashioned from a handkerchief. The sound of an ambulance was heard, not a simple siren like at home, but those two tones you hear from emergency vehicles careening through the streets of Europe (deh-dah, deh-dah). So I went on down the steps, turning toward the British Museum, reflecting on how much adversity Father Davenport had to cope with in this parish. Once I had passed St. George's and seen a derelict asleep up under the monumental portico, lying right against the doors.

Chapter 24

John and his aunt did not come back Thursday night nor yet Friday morning. I called the Florence to invite them to a special gathering of the Barston people for lunch on Friday at Fred's Diner, an American-style place Sid thought we'd all like, but the Italian hotel manager had not heard from them. I was worried about my friends, who seemed at risk somewhere out on the road and suddenly inexpressibly dear, but it was our last day in London, and I tried to put them out of my mind. After breakfast, the Barston people scattered to museums and stores and other London landmarks. I took a bus to Piccadilly and Burlington House to see the Andrew Wyeth show.

Something peculiar had happened to the weather Friday morning: it was dark and rainy, but it had turned quite warm. The wind was blowing so hard that as I rode down Shaftesbury Avenue, I saw people wrestling with their umbrellas to keep them from turning inside out. It was actually too warm for a raincoat, though you needed a raincoat on the street, with the cars and buses spewing up water and drenching pedestrians. From the top of the bus, I drank in the sights of the busy, crowded street, not thinking about the past or the future except when I should happen to see a small insectival car, or a black Rover, or a person with moss-colored hair, at which times I'd experience a small turn in the chest and wonder, briefly, where am I going? What will it *come* to?

After the exhibition, I stopped at Hatchards, permitting myself to buy three English novels in lightweight paperback editions. Then I took the Tube back to Bloomsbury and found Fred's Diner, which was near St. Cuthbert's on Southampton Row. Although Carol Beckwith had pledged to keep trying to reach them at the Florence, Mrs. O'Leary and John weren't there, but all the Barston people had made it, plus Anna, the breakfast girl, who had been invited as our special guest. This was ostensibly because Fred's Diner was "American," and she loved America so much, but mainly because some of the Barston people thought Anna worked for slave wages at St. Cuthbert's and needed a treat.

Fred's Diner was long and narrow, like a boxcar. "Fred" had tried to replicate an American diner. The tables were chrome and Formica, and each had bottles of French's mustard and Heinz ketchup. The walls were decorated with black and white photographs of stark American subjects like gas stations and eighteen-wheelers, even some romping football players. We had to roam through the diner, looking at each photograph, gleeful at the discovery that one of the football stars on the wall was Jimmy McAllister, a famous pro quarterback who had graduated from NCLU. (Our school was usually referred to as a "football powerhouse" because, even though it was only in a minor division, it had produced a surprising number of pros, a fact that seemed more interesting now that it was recognized in London.) With Anna in tow, we studied the photographs for further local references. Of course, Fred's Diner didn't *really* look American. There weren't any calendars from the local bank or garage, nor were there novelties for sale next to the cash register. Nevertheless, it was jarring to see American products in London, as when you went in Fortnum and Mason and saw the staff in frock coats using feather dusters on Tex-Sun grapefruit juice or Jiffy peanut butter. No, Fred's Diner was art, like a George Segal sculpture of a bus station, but it was good art, and bright and cool on this dark, warm day. It seemed to have an American air conditioner.

The food at Fred's was shockingly expensive. What they had, basically, was hamburgers, at two pounds fifty each (five dollars!), and when you added things to go with it, baked beans, or French fries, "you were looking at ten, twelve dollars for lunch, which was a far cry from McDonald's," Carol Beckwith said in consternation, but what the heck, Sid said, it was our last day in London. Presently our waiter, who was from Pakistan or India, began bringing the hamburgers, which were huge charcoal-broiled things you could hardly get your mouth around. Those among us who had had to resort to hamburgers at other places in England these past three weeks testified that those hamburgers had been horrible, while these, on the other hand, really were American-style, although it could be argued that Fred went too far in the direction of abundance, even opulence, by providing a rotating rack with a wide selection of condiments, including a corn relish that Carol Beckwith would have sworn only her Aunt Jane knew how to make. None of the people from Barston cared for hamburgers, as a general rule, but everybody said they loved *these* hamburgers that had been replicated in London.

Charles was taking a kindly interest in Anna, who had interrupted her university education to come here and work. She wanted to go to America, so why not go to Barston, he asked? His description of the various curricula and the financial aid packages sounded quite alluring.

"And Barston's a nice little town," Allison assured the New Zealander. "We've always lived on the East Coast and I didn't know whether I could adjust, but what I really love about Barston, apart from the mild winters, is that there's no traffic, literally none, except around noon, when everybody goes home to "dinner," as they call it. Then there might be four or five cars at a traffic light, but you never hear a horn. If somebody doesn't move right away when the light turns green, the people behind him just sit there and wait! Our house is about two minutes from campus, and I can get the boys to soccer practice at their school in five minutes. It's just spoiled me. When we went up to Boston at Christmas to visit my mother, I did some driving, and it was like being dropped in a shark tank."

"It's a fine town," Sid Beckwith chimed in. "Of course, I've been there most of my life, except when I was in the Army."

Carol Beckwith told Anna about Barston's other claim to fame, apart from football: peaches. All the peaches grown in Louisiana, or all the peaches worth mentioning, were grown right there in Barston. Barston's peach industry used to comprise four or five distinct farms, but now it consisted of one single farm run by a Mr. Chatham. Everybody knew Mr. Chatham at the peach farm, but Carol revealed something I hadn't known, that Mr. Chatham, a genial person who always joked with you in a farmer-like way when you went out to buy something, wasn't really a farmer—he was a retired professor. He had taught petroleum engineering at NCLU, and his hobby had been growing peaches according to the latest scientific methods, but then his interest in peach-growing had overtaken his interest in oil, and he bought that farm.

Mavis told how everybody went out to the peach shed during harvest season and bought "overripes." This term had to be explained to Anna. It applied to peaches too ripe to be shipped out for sale, or those with some small defect, a worm-hole or a bruise, which wouldn't, however, prevent you from taking them home and enjoying them on the spot after a little creative peeling and slicing. Barston peaches were the best. Harrods ought to carry them, I suggested.

"But to get good overripes, you have to go out early in the morning," I said, mentioning how pretty the orchards looked at that time of day. Peach trees looked like turned-out umbrellas, I told her. And the peach shed was charming. It was similar to a warehouse but open all across the front, elevated by three or four steps. Looking up the steps into the open shed, you could see men and boys back there in the semi-darkness, crating peaches. NCLU students sometimes worked there part-time, but they didn't seem to be "work-ing"—they seemed to be performing roles in a diorama.

"You'd love the flowers in Barston," said Lucy, who was a famous gardener, her little house on Seventh Street having a flower garden that was coterminous with the front yard. Louisiana's climatic conditions were discussed in relation to New Zealand's, and the ladies quizzed Anna on whether such Louisiana specialties as azaleas and dogwoods could grow "down under."

"You know, we ought to keep this group together," Sid said convivially. "Carol and I want y'all to see our slides when we get them developed, and we'd like to see all yours. We could have some interesting evenings. We could get John and Mrs. O'Leary to come."

There was a worried silence as we thought of them out on the road.

"They'll be back," Edwina said stoutly. "They probably just decided to spend another night somewhere."

"I'm worried about car trouble," I put in.

"I like your idea, Sid. We could make it a club and meet regularly," said Charles. "Hear, hear," he added, gently rapping his spoon on his water glass, probably already planning a newsletter.

"We could call ourselves the Anglophiles!" cried Lucy.

"You really must come to Barston," Sid Beckwith said to Anna, who seemed interested. "We'll take you to visit the broom handle factory," he added with a wink, alluding to an actual business in Barston which was often cited, with ironical intent, as proof that Barston bustled.

Fellowship at lunch was so intense that everybody wanted dessert and coffee, even those women who were usually horrified at the idea of dessert because they were trying to diet. The foreign waiter, who seemed very nervous, as if this were his first day at Fred's, or even his first day in England, recited the available "sweets." Pecan pie was one of these (of course he said "pe-CAN," in the risible non-Southern way), and we speculated on what the English, or whatever nationality Fred might be, would make of this Southern delicacy. I liked the pie, which was served in large, sticky wedges, but then I was in that voracious state brought about by fatigue where anything tastes wonderful—just goes down the hatch and disappears, like what you eat in a museum coffee shop after seeing the museum, "fuel food," I call it, which can't possibly be fattening. But the women from Barston argued vociferously about it, each one having a favorite pecan pie recipe (even Allison, a newcomer to this field) which they claimed would produce better results in some way: less sticky filling, flakier crust. Carol Beckwith, the pie's harshest critic, denounced it as "gummy." The pecans themselves also came in for some criticism because they were so soft and small. Where on earth had they come from? Not Louisiana, certainly, where pecans are meaty and two inches long. These were pee-wee pecans from some British colony or minor protectorate.

∾ ∾ ∾

Outside we were struck again by that warm, turgid weather. "It's a bloody 'eat wave," Sid quipped. The sidewalks were wet, like those muggy winter days at home when it's not raining, but the humidity is so high that the pavement never dries and leaves stick to it. We walked together in a large gaggle back toward St. Cuthbert's—I wanted to deposit the books I had bought, also jettison my raincoat, which felt stiflingly hot. Our progress was slow. Mavis and Lucy walked very slowly, as did Allison, and their umbrellas kept getting entangled or threatening to put out somebody's eye.

"Remind me what kind of car John's in?" Sid asked me.

"A Vauxhall Chevette. With a hatchback. I call it 'kitchen-sliced,'" I added for the ladies.

I looked for the little orange car in the confusing swirl of traffic around Russell Square. I also peered at black Rovers, having for the past couple of days been visited by the vague fantasy of MacPherson's black Rover coming to a stop at some curb and the door opening and myself (like a sleepwalker) getting inside. But it was a taxi that drew my attention on Bedford Place, a taxi whizzing past with a passenger who looked like Rajiv. It couldn't be, of course. But the taxi stopped down in front of St. Cuthbert's. The door opened and the passenger emerged. Why, it *was* Rajiv, wearing his white pajamas. This looked perfectly natural in London, where the exotic was the norm.

"I know that person. That's Mrs. Glover's helper, the student who's staying with her," I said, running on ahead.

"Rajiv, good heavens! Where is Mrs. Glover?" I said as soon as I was close enough, looking down into the back seat of the taxi, which seemed empty but where Mrs. Glover might appear, like a revenant or Tinker Bell.

"She is at home. She is resting now," he said. "She has asked me to give you this."

Rajiv had been holding something to his breast—a white paper bag—and now he put this bag in my hands. I thought it might be a picture when I first saw it, one of her North Sea studies, perhaps my beach, but it was heavy and thick. Nothing had this density but a manuscript representing many years of work.

"Mrs. Glover knows you will take very good care of this," Rajiv said.

"Wait! What am I supposed to do with it?" I cried, for he was getting back in the taxi, saying to the driver, "Charlotte Street."

"Won't you come in?"

"My uncle is expecting me—I must go. There's a letter for you there. Good-bye!"

"What is it, Caroline? What's happened?" said the Barston people, jostling around me on the sidewalk.

"I think it's a manuscript from Mrs. Glover. I don't know yet what it is!" I pulled it partway out of the sack. The top page was the letter from Mrs. Glover in handwriting so spidery it looked like a code. The next page said, "A Small Town Girl, by Emerald Glover," and then there were hundreds more pages. I flipped through the pages, but nothing really registered.

"Whatever it is, it will surely need a lot of editing," Edwina observed with scholarly lust, and Charles said,

"That's a very valuable manuscript. Let's get it inside." And I remember thinking, as I carefully shifted the pages back into the sack, away from the light and the fearful Louisiana-like humidity, I don't have to worry about my job. Charles couldn't possibly fire somebody in possession of a manuscript such as this, raw material for who knows what and in itself a potential acquisition for the Rare Book Room. Emerald Glover was the most exciting thing going at NCLU right now, a producing author, a writer of our own. Smollett was put in the shade, and poor Lady Hermione, I thought, going up the steps with my manuscript, that pale poetess had become as wispy as a figure in a Book of Hours, whereas Mrs. Glover was very much part of the modern world—why, she was scheduled to be on the telly!

I went into the telly room, far too impatient to see what I had to go all the way upstairs, and Charles followed me. The others tactfully left us alone, guided away by Edwina, who of all people understood the solemnity of this occasion. I sank into a chair and pulled out the letter.

Dear Caroline,

I considered coming myself. I even began to pack for the journey, but I grew tired and had to go sit by my fire. It is too late for me to go away from here, to go back to America. I shall stay in my home, with my flowers. I shall do my work.

I have felt new life this last week. Your interest in me, your interest in my work have been as—well, as the sun and rain to my garden. It seemed to me for the first time in many years that something I have done might be of value to someone else. I resurrected this work, over which I laboured for many years without a feeling of accomplishment. I found myself working again, and this past week I have known the joy of completing it. I hope I do not ask too much if I request that you take this manuscript back to

America with you and send it somehow (I don't care how) to Mr. Farquhar in Philadelphia. From what you have told me, Mr. Farquhar is the publisher in this world most likely to take notice of my work. I can rest now, knowing that it is in your hands.

Meanwhile, I have received the gift of another story, something I thought should never again be mine. It came to me when Dora came through the door, that day not too long ago in actual time but an age ago, in my heart. I know again the exaltation of creation. You have my everlasting gratitude for bringing this joy to me, my dear.

Now, go home and write about me. NO—go home and write about yourself. And come again to Rutland Cottage.

Your loving friend,
Emerald Glover

"Oh, how sweet," I cried, passing the letter to Charles, who, out of some extreme of scholarly courtesy, had refrained from reading over my shoulder. He had been pacing around like an expectant father.

"It's a new novel, or a diary, or an autobiography," I said variously as I thumbed through the manuscript, trying to pin down its nature. The manuscript was a patchwork. Some of it was typed, but the final pages were handwritten. Many of the earlier pages were brown around the edges, but some of the pages in the first part of the manuscript were brand new. Scissors and paste had been used, and the entire manuscript, front to back, was full of blots and corrections and emendations and glosses. It looked like a novel told in the first person, and the first part seemed to be about Louisiana, the latter part set in London. The first glimpse of London. Something about Trafalgar Square. Something about the Duchess of York. Tea with Lady Ottiline. I *yearned* for my chair at home, my little shell reading lamp.

"Oh my dear Caroline, this is perfectly marvelous," rhapsodized Charles, walking back and forth, eyes shining. I lifted the weighty manuscript up to him so he could have a look. It dawned on me now that this was the only copy of a document of great historical importance. I compared my first trip over to the British Library in search of Emerald Glover materials to a treasure hunt. I thought at the time (mistakenly) that I had not found very much, but this, this! This manuscript was a find like the Koh-i-Noor Diamond.

"What if I lose it? Or what if something happens to it?" I cried.

"The first thing you need to do is make a copy," Charles said. It was not necessary that he mention the first version of Carlyle's *French Revolution*, which was accidentially burned. "Why don't we take it round to the British Museum?"

"No," I said instinctively, knowing the reputation of that great institution for the ruthless acquisition of irreplaceable treasures, fearing that "A Small Town Girl" might somehow be confiscated by a guard. "I mean, it seems to me I saw a little shop on Great Russell Street that does copying. I think it might be faster, and cheaper."

"You know what," Charles said speculatively, pacing away and then back, pulling on his thick brown mustache. "Let's take it to Barrow and Long. I'd like Nigel Barrow to have a look at it."

"Who's Nigel Barrow?"

"My publisher. Barrow and Long did my last two books. They're good people. Nigel can give us an opinion."

"Mrs. Glover asked me to deliver this to Philadelphia. She has strong ties to Farquhar and Sons in Philadelphia. I don't think she'd want me to take it to another publisher."

"We're not going to hand it over, Caroline," Charles said, looking amused. "We'll just let Nigel see it. You'll need a London publisher sooner or later, in any case. You need to tie into the BBC series, don't you see. Besides, Nigel will have a copier and a secretary to do the copying while we have tea."

Charles spoke in a jolly, affectionate way and did not attempt to touch the manuscript, which I was clutching to my breast. Before I knew it, Charles had hailed a cab, and we were being thrust down Great Russell Street and over to Shaftesbury Avenue. I was worried. What should I do with the copy once we got it? It couldn't go on the same plane as the original—that much was clear. What if we crashed? Perhaps I should fly straight to Philadelphia, I suggested, suddenly seeing the scheduled trip back home (to Gatwick, to Atlanta, to Middleton, to Barston) and a subsequent flight to Philadelphia as rife with opportunities for crashes and fires.

"You don't have to do that. Let's mail one to Philadelphia. If it doesn't arrive, you can take yours," Charles proposed.

Meanwhile, we were plunging through the crowded streets of London, then burrowing into various alleys and shooting out of them like a killer cab, sending pedestrians scattering this way and that, but at last, we were disembarking at an old stone building and going inside.

Barrow and Long had offices behind a simple door. Nigel Barrow was a bony, well-spoken man in shirt sleeves. He and Charles seemed to be old friends. I was very nervous as we took seats in his office, which was shabby in a distinguished sort of way and overlooked a green garden or square. I believed Mr. Barrow would never have heard of Mrs. Glover and would stare at the manuscript, obtuse to its value, but I needn't have worried. He had heard of her, possibly from the *Hedgerow* or maybe even from MacPherson himself, whom he actually knew. He was not MacPherson's publisher, but he spoke of that publisher and MacPherson familiarly as if they were members of a club. I felt pride in Charles, who was also in this London club at the same time as he was one of ours at NCLU. I was encouraged to tell Nigel Barrow the whole story of Emerald Glover, beginning with the picture in the Strachey biography and ending with the receipt of this manuscript not more than an hour before. I allowed Mr. Barrow to hold the manuscript and riffle through it.

"We'd be very interested, very interested," Mr. Barrow said. "MacPherson's interviews always fan up public interest. Perhaps a softcover."

"Mrs. Glover asked me to deliver this to Farquhar and Sons in Philadelphia," I said earnestly, moving toward the manuscript, whereupon Mr. Barrow and Charles explained to me that publication by Barrow and Long in no way precluded publication by Farquhar and Sons. I was made to see that Mrs. Glover would be delighted to have an English publisher. Of course, it all hinged on a careful reading by Mr. Barrow to ascertain whether "A Small Town Girl" had genuine literary merit, although he spoke as if that were a foregone conclusion.

Mr. Barrow went to a cabinet containing decanters of port and sherry. We celebrated this moment with a glass of sherry, Mr. Barrow actually going on to express interest in what I might write about Mrs. Glover or even another subject, speaking to me as if I were a real writer. Warmed by the wine, I ventured to reveal my intention of writing Mrs. Glover's life story, which occasioned another round of sherry, and my dear colleague Charles, dearer by the moment, toasted that volume as if it were already in existence, as indeed, at that moment, it actually seemed to be.

We repaired in due course to some cloakroom or anteroom which housed a gigantic copy machine. Two copies of "A Small Town Girl" were called for: one for Mr. Barrow to appraise (and then, to the joy of all, publish), the other to be mailed by his very dependable secretary to Philadelphia. But the job of copying the manuscript was not entrusted to a secretary. Mr. Barrow himself placed portions of the manuscript in the correct slot of the mammoth copier and kept track of the original and each copy as they came through. This wasn't one of those humdrum copiers for amateurs, where you copy pages one by one. No, this was a fast, professional machine that took a stack of pages and, ingesting them somewhere deep inside itself, flipped out page after page of copies by some mysterious process like the birth of a baby. I stood by, faint with anxiety (it would be now, with these irreplaceable pages, that we would hear a sickening crunch, and Mr. Barrow would frantically open the machine to find a damp-looking wad). But this was the only way to ensure the manuscript's survival, and I felt much as the mother of an only child must have felt, back in the early days of the small-pox vaccine, when Dr. Jenner made the scratch.

When we got back to the hotel, manuscript intact, it was almost time for dinner, and there was growing anxiety about John and Mrs. O'Leary. It was openly acknowledged that renting a car and driving around the countryside was not without peril. Only a morning or two ago at breakfast, Sid had reported on a story he had read in the *Times* about an American man who had killed his family in a rental car. Well, he hadn't literally killed them, but he had pulled out on an A road and been run down by a lorry. His wife and two daughters had been killed outright, but he (poor man) had survived. Every American who read or heard the story would know that the man had looked left before pulling out, not right, and that it was all his fault. I had heard other tales of accidents in Britain having to do with driving on the left or with the road crews always working on the narrow roads. Why, just this week, I heard a story about a man who came over a hill and ran smack into a British bulldozer, shearing off the right side of his car. And then there was another cause for alarm: the weather was really terrible—warm, windy, and turgid, just like the weather in south Louisiana right before a hurricane. It was easy to imagine the Vauxhall blown off the road in a ditch, its little wheels spinning.

Just how you could locate people out in the country-side was the question that Sid and Carol Beckwith, Edwina, Charles, and I discussed intensely in the lobby of St. Cuthbert's. Edwina had fetched John's postcard from our room and it was examined for clues, although it told nothing beyond the known facts that they had been in Edinburgh on Monday and intended to be back Thursday afternoon. We stood in the lobby pooling memories of remarks they had made, trying to piece together an itinerary. For the first time, Scotland Yard was mentioned.

"Miss Landry," Mr. Sparks called out flirtatiously from his open office. "Telephone message for you!" He was excavating for the message in the jumble on his desk. "Someone named John?" I asked breathlessly.

"John? No, I don't think so. Another of your suitors." The aggravating Mr. Sparks still had on his baggy brown corduroys but had changed out of his Irish fisherman's sweater, I saw as I waited. Now, despite the heat, he was wearing a green sweater with leather patches on the shoulders, a commando sweater.

"Robert. A Robert called you," said Mr. Sparks, holding up the note with an air of triumph.

"Really? When?"

"About an hour ago, I should say. Maybe longer."

I dialed the number on the note, smiling brightly at Mr. Sparks in the hope that he would discover urgent business elsewhere, but he stayed where he was, desultorily rummaging through slips of paper on the desk, wearing that sweater which, like his other sweater, was ironically designed for a life of hard, daring work.

The phone rang with that odd double ring, unlike phones in America.

"Hello," said a woman's sultry voice.

"Hello, this is Caroline Landry. I'm returning Mac—Robert's call," I said, meeting Mr. Sparks's amused glance.

"Hold on. I'll get him."

Plonk. Had that been Chauncy? I couldn't be sure. There was always something to wonder about with MacPherson.

"Caroline," MacPherson's voice said.

"Hi. I got your message."

"We just got back from Manchester. Elizabeth's here, from the show. Just going over scenes. It won't take long. How about dinner?"

"Umm, I can't, I'm afraid. We're all gathered here waiting for John and his aunt." I had turned and was looking down the long lobby to the open door. Sid was standing out on the stoop in front of the hotel, looking down toward the Florence like stout Cortez in Keats's poem. His hand was shading his eagle eyes from the drizzle, though, not the sun. "See, they were due back yesterday. But you could join us over here."

"Have you thought about staying in London to work on the edit?"

"Umm, not really. It's been a rush. I've been so busy."

"Well, when you get home. What's your number there? Never mind, no pencil. I'll find it. I'd better run now. Take care. Safe flight. You're the best."

I opened my mouth to tell MacPherson about the manuscript—that was the big news!—but he had hung up before I could get it out. He had vanished, in that way he had. I knew he wouldn't come; I seriously doubted whether I would ever see him again or even hear from him (but who knew?) I imagined having to look in the PBS schedule to find out whether *Lives of the Novelists* was coming on. But that seemed like a minor matter at the time. I believed that MacPherson would have found me some sort of job and somehow solved the tricky problems of visas and work permits had I just called back, but the possibility of staying in London seemed so distant, like the image of the city in that old print about Greenwich. Staying was not in the picture anymore, once "A Small Town Girl" was put in my hands. I had my work cut out for me; I had a job.

❀ ❀ ❀

At long last, the Vauxhall hove into view down the street, and John and Mrs. O'Leary got out stiffly, like people emerging from the hatch of a submarine after a long underwater expedition. John looked exhausted in his rumpled windbreaker. They had just come from Northumberland. They had gone back to Rutland Cottage to see Aunt Emerald, he said. His Aunt Dora had wanted to go back.

"Why didn't you call? We thought you'd be back yesterday. We were so worried!"

"I did call your hotel. Didn't you get the message?" said John, hugging me, surprising me with a kiss.

That night we all ate together at the *ristorante*. I told John and Mrs. O'Leary about getting the manuscript, about which they had known nothing. The Barston people pressed them to tell us about their journey to Edinburgh. John told me *sotto voce* that he had something extraordinary to tell me after dinner. But for the most part that evening, we talked about what awaited us on the other side of the Atlantic. As is often said, everything is different on a journey once you have turned your face toward home. Edwina described the umbrella that she had bought Ernest from James Smith and Sons. Allison brought up the subject of the engagement party she planned to give Edwina and Ernest. Pocket calendars were taken out, dates in September discussed. Carol Beckwith worried about the possibility that the power had failed some time during the past three weeks and the air conditioner gone off, allowing the books to mildew, something that had happened on one of their previous trips. Suddenly I thought of my cat Ottoline, really *thought* of her, the way her head feels when you stroke it, how she purrs and closes her eyes, and I remembered how worried I had been the day I left her that she would scratch the Harkriders' furniture, or that she would fail to use the litter box in its strange location and do something unforgivable under a bed.

After dinner, the people from Barston were heading for a famous pub on Fleet Street. Mrs. O'Leary, who had apparently renewed her vow of temperance since that first night at Rutland Cottage, did not want to go. "I'm worn out, traipsin' around Britain for almost a week. I wouldn't a missed it for the world, but now I need to rest," she declared.

And so it was that John and I walked her back to the Florence and then set out to join the others at the pub. But there had been another revolution in the weather. Now it was colder, and the wind was clearing the sky. Walking over to Fleet Street, John and I found that neither of us wanted to go inside a dark, noisy pub, not when there was this London twilight, so fresh and bright! It hardly needed to be discussed by John and me, this business of twilight walks. This is what we liked to do, and now we could talk.

"So tell me about going back to see Mrs. Glover. I was really surprised."

"Oh, Caroline," John said, shaking his head. "Dora was worried about Emerald. Kept talking about her in that big house, being short of money. She wanted to take her home."

"I heard them talking about it."

"Aunt Emerald wouldn't budge, though. So Dora *bought* the house. Yesterday we went to see a realtor and a lawyer in Pelwichton, and Dora bought the whole damn property. She arranged for a live-in caretaker and God knows what else."

"Good grief! How did Emerald take it?"

"She didn't have much choice. You know how Dora is—she could overturn a tank. Emerald finally agreed if Dora and I would agree to come back next summer, if *you* would come."

"Good grief!" That was all I could think of to say. "Good grief!"

We walked in the wind, clasping hands at the immensity of this. John filled in more details. Dora's banker in Jonesfield had been after her to invest some of her money. She had had some three hundred thousand dollars in her checking account alone.

"Good grief!"

You seem to have the city to yourself at the hour of eight-thirty or nine, and we walked up Fleet Street, which at some point becomes Ludgate Hill, on toward St. Paul's. It is a very long way, but you can walk from Bedford Place in Bloomsbury to St. Paul's Cathedral on a route past all the newspaper offices that goes up hill in its later stages and which really seemed, on that evening, like a stairway to heaven. We never saw a soul in the old stone streets, the sky growing brighter rather than darker, the wind colder. The thing about London, I thought, is that you're always exposed to the elements in a way you're not at home. I was so tired that sometimes I thought I wasn't going to make it to St. Paul's. But the famous dome was in sight up ahead when suddenly I stopped, unable to put one foot in front of the other one more time and burst into tears.

John was alarmed by this collapse, though it made perfect sense to me.

"I never got to sit in St. James Park and listen to a band," I finally managed to say, and John, with a firm grasp around my shoulders, somehow attracted a taxi. I climbed in the back, most grateful, almost dead with fatigue.

Chapter 25

The next morning, I woke up with the worst sore throat of my life. And it was *six o'clock*, such a ghastly hour because we were leaving for Victoria Station at eight-thirty, and I had not even started to pack. I felt horrible. My head ached, one nostril burned somewhere up deep inside, and every time I swallowed, I felt as if the top of my head were going to blow off.

I got up, unsteadily, and went to the window. I peeked behind the orange curtain. London seemed to be gone. There was a thick white fog or mist; I could hardly see the terrace across the street. In the dark of the room, I could just make out Edwina, lying log-like in her bed, snoring. (She did not need to get up early, having already packed her suitcases, which were standing by the door.) I contemplated the sink. Perhaps I shouldn't wash my hair with this throat, I thought; then I thought of the long flight home, the presence of John, the next moment finding myself under a glassful of ice water. A few minutes later, my throbbing head bound up in the skimpy hotel towel as if in a poultice, I surveyed the dim room. I had so much more stuff all of a sudden! There was the manuscript. Then I saw the stack of programs and museum guides in one chair, the bag of paperbacks from Hatchards in another. On the dresser was my loot from the stationer's—the three Cambridge Reporters notebooks and the other little notebooks. Then there were clothes—my new raincoat, the red Fair Isle sweater and hat, the dresses I had bought, various gifts for Mother and Grandmother (just little things, but things which now seemed bulky and intractable), and—heavenly days—the Benedictine poster in a long cardboard tube. Even the tiny paper bags with museum postcards now seemed heavy and unwieldy. I must have been crazy to encumber myself with all this, I thought as I heaped it together on the bed. There just wasn't room! I considered trying to ship some things—I had heard comedic accounts of the last-minute boxing-up of treasures acquired abroad, the taking of boxes to foreign post offices—but there wasn't time for that, there just wasn't time!

I had to stuff and wedge, wedge and stuff, until I fell back, exhausted. By the time Edwina woke up, everything was in either the medium-sized suitcase or the carry-on bag except the manuscript and the tube, which I would just have to carry in my arms.

Presently Edwina arose in her usual good spirits. "Where did you and John get off to last night?" she asked, ripping open the orange curtains.

I just smiled, coughing gently and pointing to my throat.

Edwina prescribed hot tea, and later, down in the breakfast room, Mavis and Lucy also performed a medical examination, diagnosing fever and upper respiratory infection, possibly even a strep throat. They located various medicaments in their pouches and soon had me sucking on an evil-tasting lozenge. Against my better judgment, I took a large, powerful-looking antihistamine capsule they pressed on me that promised to work all the way home.

The hotel seemed to have a completely new set of guests that morning. The "playwright" was not there, nor was the Japanese teacher; I did not see the girl in the leopard-print dress. The largest table was occupied by a new American family headed by a tweedy-looking professor. His wife wore no makeup and had painfully short hair, and they had four little children who looked pure and well-behaved, the kind of children who weren't allowed to watch anything on television but *National Geographic* specials and *Little House on the Prairie*. I knew by some sixth sense that they had been all through Europe, camping out in the cold, for all of them had terrible drippy colds, which is what my sore throat, my earache would blossom into, I thought gloomily. I also noticed a group of Scandinavian students with only the most rudimentary knowledge of English trying to order breakfast in English from Anna. "Toast und mar-me-läde," one of them was saying in that up-and-down zigzag way of the Scandinavians, which foray into the English language caused the others to laugh uproariously. But breakfast this morning was a rushed affair, with no time to linger over tea and observe the other guests. We had to check out, pay our bills, get our things downstairs, locate a cab. On our way out of the breakfast room, we said good-bye to Anna, reiterating invitations to come to Barston and promising to show her New Orleans, trying to convince her that she was our friend for life, no mere employee, though Mavis and Lucy undercut this democratic effort by taking money out of their purses and pressing it on Anna, who turned bright red.

Somehow I got my bags downstairs—they seemed to be filled with boulders—along with the weighty manuscript, which kept shifting around in the sack, sometimes pinching the tender flesh around the bend of my elbow, and the obnoxious tube, which would not stay still in the crook of my arm. Mr. Sparks was in the lobby, responding to our fervent good-byes in his bored, lofty way, taking scant notice of a group of red-eyed people who had just struggled into the lobby with about ninety pieces of luggage, straight from Heathrow or Gatwick, definitely Americans. I did not bother to chastise Mr. Sparks for not delivering John's message. We had to bump past the new arrivals' luggage with our luggage, then maneuver out the door to the porch, where it was freezing cold and fuzzy looking. Sid was marching back and forth, looking for the cabs Mr. Sparks was supposed to have ordered for us.

Everybody's possessions had multiplied. As the people from Barston assembled on the sidewalk, divided up, and loaded into taxis, which had finally come, everybody had at least one shopping bag with items too cumbersome or fragile to pack, and there were five or six tubes that had to be maneuvered to avoid putting the other peoples' eyes out. We could hardly breathe in the taxi, and I felt faint and miserable as we spun away from St. Cuthbert's and around the corner, shot down the streets. This was too fast, too precipitate! London looked quiet and majestic in the fog. You saw gray and green, and then, in the geraniums, the buses, the telephone booths, heart-breaking flashes of red. Incredibly, people were just walking down the sidewalks, carrying their black umbrellas, showing no awareness that they were the most privileged people on earth.

Victoria Station was loud and bright. Just inside, I was moved to tears by the sight of a clean-looking derelict rummaging around in a garbage can. Up some escalator, in a room where you could check your bags on through to Gatwick and not have to bother with them on the train, I found John, who was already there with his aunt.

"What's wrong with you, young lady? You look peaked," Mrs. O'Leary said sternly to me.

I made a gargling sound and pointed to my throat. I felt so ill by this time I would just as soon have given away my bags were it not for the new suit. But John, bless him, seized them; I sank in a chair. Allison was bringing me a Styrofoam cup of hot tea. Mrs. O'Leary unsnapped her purse and pulled out a bottle of aspirin to dose me with.

"I'm dying," I told her, sipping the dirty-tasting tea. More and more travelers were assembling in this upper room. Behind me, two or three different bass voices were arguing in a fierce-sounding foreign language; I looked around and saw a knot of black men in tribal garb. I also saw other people from the NCLU charter flight who had not stayed in England these past three weeks but had gone to other countries. They looked tanned and healthy, standing around talking, holding plastic shopping bags that looked completely different from the shopping bags of the great London stores. I overheard snatches of conversation centering on the sunny weather in these alien places. "How have you stood this godawful weather?" said one woman who had a dark tan, laughing loudly. "It was gorgeous every day in Greece!"

When the train arrived, we crowded down to the platform, and once in my seat on the train, I fell asleep, waking only when we yanked to a stop at one of the red brick stations, going right back to sleep. I wasn't missing anything in the way of scenery. The mist obscured everything outside the window but the signs giving the name of the stops in big black print and the shapes of a few black trees.

I thought I wasn't going to make it from the train to the plane—it was a long way up escalators and down concourses, through crowds. John kept bounding off to look for a wheelchair or one of those contraptions like a golf cart for me to ride on, but nothing was available. I could not go fast enough, and there was the awful feeling that we were going to miss the plane, and I was dying to get on the plane, if for no other reason than to sit down. But at long last, we reached the right waiting area. The other people on our charter flight were calmly sitting in the rows of chairs, as if they had been there for hours, waiting to see a doctor.

At that moment, our flight was announced, a man's voice saying something like, "Flight 555 leaving from Gate 15 in five minutes. Check your boarding passes, please," just this dry information, but the announcement was strangely pleasing. The reason, I realized, was that the speaker had an American accent. Every official voice I had heard in the last three weeks had been British, which had been more of a trial to my spirit than I realized. The British voice made so much of every word; it was so exaggerated and emphatic, so ornamented, like a madrigal, I thought woozily. But this American voice was plain and simple; it was a normal voice. I didn't feel inferior when I heard it, as if I'd been born on the wrong side of the ocean.

England was so small, I thought, as we moved toward the door that would lead to the plane. I could see why people had wanted to go out to India, or Ceylon—even America, some place with more space.

I felt faint. My knees buckled. I was on the floor, striving to get back up but feeling deliciously sleepy, much preferring to lie down.

"Excuse me, is there some problem?" said the airline employee with the comforting accent, somewhere above me.

"She's sick, young man. Can't you *see?*" Mrs. O'Leary said.

"Leave me here, please," I said. My thinking was that I'd just nap on the floor there a while.

"I believe she's fainted. I'll carry her," I heard John say, and as I rose in the air, I was seeing John's back as he carried Mrs. Glover down the top of the ridge, feeling perhaps that I was Mrs. Glover as I wafted along in John's arms, through a door, then through that accordion-like tube into the plane. We were the last ones on—the engines already whined— and as soon as we passed by the gaping flight attendants, the plane started to move. I was conscious of the Nicholsons, grand in their seats, like ambassadors, looking at me curiously, but I was too dizzy to explain why I was floating in, not walking. The seat John laid me in was between two incurious strangers, thank God. We were in England now, but the airplane was rolling, wheeling around, rolling, gaining momentum, shooting forward, rising up out of the fog into thin air, as if we had been going down white water rapids on a log raft and suddenly shot out over some falls. We were in England, but I was going inexorably up—away, away. We were flying up in the English empyrean, away.

I felt agitated and confused for a while and believed that I could not remain for long in a place so confined as this narrow seat. But presently, I relaxed, perhaps because of the antihistamine, which I believe was interfering with my thinking, and also the monotonous drone of the plane. In a while, I felt irradiated by a surprising calm, my mind overtaken by images of the day we had gone to the beach. I felt as though I were walking toward the dunes at the beach, going up the path between the long, waving grass in joyful expectation of the sea. I had been excited then, but I had also had a curious sense of peace. There had been the feeling that anything was possible, everything was possible; and even then, I had had the odd conviction that this feeling, this place, was something I would be able to draw on any time I wanted to, like the tree in Jeremiah. It was as if I lived in that white house out to sea now, I thought, picturing myself at home, thinking in the chair under the shell lamp, pausing to write.

I have to write this down, I thought, just before I fell asleep.

About the Author

JULIE L'ENFANT writes both fiction and critical studies. Her first novel, *The Dancers of Sycamore Street* (1983), was republished in 2019. Her previous books include *The Gag Family: German-Bohemian Artists in America* (2002) and *Pioneer Modernists: Minnesota's First Generation of Women Artists* (2011), both winners of a Minnesota Book Award. Her most recent book is *Hazel Belvo: A Matriarch of Art* (2020). She was a professor of art history at the College of Visual Arts in St. Paul, Minnesota.